The
GLASSBLOWER'S APPRENTICE

Books by Peter Pezzelli

HOME TO ITALY

EVERY SUNDAY

FRANCESCA'S KITCHEN

ITALIAN LESSONS

VILLA MIRABELLA

THE GLASSBLOWER'S APPRENTICE

THE GLASSBLOWER'S APPRENTICE

PETER PEZZELLI

West Passage
Publishing

West Passage Publishing Company
P.O. Box 3228, Narragansett, Rhode Island 02882

10 9 8 7 6 5 4 3 2 1

To Alice

Mille Grazie

I owe a great many thanks to those who helped make the creation of this book possible: To my wife, Corinne—who long ago started all this when she gave me that typewriter, and has been my inspiration ever since—and to my children, Andrew and Gabriella, and my mother, Norma, all who patiently took part in the seemingly endless process of reading what I wrote and then rereading what I rewrote then proofreading what I rewrote again; To Edith Greene, ace copy editor; To Cindy Baron, for creating such a beautiful cover illustration; To Sundance, and this with a fond farewell, for his unfailing enthusiasm and loyalty; To all those readers who took the time to write me a letter or e-mail, or post a message on my website, encouraging me to keep writing. To the many hands that printed and packaged and carried this book with great care just so that it could find its way into yours.

And, of course, first and lastly, greatest thanks and praise to the Editor, who always and in all ways has the last word.

Ferragosto

CHAPTER ONE

"Faaabioooooo!"

The singsong voice carried across the whole of Mont'Oliva, scampering through the streets and alleyways of the little village like an exuberant child at play. Chased by the hot breath of a late afternoon breeze, it skipped by the open doorways where the old women sat on the stoops, knitting and gossiping, then out onto the dusty piazza to the fountain where the little children cooled themselves by the water. From there it scuttled past the steps of the church and bell tower standing tall and dry and ominous, then back again between the houses with their gritty stone walls bleached white by the Italian sun. At last it went scurrying along beneath the lines of drying laundry flapping like flags overhead before finally coming full circle to its source.

Standing on the terrace outside her house, Liliana Terranova, the voice's owner, surveyed the table where she had just laid out a plate of sliced tomatoes and mozzarella, a bowl of olives, a basket of bread, and a bottle of mineral water. After setting out the plates and napkins, and fussing with the tablecloth, she paused and inclined an ear to the window above her, awaiting a response to her call. When none was forthcoming, she looked up and cupped a hand around her mouth.

"Faaaaabiooooo!" she called once more, this time a little louder and more insistent.

Perturbed when this second attempt met with no better result than the first, she stood for a few moments more with hands on hips, tapping a foot in mild consternation.

"Ay, *figlio mio!*" she cried in a decidedly less singsong voice that no doubt carried well beyond the confines of the village.

Upstairs in the house, seated on his bedroom floor with legs spread wide, a set of earphones drowning out any sound save for the music playing on his iPod, Fabio Terranova paused for a moment and straightened up. Oblivious to the world outside from which his mother was calling, he had been there all along in his room, stretching for nearly an hour, a rigorous daily routine he followed without fail.

A thin sheen of sweat glistening on his brow, his legs still splayed, his head and back and shoulders in perfect alignment, Fabio breathed easy and rested for a time. Turning his head, he let his gaze methodically take in his surroundings. It first alighted on the mirror above the dresser where he saw displayed the ribbon he had received as a six-year old after winning his first dance competition, the very first he had ever entered. Many more from other competitions in the ensuing years adorned the rest of the mirror's perimeter. Farther over, on the shelf to the side of the dresser, stood a small battalion of trophies, and beyond that the wall was papered with photographs and press clippings of his ballroom exploits. The message, from all he observed, was clear: It mattered little whether he danced solo or with a partner; wherever and whenever he danced, Fabio Terranova danced to win. The results spoke for themselves.

Fabio's survey of the room continued. On the wall over his bed hung a poster of Fred Astaire twirling Ginger Rogers, beside it another of a rain-drenched Gene Kelly swinging around a lamppost, and a third of Michael Jackson moonwalking across the stage. Dancing was Fabio's passion, his obsession really, and wherever he chose to look he found inspiration and encouragement for his vision of perhaps one day finding his own image displayed on a poster. Ever since he was a little boy, surrounding himself with constant reminders of this goal was the way he had arranged his little piece of the world. Now just a few months short of his twentieth birthday, he worked at his flexibility and every other aspect of his dancing skills with the fanatical devotion of an aspiring athlete or anyone for that matter who was chasing a dream.

Fabio took a deep breath, held it for a moment, and then slowly exhaled, releasing the tension from his muscles. "You're the best," he told himself as he extended his torso over the floor and relaxed back into his stretch.

It was just at that moment, as he was about to lose himself once more in the music, when a woman's shoe suddenly sailed through the open bedroom window, glanced off the dresser, and struck the back of the young man's head. The shoe knocked the earphones from his ears before it plopped down unceremoniously on his lap.

Though not at all injured by the projectile's impact, a wincing Fabio gave a cry of indignation at the assault. He sat there for a moment, rubbing the back of his head before giving in to a smile when he regarded the shoe. With a chuckle he grabbed it, eased himself to his feet, and went to the window. Nudging aside the curtains, he leaned outside and looked down to the terrace where he beheld his semi-barefoot mother looking impassively back up at him with arms crossed.

"*Scusami, Signora,* " he said haughtily, wagging the shoe at her for effect, "but does this shoe belong to anyone I know?"

"Ah, so you weren't dead up there after all," Liliana replied nonchalantly. "I'm so relieved."

Fabio eyed her with an impish grin. "You know," he told her in an equally impish voice, "if this had been high-heeled you might have taken my eye out."

"That's why I wear flats," she replied, "what kind of mother do you think I am?" Then, gesturing to the table, "Now that I have your attention, *carissimo*, why don't you come down and have a little something to eat."

"I'm not hungry," he told her.

"But you will be later. Come down now."

"When I'm done stretching," he answered.

"Enough stretching. Come down and eat!"

"When I'm done, Mamma," he told her patiently before pulling himself back inside.

"Don't be long," she called after him. "And give me my shoe back!"

Fabio casually tossed the shoe back out the window the way it had entered. Apparently it landed on an inconvenient spot, for he heard his mother lamenting, *"Mannagia la miseria!"* as he sat back down to continue his routine.

Later, when he had finished stretching, Fabio slowly rose from the floor and stood for a time before the full-length mirror affixed to the bedroom door. Gazing at his reflection, he began to take careful inventory of himself. This was less an exercise in vanity—though he did possess an ample quantity of that particular attribute—than a thorough and, to him, very necessary period of self-assessment. He did not need to wonder if he was handsome of course; that much was self-evident. One needed only to consider the dark, captivating eyes, the thick, jet black hair, and the finely chiseled profile. Added to these, Fabio possessed an athlete's physique, slender but well-muscled. But all of that was not enough, which was why Fabio scrutinized every part of himself, searching with cold detachment for areas of possible weakness: his posture, the angle at which he held his head, the tone of his chest and arm muscles, and above all else the air of confidence he exuded. Without this last, intangible quality everything else could fall apart in the judges' eyes and, worse, in his own. In his young life he had already watched more than his share of up and coming dancers come undone by nothing more than a lack of faith in themselves, dancers often equal in physical talent to him, equal in almost every way save for this one element. Fabio well understood that, for what he hoped to accomplish, doubt was deadly, and so he took great pains to chase every notion of it from his mind.

By the time Fabio finally showered, dressed for the evening, and made his way downstairs, his aunt, Zia Pasqualina, had stopped by. When he walked out to the terrace, a small valise in hand, he found her sitting at the table, chattering away with Liliana. At seeing her nephew, she threw her hands up in delight.

"There he is, *finalmente!*" she exclaimed. "I was wondering how long I was going to have to wait to see the famous dancer."

At that Fabio stopped, dropped the valise, and struck an upright, rigid pose like that of a matador who has just entered the ring. His eyes suddenly smoldering with dark but comic menace, he snatched his aunt's hand, swept her off the chair, and gathered her into his arms.

"Not famous yet, Zia, " he told his aunt, pulling her close, "but give me time." Then, rolling his eyes, he added breathlessly, "I think I feel a tango coming on."

"Careful, Fabio, you'll hurt her!" cried Liliana.

"*Dio mio!*" his aunt laughed helplessly as Fabio suddenly whirled her across the little terrace, paused, and whirled her back again to the table where he dipped her for dramatic effect before gallantly easing her back onto her chair.

"*Ma tu sei pazzo!*" cried Pasqualina, her cheeks bright red from the escapade. Then, laughing to Liliana, "He's crazy, this son of yours. Handsome, but crazy!"

"Dance, dance, dance," sighed Liliana. "It's all this one ever thinks about."

"What else is there for me to think about, Mamma?" asked Fabio, settling down at the table with them.

"You might think about getting a job someday soon," his mother offered.

Fabio chuckled and held up his hands, gesturing about at the little village surrounding them. "Where?" he wondered aloud. "In this thriving metropolis?"

Liliana gave another sigh and shook her head. "Do you hear how he talks to his mother?" she complained.

"Oh, leave him alone, Liliana," Pasqualina chided her. "He's young. Let him live. He has his whole life to worry about a job. So, Fabio, where are you going tonight all dressed up?"

"It's the last weekend of Ferragosto," he told her, "so I'm going to Formia."

"And what's in Formia?"

"Seven Up," said Fabio.

"And what is Seven Up, and why are you going there?"

Fabio smiled. "It's a dance club, Zia, the best in the whole province," he explained, "and I only dance at the best."

"Dance, dance, dance," clucked Liliana.

Pasqualina chuckled and nodded to the suitcase. "And what's with that?" she asked. "Are you planning to sleep on the dance floor tonight?"

"No, Zia," said Fabio. "I'm staying at my friend Enzo's apartment tonight. He's taking me to the train station tomorrow."

"And where are you going tomorrow?"

"To Milano," a rueful Liliana answered for him.

"Milano?" said his aunt. "And what will you do there?"

"What else," said Liliana.

"I'm going to audition for *Dance Italia!*," said Fabio excitedly. "All the best dancers in Italy go there—and I'm going to show them who's the best of the best."

"So maybe we'll be seeing you on TV someday soon?" cooed Pasqualina. "How exciting!"

"Not maybe," said Fabio, brushing a speck of lint from his slacks. "Definitely. And then it won't be long after that when I'll be going to America."

"And why America?"

"Because, Zia, that's where the best of the best go," Fabio told her with much conviction. "Just wait. Someday you'll come to New York and see me up on the stage on Broadway, or maybe in the movies, dancing with the most beautiful women in the world!"

"Like Fred Astaire," said Pasqualina dreamily. "Wouldn't that be something. Your father would be so proud."

At that Fabio gave a wistful smile and fell silent before looking out over the red-tiled rooftops of Mont' Oliva. Set amidst a cluster of houses near the highest spot in the village, the Terranovas' little terrace afforded a lovely view of the valley down below where the vineyards and groves of olive trees knitted into the rolling terrain stretched out in precise crisscross lines like bristles on a brush. Beyond them in the distance the sandy sunburned peaks of the Apennines rose roundabout, guarding the horizon like ancient fortress walls. Closer to home, a solitary figure could be seen emerging from one of the vineyards. His work done for the day, he made his way down the dusty path that led to the road where he was soon joined by another man, the pair trudging back toward the village with shirts flung over their shoulders. It had been a blistering hot day—typical for late August—but now the breeze through the valley had kicked up in earnest and things were mercifully cooling as the sun fell off to the west and the shadows of the trees and the houses lengthened.

Fabio poured himself a glass of mineral water and took a sip, keeping an eye all the while on the two men ambling along the road. For a moment he was a small child again, sitting as he often did on the edge of the terrace, watching and waiting to see his father come walking home after a long hot day of toiling away in those same vineyards. "Papa!" he would cry at seeing him come into view. Then Fabio would be off like a shot to meet his father halfway as he made the long weary trudge uphill to the village. At the sight of the little boy careening his way, Franco Terranova would inevitably stop and open wide his arms just in time to catch him as he leapt into his powerful embrace. Smelling of earth and sweat, the black and gray stubble on his face rough against his son's cheek, he would flip the boy up onto his shoulders and, weary as he might be, make the rest of the trek home with Fabio riding there like a conquering hero.

"So, Fabio," Zia Pasqualina was saying, bringing him back to the present, "what do you think, will you still bother with us anymore someday after you've become rich and famous and you're living in New York?"

"I doubt it, Zia," Fabio kidded her, giving a disdainful sniff for effect. "I'm sure I will be much too busy. You know how it is, signing autographs, posing for pictures, all the usual stuff celebrities do."

"What, too busy even for your mother?" cried Liliana, reaching out to give her son a slap across the top of the head. She missed intentionally, of course, for she could never dream of hurting the apple of her eye—the occasional thrown shoe notwithstanding.

"Ayyy, careful!" laughed Fabio, ducking below his mother's hand. "You'll mess up my hair."

Now it was Pasqualina's turn to give a wistful smile and look out across the valley. "But you are right, Fabio," she told him, her gaze fixed on some point off in the distance. "You *will* be too busy. So don't look back, not ever when you finally leave here. This place is a cage, a very pretty cage, but a cage all the same, and it's full of pretty traps. So get out there in the world and make your mark if you can. Don't give this little molehill a second thought until you get everything you want. And don't you worry about us, either, we'll always love you and we'll always be here for you if you need us."

"Hey, what are you trying to do, Zia," said Fabio, giving her a playful poke, "make me cry?"

"Hah!" laughed Pasqualina, coming back to herself. "That I would never want to do." With that she got to her feet and gave her nephew's cheek a pinch. "And now, *bellissimo*, it's time for me to go," she said. "Your uncle will be wanting his supper."

"Ciao, Pina," said Liliana.

"Ciao, Liliana."

"Tell Zio I said hi," said Fabio.

"And you do what I told you when you get to Milano, *capisci*?" replied his aunt.

"*Si*," said Fabio with a solemn nod.

After Pasqualina went on her way, Fabio and his mother sat for a few moments in silence. As he listened to the breeze whispering across the rooftops, Fabio looked down to the valley, hoping to catch sight of the two walkers on the road to see who they might be. By now, though, the pair were lost from view, so he sat back and folded his arms, thinking back to that long ago afternoon when he had sat there waiting and waiting, but his father had never come home.

"How old would Papa be right now if he were still alive today?" he wondered aloud.

His mother did not respond right away, even though she readily knew the answer to his query. "What makes you ask?" she said at last.

"I was just thinking about him, that's all," said Fabio.

"He would have been fifty-nine," Liliana told him.

"Fifty-nine," Fabio repeated. "So he was forty when I was born. That's not old, I suppose, but it's not really young either, is it? Why have I never thought about that?"

"You're father and I married late," said Liliana with a shrug, "and *he* died early. There's nothing really to think about. That's just the way things get arranged sometimes in life."

Fabio paused to consider her words. "Do you think Zia was right?" he said after a time. "Do you think he would have been proud of me?"

"Your papa?" laughed his mother. "You were his whole world. Of course he would be proud of you. He *is* proud of you, as a matter of fact."

At that Fabio smiled. "But do you think he would have liked it better—I don't know, let's say if I played *calcio* instead of dancing? I was always good at it in school, you know. I could have been a great *portiere*."

Liliana gave a dismissive wave. "The world is full enough of people who like to run around and kick soccer balls," she said. "Your father knew that you too could have very easily been one of them if that was what you wanted to do. But he also knew that you have a very special gift, *figlio mio*, one more important than being able to throw yourself on the ground to keep the ball out of the net."

"I don't know about that, Mamma," Fabio pointed out with a chuckle. "Keeping the ball out of your own net is pretty important in this country."

"So is following your heart and using the gifts God gave you," she replied. "Or at least it should be. You see, Fabio, you have something beautiful inside, something that everyone else can see right away when you dance. It's like when you look at a really beautiful painting or a statue, you know right away that no matter what kind of crazy life he might have been living, something wonderful must have been going on inside the artist who created it, even if he didn't know it himself. And like any artist, you give part of it away to whoever looks at what you do, you share with them that wonderful thing going on inside you."

"So, you're suggesting I should take up painting?" said Fabio, giving her a sideways look.

Liliana rolled her eyes and looked upwards with hands folded, as if praying for patience. "What I'm suggesting is that you had better watch yourself when you go to Milano tomorrow," she told him. "*Sta attento!* And I don't care how much of a big shot on Broadway you become someday, you'd better not ever forget your mother. Now eat something before you go. You're too skinny. People will think that I don't feed you."

Fabio took his mother's hand and kissed it. "Don't worry, Mamma," he told her. "Everybody knows you take good care of me." Then, as he pushed away from the table and stood, he said, "I should be going now. Enzo will be waiting for me on the piazza."

Liliana eyed him sharply. "So, you are going out tonight to have fun with your friends," she said. "And then what? How many days will you be away in Milano?"

"Three," Fabio told her. "The auditions are on Monday, and then the call backs will be on Tuesday."

"And how do you know you'll get a call back?"

"Mamma, please," said Fabio, rolling his eyes as if this was the most ridiculous question he had ever heard. Then he grabbed his valise and was off to the piazza.

CHAPTER TWO

"Ciao, Fabio!" came a voice from one of the windows above as he wound his way through the narrow streets. Fabio recognized it immediately and inwardly groaned.

"Ciao, Bettina," he replied, barely slowing to look up at the girl as he passed.

"Where are you going tonight?" she called.

Reluctantly Fabio paused and turned around. Bettina, he well knew, had been pining away in vain for him since the two were school children. In all those years, Fabio had rarely given her a first glance, never mind a second. She was a plain-looking girl, not at all ugly, but simply not up to his standards; Fabio had his sights set much higher. Besides that she was like most of them in the village, girls whose only thoughts in life were for having a ring on their finger and a baby in their arms, content to pass their days watching the sun rise and fall over Mont'Oliva. Perhaps one day—though he could scarce imagine it—he too would desire that kind of settled, monotonous, mind-numbing life, but for now Fabio had no intention of letting himself get tied down in that way. There were far too many places he wanted to see and far too much he wanted to do. And so he gave the girls like Bettina little more than a morsel of his attention when situations such as this arose. In his mind he was not being rude or cruel. He was only sparing them needless pain.

"Eh, no place special," he told her. "Just out for the night."

With elbows resting on the window sill, her chin propped up on her hands, Bettina gazed down at him with affectionate eyes. "And what's with *la valigia*," she asked, nodding to Fabio's valise. "It looks like you're going away somewhere."

"For a few days, that's all," answered Fabio, turning to go. "Ciao, Bettina."

"Ciao, Fabio, *sta attento!*" she called after him, her voice dripping with disappointment at the prospect of his leaving. "Be careful."

Breathing a sigh of relief, his aunt's warning still fresh in his mind, Fabio continued on at a brisk pace—lest he encounter any other pretty traps lying in wait for him—until at last he stepped out onto the piazza. Up ahead he saw Enzo and his other friends milling about the fountain. It was just then that, from off to one side, a soccer ball suddenly came rolling his way and glanced off the side of his foot.

"Ayyy!" Fabio cried indignantly at the group of young boys gathered by the side of the church where they had been playing an impromptu match. "Watch out for the shoes!"

"Eeeek!" teased one of the boys in reply. "Look out for my pretty boy dancer shoes!"

At that Fabio shot the boy a most malevolent glance before turning quickly to Enzo and the others to give them a wink.

"*Guarda, guarda!*" his friends whispered merrily amongst themselves. "Watch what he does now!"

Without another word, Fabio pirouetted in place a full three times *al* Michael Jackson before laying his foot, shoe and all, squarely into the ball. The unsuspecting boy could only gape helplessly as it came whistling back across the piazza, whizzing within a whisker's breadth of his ear before slamming against the far wall. The sheer power in the kick and the rush of air as the ball passed was enough to topple the startled lad backwards.

The piazza erupted in laughter.

"Now remember what I say," said Fabio, wagging a menacing finger at the boy, who was soon sitting upright, rubbing his ear to make certain that it was still attached to the side of his head. "Watch out for the shoes! *Capito?*"

The boy did not have the temerity to reply, but the look on his face was enough to convey that he well understood the message.

With an air of great self-satisfaction, Fabio ambled the rest of the way across the piazza to join Enzo and the others. There he sat on the edge of the fountain and indulged himself in a cigarette, a rare deviation from his maniacally disciplined regimen, but it *was* the last weekend of Ferragosto after all. Taking a long drag, he slowly exhaled a stream of smoke while he inspected the side of his shoe for scuff marks. Enzo meantime came and sat by his side.

"So, *Generalissimo*," he asked, rubbing his hands together in gleeful anticipation, "what is our battle plan for tonight?"

Fabio regarded his friend for a moment and smiled. Enzo and he had been partners in crime since the two were toddlers, frolicking about that very same fountain beneath the watchful eyes of their mothers. They were an odd pair, really. A born follower, Enzo possessed none of Fabio's easy self-confidence, or sense of style, and certainly none of his physical prowess. Indeed, he was a rather pudgy sort, though not terribly so. He simply had that look about him of pleasant dishevelment which contrasted sharply with Fabio's inevitably precise bearing. That summer he had decided to grow a somewhat comical looking mustache which he had imagined would increase his appeal with the opposite sex, but of course had the contrary effect. Despite these shortcomings, which in someone else might otherwise have proven too much to tolerate, Enzo did possess certain virtues that Fabio appreciated. For starters he was good-natured and good company—*simpatico*, one might say—and he was willing to put up with the condescending barbs and fits of pique and arrogance to which Fabio was occasionally given. Added to these noble qualities, Enzo also owned a car and had recently rented a small apartment on the outskirts of Frosinone where he was planning to attend university. The availability of the former, but particularly the latter, was, on that night, a matter of acute interest to Fabio.

For his part, Enzo enjoyed in return the very tangible benefit of being able to mingle with the *ragazze,* the young ladies who inevitably gravitated to Fabio whenever the two prowled the nightclub circuit together. There Enzo would stand dutifully by his friend, watching and waiting, ever hopeful that he might endear himself to one of the lovely rejects whose charms had been insufficient to win over Fabio. In this regard he had had very little luck to date, none in fact, but simply having the opportunity from time to time made tolerating Fabio's volatile temperament worthwhile. So it was in some sense a friendship of convenience for both, but Enzo truly loved Fabio like a brother, and was as loyal to him as a Dalmatian.

Fabio put an arm around his friend's shoulder. "The battle plan, *Capitano mio,*" he chuckled in reply, "is the same as it always is. We are the *Conquistatori.* First we find Aldo, then wherever we go, we descend on the dance floor and take what we want!"

Enzo once more rubbed his hands together, giddily contemplating the romantic prospects of the night to come. Then he paused and gave Fabio a sideways glance.

"What do you think?" he asked slyly. "Will Caterina be there?"

At the sound of the name, Fabio did not at first reply, but simply gave a low growl the way a tiger might when, after days of fruitless hunting, it finally catches the scent of its prey. Caterina was a stunning ballroom *ballerina* he had met three weeks earlier at a competition in Gaeta. He first laid eyes on her as he was stepping off the dance floor and she was stepping on, her sheer sequined gown shimmering like moonlight on the water. Fabio himself had just finished what he considered a lackluster rhumba with his own partner, Fillipa, in whom he had not been particularly pleased for some time, and was in a foul mood. That soon evaporated when the music began to play and he observed Caterina beginning to dance.

Fabio could not help but be taken with her, mesmerized as he was by the graceful movements of her long, beautifully toned limbs and the swaying of her dark, silky hair. Though still unrefined, she danced with a beguiling sort of controlled fire, oozing style and sensuality with every turn, every effortless step across the dance floor. Sadly—or perhaps fortunately for Fabio—her partner, a young man of his own age, was clearly not equal to the task of leading such a ballerina. He struggled to stay ahead of her throughout the dance, and their performance as a whole was subpar. They were an obvious mismatch, and Fabio marveled that the two should have ever entered such a competition together. Then again he also understood that such pairings were often arrangements of convenience born of necessity, each dancer using the other as a stepping stone to some other destination—or partner more precisely. Fabio considered Fillipa. Lovely as he might have found her in the beginning, he needed but a moment to conclude that he had stepped across as many stones as he possibly could with her. It was time for him to move on.

And so, the very first moment the opportunity presented itself after the competition, Fabio was quick to approach Caterina, ostensibly to offer congratulations on her performance. Under this pretense, he smoothly segued to an introduction. Caterina's eyes, darkly luminous like his own, had sparkled when her gaze met his, and there was electricity in her touch when she offered her hand, telling him all he needed to know. Fabio was instantly smitten, and from that moment forth thoughts of her dominated his every waking moment.

In the days that followed the two would meet again but once, and only briefly, for coffee. Caterina lived across the Italian peninsula in a village outside Pescara, far from tiny Mont'Oliva, but she had been as instantly taken with him as he with her, and the pair communicated at all hours online, sharing their dreams of dancing, and their dreams of each other. For his part, without ever having once stepped out onto a dance floor with her, Fabio already had plans to take Caterina with him when at last he went to America after his triumph to come in Milano. He was certain that in Caterina he had found that perfect ballerina for whom he had been searching. Suddenly it was as if he could see his entire life unfolding before him. In his fevered imaginings, he and Caterina were together always, forever wrapped around one another, both blissfully lost in a perpetual dance. Was it love he felt, or just a wildfire that would die out as quickly as it had been kindled? Fabio could not say. All he knew for certain was that he had to make her his.

"She said she would come," Fabio finally replied, getting to his feet.

"Then what?" said Enzo.

"Then I will take her in my arms and make love to her on the dance floor like no one has ever seen. And then later, when I take her home with me..." Fabio's voice trailed away in another puff of smoke.

Enzo gave a sigh of resignation. "And then I'll be sleeping on the couch," he finished.

At that Fabio smiled and patted his friend on the shoulder. "*Andiamo*," he said nodding across the piazza to where Enzo had left his car. "Aldo will be waiting for us at *il muro*."

Though a sizable assemblage was gathered there, Aldo, the third member of the conquering *Conquistatori*, was nowhere to be seen when the duo arrived at *il muro*, a short section of wall lining the road just outside the village. The wall overlooked a sheer, rock-strewn embankment that tumbled down to the river flowing through the valley below. It was a popular spot with the *giovantu`*, the area's young people, who liked to congregate there especially on warm summer evenings like this one. Just out of sight of the ever watchful eyes of the village elders, it was the one place where they could go to mill about in peace, puffing their cigarettes while they talked and laughed about the things teenagers around the world talked and laughed about away from their parents. Seated on the wall, tossing pebbles over the side, they could lazily stare far down the valley, watching the headlights of the cars winding their way along the river, or those descending the adjoining road directly across the street, a treacherously steep route that led up over the mountain pass to the coast. A favorite pastime was playfully speculating on whether the brakes of approaching motorists would hold before their cars plummeted downhill to the junction at the wall where they would have to stop and turn right or left.

"Where is Aldo?" asked Fabio to no one in particular when he and Enzo stepped out of the car. The question was greeted at first with silence and then with a communal shrug.

"He was here a little while ago," Tomasso, one of the boys, finally offered, "but I think he went home."

"Where are you going tonight, Fabio?" asked one of the girls.

Fabio did not answer right away, but instead looked out across the valley, his mouth squirreled up in an expression of mild consternation as he contemplated the horizon. By now darkness had fallen over the valley and all that was left of the sun was a faint smudge of purple and orange across the mountaintops. The night was still young, but it would not stay that way forever.

"Formia," he said at last. "Aldo's supposed to come with us." He turned and gave a nod to Enzo. "What do you think?" he asked.

"I tried texting him a little while ago," replied Enzo, holding up his cell phone. "I'll try again, but I think he turned his cell off."

Fabio turned the matter over in his mind for a few moments before looking back at the others. "Did Aldo walk home by himself?" he asked.

"No," said Tomasso. "He left with Violetta."

Fabio gave a grunt, as if to indicate that some suspicion of his had been vindicated. "Ah, Aldo and Violetta," he snickered. "That explains it."

"Explains what?" said Enzo.

"Why Aldo won't be coming with us tonight," said Fabio. He motioned for Enzo to get back in the car. "*Andiamo, capitano mio*," he said. "It's time to go to Formia."

"*Subito!*" cried Enzo with a crisp salute. "*A Formia!*"

"Tell Aldo he doesn't know what he'll be missing!" called Fabio to the others when they were settled into the car. Then Enzo revved the engine and drove them away up the road that led through the mountains to the ocean beyond.

CHAPTER THREE

The cars were already lining both sides of the road outside of Club Seven Up when the two finally arrived in Formia. The moment Enzo found a parking spot and brought the car to a halt Fabio jumped out, stretched his arms over his head, and turned his face to the balmy breeze gently puffing off the Tyrrhenian sea. He closed his eyes for a moment, letting it caress his cheek and hair as he breathed in the scent of the ocean, the air so different from that of the mountains. It filled him with a sense of liberation. With a contented sigh he gazed up at the blue-gray clouds racing across the face of the half moon before inclining his ear toward the club just down the road. Despite the roar of the waves crashing onto the nearby beach he could hear the thumping of the music rising from within, the relentless rhythm calling to him like distant drums. His insides churning with nervous anticipation, he turned to Enzo, who by now was already at his side with comb in hand.

"I have a feeling it's going to be a very good night, *amico mio*," said Fabio. "Are you ready to take what is ours?"

Enzo hurriedly dragged the comb through his tousled hair and did his best to smooth his mustache before shoving the comb into his back pocket. "Ready!" his said excitedly.

"Then *avanti*!" cried Fabio.

"*Forza i Conquistatori!*" cried Enzo.

When the two walked through the entrance to the outdoor discotheque and beheld the tightly packed throng, it seemed for a moment as though they were looking not at a collection of hundreds of individual bodies, but instead one single organism that pulsed and moved to the rhythm of the music. The heat of it hit them in the face like the steamy breath of some enormous beast, the mouth of which they eagerly stepped down into. Enzo, his eyes wide as saucers, struggled to watch where he was going as Fabio led him through the press of the crowd. It was no easy task; wherever he looked his gaze fell upon one enticing young female after the other. They were everywhere it seemed, so many of them splendidly arrayed on that hot summer's evening in one beguiling stage of near undress or another, each one more beautiful than the last. It was the last sizzling Saturday night of Ferragosto, the cherished weeks of August vacation, and the ladies were ushering it out in fabulous style. It was their show after all. With laughter and screams of delight, they took to the dance floor in groups while others huddled together on the sidelines, sipping their drinks, talking and scheming amongst themselves while casting furtive glances at the eager young men ever eyeing them from nearby.

For his part, though, Fabio was all but oblivious to the frenetic scene. He waded through the crowd, past more than one pair of admiring female eyes, before coming to a stop at the center of the gathering to get his bearings. There he stood, slowly scanning the crowd in every direction with methodic intensity. He was searching of course for Caterina, but she was nowhere in sight. The first misgivings that perhaps she had not come to the club that night were just beginning to scratch at his psyche when he suddenly spotted her staring back at him from amidst the crowd on the elevated dance floor. She had obviously been watching for him, for she flashed a smile of satisfaction the moment their eyes met before immediately turning away to face her dance partner of the moment. The lucky young man was trying at every opportunity, with only minimal success, to keep his hands on Caterina. With Fabio now looking on, she finally allowed herself to spin into his embrace and pressed herself close to him, bringing her lips a tantalizing, tormenting inch from his before pulling once more away. The teasing display had the intended effect on Fabio, and he gave another low growl, like that of the tiger who has finally spotted its prey.

"*Accendino?*" came a soft voice, momentarily snatching his attention away from the dance floor.

Fabio turned and discovered a rather attractive young woman standing a few steps away. With a casual toss of her lovely blonde hair, she gave him a suggestive nod and held up a cigarette, waving it at him to indicate that she needed a light.

"*Accendino?*" she repeated, her gaze as sultry as her voice.

It was an old tactic, Fabio well knew, a convenient invitation women often used to break the ice after happening upon a man they had found to be of interest. Interesting as *she* might have been, Fabio's first inclination was to direct her to Enzo standing at his other side with lighter already in hand, no doubt eager to act in his stead. But then another idea occurred to him. Two, he decided, could play at Caterina's game, so Fabio turned to the dance floor and shot her a teasing look of his own before turning back to the young woman still awaiting his response.

"*Si, certo, signorina,*" said Fabio, snatching the lighter away from Enzo. With a cordial grin he held it up, letting the woman take his hand.

Her gaze never leaving his, she guided the lighter's flame toward the tip of the cigarette now resting suggestively between her lips. When it was lit, she kept a gentle hold of his hand just long enough to give a little sigh and blow a puff of smoke across his fingers, extinguishing the flame.

"*Grazie,*" she said breathlessly, releasing him at last.

"*Niente,*" said Fabio. He snapped the lighter shut, handed it back to Enzo, and gave her a smile. *"Che bella notte,"* he said. "It's a beautiful night."

"Bellissima," she agreed in a tone that indicated that there was every possibility that the night would only get better.

"Come ti chiami?" asked Fabio, inquiring as to her name even though he had not the slightest interest.

"Serafina," she replied after exhaling another puff from her cigarette. *"E tu?"*

Before he could further pursue his conversation with the arresting Serafina, Fabio felt the sharp stab of an elbow digging him in the ribs.

"Cos' e`, Enzo?" he grunted to his friend. "What's the matter?"

Enzo gave a little cough and gestured with his thumb for Fabio to look behind him. Fabio turned to find standing there a much displeased Caterina observing him with arms crossed. With daggers in her eyes she shot a withering look at Serafina, who of course returned fire with one of her own. Then Caterina turned back to Fabio with a look of acute annoyance.

Apparently, two were not allowed to play the game after all.

Fabio could not help but be pleased that his little gambit had worked to perfection. All the same, observing as he could the ire in one woman's eyes and the defiance in those of the other, he felt a bit uneasy, something akin to what a referee must feel when standing between two angry prize fighters itching for the ding of the opening bell. This apprehension grew stronger when Caterina took a menacing step toward Serafina, leading him to believe that an outbreak of hostilities was imminent. To his relief, however, she went no farther. Instead her expression suddenly softened and she gave him a sly, sideways look. Then with an impish pout she put two fingers to her lips, as if she too were holding a cigarette.

"Accendino?" she said in a playfully seductive voice.

Fabio did not reply right away, but instead allowed himself

a moment to let his eyes take all of her in. Commencing the journey at the tip of her shoes, his gaze roamed up the sleek contours of her legs and thighs to the impossibly short leather skirt clinging desperately to her hips. From there it meandered across the smooth plain of her bared midriff where it lingered for a moment on the jewel adorning her navel before climbing higher still to alight on the silk halter top caressing the curves of her breasts in the most delightful way. All in all it was a beguiling ensemble. Devastating in its simplicity, it suggested everything, but promised nothing, and by the time his eyes once more reached hers, the *Conquistatore* was conquered and Fabio was putty in her hands.

"Why would you need one," he breathed at last, "when you're already on fire?"

The remark obviously pleased Caterina, for without another word she seized him by the hand and began to drag him away to the dance floor.

"*Arriverderci*, Serafina!" laughed Fabio over his shoulder, only too happy to let himself be pulled along.

Not at all amused by the unfavorable turn of events, Serafina scowled in outrage and petulantly flicked her cigarette down at Fabio's heels before he disappeared into the crowd. With a huff she reached down into the tiny purse on her hip and soon pulled out a replacement. When she looked up, she found herself facing Enzo. With Fabio now out of the way, he had remained close by with hands in pockets, haplessly wondering all the while what his chances might be of somehow turning the situation to his advantage. Not particularly accomplished in this sort of endeavor, he gave a nervous cough as he struggled to conjure up some witty remark with which to charm her. With none springing immediately to mind, he simply looked at her and shrugged, as if to say that he understood how she felt. In return for this gesture of almost genuine empathy, he received from the young woman a look of acute disdain. Ever hopeful all the same, Enzo gave her a sheepish grin, nodded at the cigarette in her hand, and held up his lighter.

"*Accendino?*" he said with all the charm he could muster.

It was not nearly enough, of course, and Serafina stomped away in a fury, spewing a trail of fearsome invective in her wake. Left holding the lighter, Enzo could only breathe a wistful sigh as he watched her go. Then he chuckled, gave her a farewell salute, and hurried off to the dance floor to catch up to his friends.

Chapter Four

What a night they had!

The dance floor of course belonged to Fabio and Caterina, who inevitably stole center stage the moment they stepped onto it. How could it have been otherwise? Caterina, lovely and sinuous and daring, was the perfect match for the dark and handsome Fabio. One look was enough to see the sensual chemistry between the pair, the electricity, the almost palpable heat rising from them as they whirled about, entwining and unwinding their bodies to the rhythm of the music. It was impossible not to watch them perform, and throughout the night the cheering revelers on the dance floor would step back and gather round in a circle just to watch the two spellbound dancers have their way with each other.

Fabio was exultant. Basking in the spotlight of attention, dancing with a vivacious young woman, he was in his element and loving every minute of it. All the while, though, he burned all the more for Caterina. She was everything he had dreamed she would be on the dance floor—he would have been happy to keep dancing with her forever—but at the same time he ached for the moment to finally come when they would be together somewhere alone at last wrapped in each other's arms. And so he took little heed of the others all gathered around, cheering them on, clapping in rhythm to the music. He was far too consumed with Caterina to care about them, far too mesmerized by her every seductive twist and spin, every tempting, provocative look. It was like being struck by lightning over and over again—and craving for more. On and on it went that way, far into the night, dancing and drinking, laughing and singing, the two reveling with all the others in Ferragosto's fast waning hours. Louder and louder the music played, the dancing growing wilder and wilder, the crowd whipped into a near frenzy of drinking and carousing, all of it building to a joyful, ecstatic crescendo.

And then, all at once, almost without warning it seemed, it was over. The music, despite the pleas for it to play on, died away. The DJ bid them all *buona notte* and on cue the bartenders took to clearing the glasses from the bar while the waiters hurried out to wipe down the tables and stack the chairs. The youthful crowd, at first seemingly stunned by this sudden cessation of events, stood dazed for a brief time, like people who had been roused from an exceedingly pleasant dream only to find themselves squinting into the harsh, glaring light of the morning sun. And then it dawned on all of them: Summer was gone. It was the end of Ferragosto, and time for them to go home.

Fabio and Caterina filed out of the club with the rest of the still boisterous crowd. With Enzo leading the way back to the car, the two leg-weary dancers straggled along, she walking barefoot, her shoes in one hand and in the other a half-empty bottle of vodka she had somehow managed to charm from one of the bartenders, while he ambled beside her, his arm around her waist.

For his part, Enzo still had a considerable spring in his gait for he had danced only once that entire night, and at that only reluctantly, after Caterina had tugged him up onto the floor. "What a night!" he laughed over his shoulder when he was finally installed behind the steering wheel of his car and the others had settled into the back seat together.

"*Veramente*," agreed Fabio.

'But ooh, my aching feet," moaned Caterina, curling her legs up onto the seat. She settled back, opened the vodka, and took a sip. "They're killing me," she said with a pout to Fabio before passing him the bottle.

Fabio downed a gulp of the liquor and then slowly ran a finger down her leg. "Why don't you let me rub them for you?" he suggested. Caterina smiled and uncoiled her bare legs, stretching them out across his lap while Fabio absent-mindedly passed the vodka forward to Enzo.

"No no, none for me, *grazie*," said his friend, waving away the bottle. "You two enjoy."

"Then how about some music for the ride?" said Fabio.

"*Si*, Enzo,"said Caterina. "Something *allegra*."

Enzo obliged them by turning on the radio. When he had found a suitably lively song for Caterina to sing to, he started the car and pulled out onto the road, trying all the while to keep his eyes straight ahead as he began the long drive back through the mountains.

*

Up and up the car climbed, all the while the three laughing and singing along with the songs playing on the radio. But by the time the car made the long journey over the pass between the mountains and began to head downhill, only Enzo was left humming to himself alone in the front seat.

In the back, the vodka bottle lay empty on the floor, clinking and rolling about at Fabio's feet. Fabio was only vaguely aware of it and equally so of the thick blanket of fog outdoors that had thrown itself across the landscape, obscuring all but a small bubble of ill-illumined pavement directly in the car's path. He knew, somewhere in the back of his mind, that they were already riding down the long winding descent that led to the valley below and the road to Mont'Oliva. And he also knew that Enzo, his dependable *capitano*, had driven this road a thousand times. They were in good hands and there was nothing to worry about, so Fabio forgot about Enzo and the fog and the road, and simply let himself be held captive by Caterina, who had taken his own hand in hers and begun one by one to kiss his fingers. When she was done she gave his hand a squeeze, gently pulled herself towards him, and brought her mouth to his ear.

"*Mi ami?*" she whispered. "Do you love me?"

Fabio did not hesitate.

"*Si,*" he whispered in return, pulling her ever closer.

From the vantage point of the front seat, Fabio and Caterina were but silhouettes in the rearview mirror. However, it did not take a particularly vivid imagination to conjecture that an intimate exchange of one sort or another was transpiring in the back seat, and so Enzo, to afford the two lovers at least some modicum of privacy—and perhaps as well to keep himself awake—turned up the volume on the radio and tried anew not to look at the two darkened forms behind him that kept merging into one.

"*Mi ami?*" Caterina asked Fabio once more.

"*Si,*" he told her again. "You're so beautiful."

Caterina smiled and pressed herself against him, letting his hands roam wherever they might. "We're so beautiful together," she breathed. "Will you take me with you when you go to America?"

"I will take you with me wherever I go," he promised her. "We will always be together."

At that Caterina took his face in her hands and kissed him. Then she pulled away and sat upright. With eyes closed, she arched her head back and began to softly sing along with the radio while her body gently swayed to the rhythm of the music and the motion of the car.

Fabio felt blissfully weak all over. Though Caterina was

clearly losing control of herself, she had complete control of him. He was in her spell now and there was nothing for him to do about it—even if he had wanted to. And so he was helpless to resist when she opened her eyes once more and pushed his shoulders forcefully back into the seat.

"*Mi ami?*" she asked again, holding herself over him.

"You know I do," he told her, straining to bring his mouth to hers.

"Tell me," she insisted.

"*Ti amo*," said Fabio.

"Then show me," said Caterina. With that she sat upright again, stretched her slender arms around herself and began to peel off her top.

Down the hill the car sped.

Given the spectacle unfolding behind him, the silky brush of Caterina's hair falling against his shoulder as she leaned back against his seat, her lovely back and shoulders lit by the soft glow from the dashboard, the smell of her perfume, the music thumping on the radio, who could blame Enzo when he found he could not resist stealing a peek in the rearview mirror at the precise moment the car was careening down the hill past the sign warning them of the approaching junction?

It was just at that same moment, when he chanced to see Enzo's eyes in the mirror, that Fabio suddenly came back to himself and, looking past his friend and through the front windshield, saw a glimpse of the fog-shrouded sign whiz by. It would take him another moment, a moment they did not have, to realize that they had reached the bottom of the hill and the road out of Mont'Oliva where they would have to turn right or left, but before he could open his mouth, before he could cry out to warn his friend, *il muro* sprang into view—and poor Enzo drove straight.

The Wall of Truth

CHAPTER FIVE

"So, what do you think?" Joe was saying to no one in particular as he took the knife in hand and considered the bread roll lying on the cutting board before him. "Is it better to be an optimist, or a pessimist?"

When no one in particular responded, he plunged the knife into the roll, splitting its golden brown crust down the middle. Just out of the oven, its insides still steaming, the roll released its scent into the air already redolent with the warm, mouth-watering aroma of freshly baked bread. Barely cognizant of this olfactory delight—after six hours of breathing it in, a certain degree of habituation was to be expected—Joe began with practiced efficiency to swiftly layer the roll with provolone cheese, sliced capicola, soprasetta, and other cold cuts. When he had finished this initial phase of the sandwich's construction, he paused and turned his head slightly, inclining his ear to better hear. "Anyone?" he said aloud over his shoulder, still hopeful of a response to the question he had posited. When none was forthcoming, he turned from the cutting board and with arms crossed looked over the counter top.

It was lunchtime at his little submarine sandwich shop and a line of patrons patiently waiting to place their orders or to pick up ones they might have phoned in stretched to the door.

A sizable assemblage of Friday regulars, jabbering away while they enjoyed their sandwiches, was already squeezed in and around the odd—a kind person might say eclectic—collection of mismatched tables and chairs that served as the establishment's furnishings. Obtained over the years from yard sales and second hand stores, or occasionally snatched from the junk pile, the used furniture lent an air of comfortable dilapidation to the place. With its ancient hardwood floor and dark, elaborately detailed woodwork, the scratched and faded remnants of a bygone era, the eatery was illuminated only modestly well by two long panels of florescent lights dangling high overhead from an equally cracked and faded ceiling. A decided dinginess might have prevailed had it not been for the shop's two large front windows through which an ample flow of early afternoon sunlight inevitably streamed. Looking out as they did onto the sidewalk running the length of Main Street, the windows afforded those sitting by them an excellent view of the passing cars and the people coming and going through town. It was not the Ritz, but all in all it was as congenial a spot to enjoy one's midday repast as any to be found in downtown Wakefield, Rhode Island.

Joe, a wiry fellow with a grizzled angular face framed by a thin crop of almost pure white hair, scratched his chin in puzzlement while he considered the gathering before him. "What do you think, Pete?" he said, turning to his young assistant working behind him on the other counter.

Pete, who was himself busy preparing an eggplant sub, did not look up from his work. "What do I think about what?" he said absentmindedly as he wrapped the finished sandwich in wax paper.

"Is it better to be an optimist or a pessimist?" Joe said.

Pete glanced across the counter at the young lady awaiting the sandwich and rolled his eyes. "Every day it's something," he lamented, shaking his head as he handed it over to her.

"Come on," Joe prodded him. "Tell me what you think."

"Ask me if I care, Joe," Pete replied with a huff as he nodded for the next customer to step up to the counter.

"Do you care...Joe?" said the shop owner.

"Don't ask," sighed Pete. "I'm busy."

Joe gave a sigh of his own, leaned his elbows on the counter top, and looked out across the room. On the far wall hung a piece of paper with the words "WALL OF TRUTH" scribbled on it. All about the paper were tacked dozens of other scraps, some curled and yellow from age, bearing proverbs and snippets of wisdom taken from philosophers famous and obscure. Joe considered the collection of pith for a time before turning to his customers. "How about you guys?" he called to get their attention.

"How about what?" answered one of them, a dark-complexioned man with a mane of black and silver hair pulled back into a ponytail.

"Is it better to be an optimist or a pessimist?"

"I'm beginning to grow pessimistic that you will ever finish making my sandwich anytime soon," the man replied.

"Don't worry, Dave," Joe told him, pleased that someone had finally taken the bait. "I'm almost done, but tell me what you think. Which is better?"

"I'm an Indian," Dave replied, "so I always expect the worse. It's better that way."

"Oh, come on, Dave," said Joe with a dismissive wave of his hand. "What's being an Indian got to do with it?"

"It's got everything to do with it!" exclaimed Dave, suddenly growing visibly agitated. "How else is a man supposed to look at things after his people get all but annihilated and their lands are stolen from them?"

"But that was back in what, the seventeenth century when all that happened to the Narragansetts?" Joe pointed out calmly. "Why not just move on and leave it alone in the past?"

"What, is there an expiration date on injustice?" Dave griped, looking about for support from his fellow lunch patrons.

"Should we all just forget about history and pretend that it didn't happen? You know, it wasn't your land that was stolen, not your people who were slaughtered. You'd think different if it was—white man."

"You know, he's got a point there, Joe," said Tommy, one of the regulars at another table. The sentiment was echoed by more than one in the predominately non-Native American gathering.

Joe stood there, impassively taking in the bray of public opinion that seemed to have turned against him. He let it continue unabated for a short while before finally holding up a hand for quiet. "Okay, Tommy," he finally conceded, "maybe Dave does have a point. But let me ask you all a question. How far back do we get to go with injustices?"

"What do you mean?" said Dave, eyeing the sandwich maker suspiciously.

"I mean what's the statute of limitations?"

"What do you mean by 'statute of limitations'?" said Tommy, eyeing his sandwich more closely than its maker, before taking another bite.

"Well, look at my family," Joe began. " *My* people on my father's side descended from the Abruzzesi. Two thousand years ago they fought against the Romans for over a century to keep *their* freedom and *their* lands, and do you know what happened when they finally lost?"

"No," grumbled Dave, "but I'm sure you're going to tell us."

"That's right, I am going to tell you," said Joe with great conviction, wagging his finger at all who were bothering to pay attention. "First they burned every village to the ground. Then they crucified every man and boy over the age of ten and left them hanging all along the road leading out of the mountains. When they were done doing that, they enslaved everybody else who was left standing. So tell me, what am I supposed to do now? Should I hop on a plane and fly to Rome, go to court and sue Silvio Berlusconi for reparations? Should I hang my head all my life about an injustice done to my people so long ago that no one remembers? *Or* should I just accept that bad things happen sometimes in life and try to look on the bright side, maybe try thinking 'gee, that was bad what happened all those years ago, but maybe things happen for a reason, maybe if things hadn't worked out the way they did, I might never be here in America enjoying the life that I have now'."

Tommy mulled the matter over a moment before throwing his hands up in surrender. "You know, I guess he's got a point too," he said to the others. A murmur of reluctant acknowledgment rippled through the gathering.

Dave lowered his gaze and scowled at Joe. "There are times," he said in a low, menacing growl, "when I really don't like you."

"Eh, I know," said Joe with a shrug. "That's just because you're a pessimist. Forget about it." He held up the sub. "You want some hot peppers on this?"

"Please," answered Dave, his ire of a moment earlier somewhat dissipated at the prospect of his sandwich's completion. "But just a few, not like last time. You almost killed me. I thought my throat was on fire."

"I'll be careful," promised Joe. Then, as he went back to finishing the sandwich, "So, anybody else got an opinion?"

There were several, and so a lively debate—one in which every rule of order was ignored—soon ensued.

Later, after the lunchtime rush was over and things had quieted down once more, Joe took a towel to wipe down the tables while Pete cleaned up in the back. Before getting started he wandered out the front door and stood for a moment on the sidewalk, breathing in the bracing air of that brisk November day before taking a seat at one of the outdoor tables. Across from him at the same table sat the sole remaining customer at the shop. An older gentleman of more or less his own age, he had stayed outside despite the chilly air, hidden behind the pages of the newspaper throughout most of the earlier proceedings inside.

"It's not so cold out here as I'd thought it would be," said Joe, looking up at the sky. "It's actually rather pleasant here in the sun." Then, when this remark elicited no response, "Any good news?"

"Haven't found any yet, Joe," came the reply from behind the still raised paper. "But I haven't given up hope."

"Ah, there's always hope, isn't there, Rick," said Joe with a wistful air.

At that Enrico "Rick" Vitale folded the newspaper, put it aside, and pondered for a moment the depths of his coffee cup. "I suppose that's what an optimist would say," he replied before downing the last few drops of lukewarm brew at its bottom. Then, setting the cup down, he gave a chuckle and added, "The gang raised quite a racket today. You really had them going for a while in there."

"Eh, things were a little too quiet for my taste," said Joe. "I figured it was time to liven things up a bit." He gestured to the newspaper. "May I?"

"Of course," said Rick, sliding it over to him.

"But why did you stay out here?" asked Joe as he glanced over the headlines. "I kept waiting for you to poke your head inside to add your two cents like you usually do. What's the matter, things on your mind today?"

Rick shrugged. "Sometimes I don't bother when it gets too animated, that's all," he said. "I just like to sit back and listen."

"I know what you mean," said Joe, still scanning the front page. "Besides, it can be hard to get a word in edgewise sometimes when the crew gets worked up."

"Sometimes it's just as well if you don't," Rick observed. "How does that saying go? Better to be silent and only thought an old fool..."

"Ha! Then to speak up and remove all doubt?" laughed Joe. "Are you trying to tell me something, *paesan'*?"

"Not me, Giuseppe," Rick chuckled in return. "You're the

wisest man I know in Wakefield."

"Hmm, that's a wonderfully evasive answer, if ever I heard one," said Joe, opening wide the pages of the paper to get a look inside. "You could have been a lawyer. I think maybe you missed your calling."

"I've missed more than one," mused Rick, once again pondering his empty coffee cup.

"You want a refill for that?" said Joe from behind the paper.

Rick shook his head in bemusement. "How do you do that?"

"It's my business. So do you want some more coffee, or not?"

"Nah, no thanks," he said. "But tell me, that story about the Romans crucifying the Abruzzi men. I'm not sure I recall reading about that in the history books when I was in school. Was that really true?"

Joe refolded the paper, slid it back to Rick, and gave a shrug. "I'm a Jew from Brooklyn, so how would I know?" he said, a mischievous twinkle in his eye. "You're the one who grew up in Italy. You tell me."

"You're going to get yourself into a great deal of trouble one of these days," noted Rick.

"Bah," huffed Joe with a dismissive wave. "Sufficient are the troubles of this day—or however that goes."

"I rest my case."

Just then from overhead came the honking and gaggling of a flock of Canadian geese, their formation a perfect V against the equally perfect blue of the sky. Both men fell silent for a time, regarding the noisy bunch until they had flapped their way out of sight to the south.

"Sounds like they're having a good time up there wherever it is they're going," mused Joe with a little sigh. "Kind of makes you wish you could fly away with them, doesn't it?"

"Why, where would I fly to?" replied Rick.

"I don't know, maybe home to Italy where you came from.

What's it been, forty years since you were back there?"

"Forty-two," said Rick.

"That's a long time to be away from home."

"My home is here now," said Rick. "I've lived much more of my life in America than in Italy."

"I know," said Joe. "But you know I still often wonder why you've never gone back. What happened? Did you abscond with the church funds? Did you run away with a senator's wife? I'd like to think you killed a man, it's the romantic in me."

"Take your pick, Louie," said a non-committal Rick.

Joe gave a satisfied chuckle. "But what on earth ever made you come to little out of the way Wakefield of all places?" he asked, continuing the allusion.

"The mountains," Rick explained. "I love skiing in the winters."

"Mountains? What mountains?" scoffed Joe with feigned incredulity. "The closest ones are a hundred miles away!"

"I was misinformed."

At that, Joe's face broke out in a wide grin. "You see, that's why you're my favorite customer," he said. "You always play along. It's the reason I give you free refills of coffee whenever you come in."

"I thought it was because *I* give you a third off of everything at my shop when *you* come in."

"That is another reason," admitted Joe. "So, how are things at your place, now that you bring it up?"

"Eh," grunted Rick, "the same, only more so." He looked at his watch and grimaced. "I need to get back soon. I've got someone coming in to interview."

"Hiring again?" said Joe, his eyebrows raised in surprise. "Glad to see you're doing your part for the economy." Then, with a hint of disdain in his voice, he added, "What's the matter, things not working out with that other one you took in last year?"

"Oh no, nothing like that," explained Rick, a bit wearily.

"He's doing fine—sort of. It's just that with Christmas coming, I'll need some help behind the counter, watching the cash register, keeping the books, that sort of thing." He paused for a moment and looked up to the sky as if expecting another flock of geese to pass. "And besides that," he went on, "I need somebody to help me start getting things organized."

"Organized for what?"

"So maybe I can pass the business on to someone else someday," said Rick. "I'm getting old, you know, I can't keep doing this forever."

"Hmm," answered Joe, nodding thoughtfully as he looked through the shop window to the back where Pete was still cleaning up. "I know what you mean. All good things must come to an end sooner or later, I suppose. But you know, it wouldn't be the same around here without you."

"You could say that about any of us."

"Very true," said Joe. "That's just life, I guess."

"There's more to life than life," observed Rick.

"Hey, I like that one," laughed Joe, getting to his feet. "I think I'll put that one up on the wall." He nodded once more to the coffee cup. "Sure you don't want a refill?"

Rick shook his head.

"Good, 'cause I didn't feel like getting back up to get it."

"But you are back up."

"Only technically speaking."

At that Rick pushed away from the table and stood as well. "Well, on that note," he said with a chuckle, "I guess it's back to the grindstone."

"Where else would we go?" said Joe with a shrug. He gave Rick a nod and a wink. "See you next time. Maybe then you can tell me the real reason why you never go back to Italy. "

"Maybe," said Rick. "And maybe then you can tell me how an Italian Jew from Brooklyn ended up hiding out in South County, making sandwiches."

"Ahh," answered Joe, laying a finger aside his nose. "Now that is a really good story..."

CHAPTER SIX

On any other day Rick might have been inclined to stay and hear Joe's story, but there was a loan officer waiting to hear his own story at the bank up the street, and Rick was disinclined to annoy him by arriving late for their appointment. It had been a lackluster year for Rick's business, a glassblowing operation he ran just a few doors down from Joe's place. With the much prayed-for Christmas shopping season yet to come, it required a not small infusion of cash to help tide things over. Rick hated borrowing money; just the thought of owing more than he could afford to pay back at that particular moment gave him a knot in his stomach. Then there was the loan application process which would entail the rather painful but requisite examination of his decidedly precarious financial situation. He was looking forward to it with as much enthusiasm as he would a visit to the dentist. All the same, having faced difficult times before, he understood that he had no choice but to bite the bullet for a little while and hold down the fort until the cavalry came to the rescue in December.

With the chill autumn breeze at his back, nudging him on, he reluctantly left the sandwich shop and walked up Main Street at a brisk gait, escorted as he went by an entourage of dry fallen leaves. As he made his way up the hill toward the bank, Rick looked down with momentary delight at them as they scratched and skittered and swirled along the sidewalk at his feet. There was, he had discovered over the years since he had first come to live in New England, something strangely irresistible in the sound of fallen leaves rushing ahead of the wind. He found in it a sort of exuberance that reminded him for some reason of children at play, and listening to them frolic was as much an autumnal pleasure to him as seeing the trees in all their fiery splendor. The sound, as it often did, set him in a better mood, for it reminded him that with every change of season there were always things great and small to which he could look forward. As he rounded the bend on his way to the bank, however, the happy spell cast by this pedestrian diversion was summarily broken when just then, from across the street, Rick's ears were assaulted by the mechanized wail of a landscaper's leaf blower.

Rick stopped dead in his tracks and scowled for a brief time at man and machine.

Oblivious to his onlooker, his own ears shielded from the obnoxious clamor by a set of ear protectors, the culprit of this outrage went about his business in an apparent state of blissful ignorance of the auditory havoc he was wreaking. Most maddening to Rick was the certainty that the landscaper's purpose in blowing about the leaves might have been accomplished with equal expedience, less cost, and far greater civility by the use of a good old-fashioned rake. For a fleeting moment he entertained a notion of crossing the street to impart this insight to the offender, but then with a sigh of resignation he let it go. The leaf blower's distressing noise was, he lamented within, simply a reminder that with the coming of each new season there were also things great and small to dread. That melancholy thought in mind, he acknowledged with only a desultory wave the tooting horn of a passing motorist, and trudged on to his meeting with the loan officer.

Later, despite having adequately secured his business

finances through the end of the year, Rick exited the bank feeling only slightly less uneasy about things than he had upon entering. He was, however, pleased to find that at least the landscaper had moved on, taking with him his mechanized horror to annoy the denizens of some other part of town. Heartened by that small blessing, he breathed a little sigh of relief and started along the sidewalk toward the bicycle shop just down the road. When he arrived, Rick walked past the main entrance and around the corner to the side of the building where he came in through the back door to the service area. There inside, a trio of young mechanics was busy at work, assembling a shipment of new bicycles while they kibitzed among themselves about whatever topic happened to have captured their interest that day.

"Hey!" cried one of them with mock indignation at seeing Rick enter. "Can't you read the sign on the door? That entrance is for employee use only!"

Rick held his hands up in a defensive gesture. "Oh, sorry, boys," he replied with equally feigned humility. "I'm just here to apply for a job. They said the applications were back here."

"Oh no," moaned one of the other two young men. "Don't tell me we're gonna have to train another newbie."

"Ha!" scoffed Rick. "Are you kidding? I've forgotten more about bicycles than you three combined will ever know."

At that the trio broke into laughter.

"So, where's your boss?" said Rick when they settled down. "I'm in a hurry, and we've got business to talk about."

"In the back, getting ready to go out for a ride," said the third of the group, getting to his feet. He leaned his head through the doorway to the storage area in the back and gave a call. "Hey, Eddie! Rick's here to see you."

"Tell him to go away," came the reply from the back room.

"Tell him I've got money for him," Rick called back.

"In that case, I'll be right out!"

The cleats of his bicycle shoes clomping against the

floorboards, Eddie emerged from the back room dressed in cycling shorts and shirt. He pulled on a wind jacket and nodded a greeting to Rick while he fumbled with the zipper.

Rick nodded in return. "It's a little brisk out there today," he said, gesturing to the shop owner's legs. "You might want to think about pulling on some leg warmers."

Eddie looked down for a moment at his lower extremities and grinned. "What for?" he said. "I haven't shaved my legs in weeks."

"Then maybe for aesthetic reasons?" Rick offered.

Eddie gave a dismissive wave. "Who do I look like, Martha Stewart?" he said. Then, with his helmet and sunglasses in hand, he beckoned for Rick to follow, and the two walked out to the front of the store. There Eddie went behind the counter and ducked down behind the cash register while Rick cast a quick eye about at the row of new bicycles anxiously awaiting their chance to take to the road. One of the bikes, a lovely red Specialized Allez caught his eye. Rick stepped closer and considered for a time its compact, tapered frame and carbon fiber fork before running his hand across the smooth, gleaming finish of the top tube. Curling a finger underneath, he easily lifted the bike a few inches off the floor. An avid cyclist—when he had the time—Rick still rode the steel frame bicycle he had purchased from that same shop nearly thirty years earlier. In its day, it was considered one of the lightest, sleekest bikes on the market, but compared to this one, his was morbidly obese.

"So, how's business?" said Rick, setting the bike back down in its stand.

Eddie straightened back up, clutching a hefty file folder across the top of which were scrawled the words "Cross Race". He gave a grunt at the query and rolled his eyes. "Same as everybody else," he said, setting the file folder atop the counter. "Waiting around for Christmas to come. I'm just hoping Santa don't leave me a lump of coal in December, if you know what I mean."

"I do indeed," replied Rick with a grunt of his own. Then, brightening, "But I wouldn't worry too much about it. You've been a good boy this year, haven't you?"

"Well, mostly," admitted Eddie with a laugh. "But I have had my moments."

"We've all had our share."

Eddie nodded to the Allez. "So, what do you think?" he said. "Time to trade in that old Bianchi and finally get something new?"

"Are you kidding?" said Rick. "My bicycle is a very jealous lady, you know. She would never talk to me again if she found out that I was even thinking about a new bike."

"Well, I certainly wouldn't want you to do anything behind her back," said Eddie with a respectful nod of understanding. "But you do know she is a little past her prime.

"Yeah, maybe," said Rick. "But I think the old girl's still got a few more miles left in her."

"Okay," said Eddie. "In that case, how about a new saddle? Yours was looking a little on the worn side last time I saw you ride."

Rick gave him a sideways look. "You aren't trying to wrangle some business out of me while I'm here, are you?" he said.

Eddie shrugged. "You did say that you had brought money."

"That I did," Rick replied. "But alas..." He gave a sigh and gestured to the file folder.

"Ah, I thought as much," said Eddie with a sigh of his own. From the file folder he pulled out a large white envelope upon which was scribbled the word "Sponsors". "So, what's it gonna be this year?"

Rick gave a shrug. "What have you got?"

"Still plenty of space for your banner along the barriers near the start finish, same as last year," Eddie told him. "Those spots are going for two-fifty, but for you we can make it an even two-fifty."

"Who could pass up such a deal?" said Rick, tugging his checkbook from his back pocket.

"More people than you think," said Eddie. "Especially these days. But I'm just kidding about the two-fifty. You help us out every year. Just give me whatever you can and we'll make sure you get a good spot."

Rick opened the checkbook and discreetly wrote out a check for three hundred dollars. He tore the check from the book and folded it in two. "There you go," he said, handing it over to Eddie. "Direct from Peter to Paul."

"How's that?"

"Never mind, inside joke," said Rick. "So tell me, who gets the loot this year?"

"Oh, the usual suspects," Eddie replied. "Some to the Community Food Bank, some to the heating assistance fund, the rest to the kids for Christmas toys."

Rick smiled. "You're a good man to be doing this race every year," he said. "I know it's a lot of work."

"You're a good man to be supporting it," said Eddie, dropping the check into the envelope. "By the way, sponsors get to race for free, you know. Why don't you give it a try this year?"

Rick shook his head. "Thanks, but I don't think so."

"Come on," Eddie prodded him. "It'll be fun."

"Yeah, like getting drawn and quartered," snickered Rick. "Besides, I haven't ridden much lately, and I don't have a 'cross bike."

"You can use mine," said Eddie. "You've got three weeks. That's plenty of time to get some riding in and practice your technique. You know we added a C race for beginners and riders of...shall we say...a certain age?"

"And what age might that be?" said Rick with a skeptical look in his eye.

"Old enough to know better," Eddie admitted.

"Well, maybe I'll give it some thought," said Rick. "But meantime I've got to back to the salt mines."

"And I've got to get out on the road," said Eddie, grabbing his helmet. He turned and ducked his head into the service area. "Hey! Huey, Dewey, and Louie!" he called in. "You guys are in charge."

"Yeah, right, Boss," came a snide response.

Eddie looked at Rick and rolled his eyes. "It's wonderful to be respected by your employees, isn't it?" he said.

At that he pulled on his helmet and the two men walked out the front door to the sidewalk where Eddie's bike was stationed with its front wheel resting atop a rack with several others. Eddie lifted the bike from the rack and leaned it against the building.

"Say, how are things going, clearing out your second floor?" he asked as he put on his sunglasses.

"Ugh, it's still a disaster up there," said Rick ruefully. "What makes you ask?"

Eddie gave a shrug. "I could use some extra space for inventory, that is if you're ever looking to rent it out."

"I might be," said Rick. "I'll let you know." He watched Eddie swing a leg over the bicycle and clip his shoe into the pedal. "So, where are you going?" he asked.

"Just out for an hour to clear my head," said Eddie. "Doesn't really matter where. I just let the bike make the decisions."

"Sounds nice," said Rick. "Maybe next time I'll join you."

"Anytime," said Eddie. With that he stood up on the pedal and began to roll away. "Thanks for the check!" he called over his shoulder.

Rick waved in return as he watched him ride away. Then, taking a deep breath, he turned his face to the sun for a moment before starting back at last to the shop.

CHAPTER SEVEN

Empty windows.

It was hard for Rick to ignore them. They were like lonely, desperate eyes following him as he made his way back down Main Street. It was not the worst of times, not quite, but it certainly wasn't the best for life along this little thoroughfare through his tiny corner of the universe. He had, of course, witnessed it all before more than once, the "space available" and "for lease" signs on the storefront windows, the sudden closure of long-established businesses, the spirit of doubt that seemed to descend like a dark cloud and take up residence in their place. The bakery, the jewelry store, the old department store down the street, and others, all of them once tightly woven into the patchwork fabric of the town, all of them simply torn away, leaving gaping holes in need of mending. But where was the thread? Who held the needle?

Rick stopped for a moment at the bend in the road and looked out across the village to the cross on the church steeple rising over the bony branches of the treetops on the far hill. He knew in his heart that somehow things were being renewed, that everything was going to turn out as it was meant to, but it was growing harder by the day to hold on to that confidence. America's strength, he had learned long ago, was its unflinching ability to tear things down that needed tearing down, and to build them up all over again from scratch. And yet, looking about at the charming old buildings lining the streets that he had come to love—mere babies by Italian standards—he could not dismiss the nervous pang of anxiety in the pit of his gut, the unspeakable fear that perhaps something more profound was happening, that something irretrievable was being lost. What, he wondered, would be torn down next? What was meant to endure? Deep inside, the wiser part of him knew the true answer to those questions, but the soft voice of wisdom was sometimes all but impossible to hear above the din of daily life. Resolving that he must try harder to listen to it, he turned his eyes once more to the cross in the distance, gave a respectful nod, and resumed his trek down the sidewalk toward the bottom of the hill where stood the little two-story building that served as the home of Vita Glassworks.

As he crossed the street to the shop, Rick saw a young woman standing outside the front door, peering in through the window. "Hello there," he called to her pleasantly.

The sound of his voice must have taken the young woman by surprise for she turned around with a start. A knit hat atop her head, her hands buried deep in the pockets of an overcoat that seemed more appropriate for mid-winter than a brisk autumn day, she made no reply but stood there with her shoulders hunched up against the breeze. As he drew near, she watched him with a steady, inquisitive gaze. Set against the dark brown skin of her face, the off-white frames of the eyeglasses she wore brought her eyes into prominence, giving her a bookish, almost clinical look, as if she were observing him from behind a microscope.

"I'm sorry," said Rick. "I didn't mean to startle you. Is the door locked?"

Still she made no reply, but simply nodded. Then in a soft, almost meek voice she asked, "Are you Mister Vitale?"

"I am," he told her.

"I am Elise Celestin," she said just loud enough for him to recognize the accent in her voice. "I've come to see you about the office position."

"Ah yes, Miss Celestin," said Rick, smiling warmly. "I've been expecting you, but you're a little early. I'm sorry if I have kept you waiting outside. You look a bit chilly."

"I haven't been waiting long, just a minute or two," she replied with a noticeable shiver. Then, with the first hint of a smile, she added, "But yes, it is a little chilly for me today."

"Then let's get inside," said Rick. "I guarantee you'll be much more comfortable there."

He unlocked the door and showed her in. The two were instantly greeted by a rush of sultry air.

"The furnace in the back," said Rick by way of explanation as he closed the door behind them. "I have a pupil working for me who's probably there right now. He usually locks the door when he's working alone and there's no one out front here to watch the shop." He led her toward the counter and gestured for her to take a seat on one of the two stools stationed in front of it. "I have an office," he told her, nodding to the door on the opposite side of the counter, "but in its present condition it's probably better if we talk out here." Then he excused himself and left her for a moment to retrieve from his desktop the resumé and cover letter she had sent him.

When he returned, Rick found both stools empty. He looked across the room and saw Elise on the other side of the shop. Dressed neatly in dark wool slacks and a plain sweater top, her coat clutched under arm, she was wandering about, looking over the glassware on display. Rick watched the young woman for a brief time, unable to keep himself from trying, as artists inevitably do, to assess her reaction to his work as she moved methodically from one shelf to the next. She moved slowly, her gaze seeming to take in each and every piece: the finely detailed vases and bowls, the whimsical bunches of grapes and strawberries, the colorful glass fish, and the ornate Venetian style decanters and matching goblets which were one of Rick's specialties. To his disappointment, as was usually the case, he found that he could discern little from her countenance. He soon gave up trying and came out to the front of the counter with the resumé and letter in hand.

"So, Elise Celestin," he said, taking a seat as she roamed out of view behind one of the display shelves, "when we spoke on the telephone I supposed from your name and accent that you might be Canadian, but your aversion to cold weather tells me otherwise."

"I am Haitian," came the reply from behind the shelf.

"I suppose that explains it," said Rick. He was about to ask her how long she had been in America when she suddenly reappeared.

"I like the Christmas ornaments and the little Nativity figures you've made," she said brightly. "They're lovely."

"Thank you," said Rick, pleased by this pronouncement. "I try to make a selection of the ornaments every year, they're quite easy for me actually. The crèche figurines are a little more of a challenge for me, though. I never feel like I've gotten them just right." He gave a little laugh. "You'd think that after all these years I would have perfected my technique with them. "

"I think they're wonderful," she said. "When did you start making glass?"

"Oh, long ago in another life," said Rick with another chuckle.

"How did you learn how to do it?"

Rick smiled inwardly at the question. For all the young woman's apparent timidity when he had first encountered her, it seemed for all the world that she was interviewing him instead of the other way around. He didn't mind—in truth he found it charming—so he gave a little sigh, arched his eyebrows, and shrugged. "My father was a glassblower back in Italy where I grew up," he told her. " *His* father was a glassblower, and so was his father before him. So..."

"So, you're carrying on the family business?"

"You might say that," said Rick.

"That's nice," said Elise. She started toward the counter, but then a shelf she had missed near the front door caught her attention. She drifted over to it and stood there for a moment, examining the small collection of pieces on display there. She reached out and touched one of them, an oddly contorted form of red and yellow hue. Others of similarly abstract style stood by it, strange twisted creations that were beautiful, but in a confused, angry sort of way. "These are really unusual," she said, her eyes showing a spark of true interest. "They are much different from your other work."

Rick cleared his throat. "That's because they are not mine," he told her. "They were done by my pupil, the one I spoke of earlier. As you can see, he has a slightly different muse than mine, but he's something of a prodigy—I think."

Elise leaned closer to the shelf. "These look almost like people," she noted, running her fingers across another of the pieces. "It's like they are trying to pull themselves out of the glass. How interesting."

"Hmm, I never thought of that before," said Rick. "But I think you might be right."

At that Elise came and took a seat on the stool opposite him. "I love your shop," she said. "Everything is so beautiful."

"Thank you," said Rick with a smile. "I just hope the shoppers next month feel the same way—if you know what I mean." With that he tugged a pair of reading glasses from his pocket, slipped them on his face, and held up the resumé. "And that, in a roundabout way," he said as he began to look it over, "is why I put the ad in the paper that brought you here today."

"Have you interviewed a lot of people for it already?" asked Elise, her voice betraying a tinge of worry. "I know there are many like me looking for work."

"You're my first," Rick told her. He felt somewhat abashed to let on that she had also been the sole respondent to the help wanted ad he had placed—a matter that puzzled him greatly given the state of the job market—so he quickly turned the conversation back to his young job applicant.

"So, tell me about yourself," Rick said. "You say that you are Haitian. That means you are an immigrant, just like myself. When did you come here?"

"When I was a teenager," answered Elise. "I came to live with my aunt in Providence." She paused, as if composing herself to tell him more, but then fell silent and fussed uneasily with the coat resting on her lap.

"And you haven't become accustomed to the cold weather yet?" Rick jested. "I'm surprised."

"No, I'm still not used to it yet," said Elise with a shy smile before falling silent once again.

Sensing her reticence to discuss further the subject of her coming to America, Rick turned his attention back to the resumé. "Well, I see that you have a degree in sociology from the university, which you received last spring," he said. "I must admit that when I placed the ad I was hoping to hire someone with more of an accounting background."

Elise was ready with a quick reply. "If you look under my experience," she pointed out, "I did work for a manufacturer in Providence as an office clerk one summer while I was going to school. I learned all the basic office functions and how to use the accounting software. I'm good with numbers."

"Yes, I did notice all that on your resumé," said Rick. "It was one of the reasons I thought I would ask you to come in." He had indeed told the truth, or at least half of it, the other reason being of course that no one else had applied. "But I must ask," he went on, "why would you want to come all this way from Providence, where you live, to work as a bookkeeper when it's not what you studied?"

"I would like to work as a social worker someday," she admitted. "But right now there are very few jobs and I need to work." She paused before adding, "As to coming from Providence, I like this area, it's different from the city, so I don't mind the ride."

"Ha," said Rick, grinning. "That means you're not a true Rhode Islander yet. Just wait. It will come to seem much farther to you someday after you've lived here a while longer. It seems to happen to everybody in this little state."

"Maybe," she said demurely.

Rick took another look at the resumé then set it aside. "I suppose I should tell you a little about the position," he said. "You say under your qualifications that you have excellent organizational skills. I must confess that that is something I myself lack." This he said, nodding to office behind him where, with the door now ajar, one could see a glimpse of papers, envelopes, and cardboard boxes strewn all about. Then, nodding upward with a rueful sigh, he added, "And it's much worse upstairs. So in between watching the cash register and getting my books and office in order, I need someone to help me go through my old records and throw out what's not important up there before the weight of it all collapses the floor and the ceiling comes crashing down on top of all this nice glass."

He stopped, gave her a questioning look, and shrugged by way of asking what she thought of the situation. A prolonged moment of silence ensued.

"I can help," she said softly, but with an unmistakable air of pleading determination in her tone, and more so in her eyes. "When would you want for me to begin?"

Rick gave a nervous cough. "Well, I was hoping to have someone start the week after next, the Monday before Thanksgiving," he said vaguely, "but of course I've only just begun to interview applicants."

He had offered this last remark mostly as a gesture to his own ego, but it struck him through to see the crestfallen look it had produced in the young woman's eyes. Unsure of what to say next, Rick sat there for a time, rubbing his chin thoughtfully as he turned the matter over in his head. He had been in earnest when he told her earlier that he had hoped to hire someone with more of an accounting background, but the more he considered things the more he realized that the mere fact that she seemed to truly like the store resonated with him in some inexplicable way. Though his inner businessman urged him to wait, perhaps run another ad and see if someone more qualified came along, the artist inside told him not to bother. And so, after letting the two debate the issue for a few moments more, he at last took a deep breath and let it out with a low grumble.

"You know from the ad that I'm not offering much of a salary," he gently warned her. "No one is going to get rich working for me."

"I don't need to be rich," said Elise simply. "I just need a job."

Rick hesitated.

"When do you think you will be making a final decision?" she asked.

Rick gave a sigh of resignation. "I think I already have," he told her. Then, leaning in her direction, he gave her a sideways look. "How would you like to work for Vita Glassworks?"

Elise was beaming. "I would like that very much, Mister Vitale," she replied.

"Then it's done," he said. "And you may call me Rick."

"Thank you, Mister Rick," she gushed.

"No," he laughed, "just plain old—"

Before he could finish they were interrupted by a great commotion coming from the small darkened hallway on the other side of the shop that led to the back of the building. They heard the sound of someone cursing, the precise words incomprehensible through the walls, followed close thereafter by the distinct sound of breaking glass. The tumult startled Elise, and she spun around to see what was happening behind her.

For his part, Rick remained more or less unperturbed. He did, however, give a little groan and roll his eyes. "That reminds me," he said. "I should probably introduce you to my pupil, your future co-worker."

No sooner had he spoken when the door at the end of the hall swung open, letting out a blast of hot air that rushed into the room like the breath of some fire-breathing beast. A darkened human form, obscured by the shadows, stepped across the threshold and slammed the door behind. It was not until the form had fully emerged from the hallway that one could see plainly that it was a young man, but one who seemed to be of an age far beyond his years. Unaware at first that he was not alone, he walked— or more accurately shuffled—with head bowed into the shop, his gait marred by an awkward limp. Shabbily dressed in worn sneakers, ragged blue jeans, and a tattered ill-fitting tank top that hung loosely from his bony frame, he muttered something to himself as he slowly approached until the sight of the others sitting at the counter stopped him dead in his tracks. His shoulder slightly hunched at an odd angle, he slouched noticeably, almost cowering upon realizing that there were others present, and he took a step back.

"Ah, there you are, just in time," said Rick in a reassuring voice. "I didn't want to bother you before while you were working. But I'm glad you are here now. Come on over, I want you to meet someone."

Without a word, the young man turned to Elise with sunken, anxious eyes. The cheek on one side of his gaunt face was oddly deformed in way that was not quite grotesque, but distorted and somehow unsettling, almost as if one were looking at his visage through a glass bottle. Obviously conscious of the defect, he quickly looked away and nervously passed the back of his hand across his forehead to wipe away the beads of sweat rolling down from the short cropped hair that covered his skull like a black cap. In doing so, he revealed a stretch of scarred, disfigured skin running up the back of his arm and side of his neck. At once he reached up self-consciously to hide it, before trying again in the next moment to cover his cheek. It seemed there was no way for him to stand at ease, and it was painful to watch for he looked for all the world like some wounded, haggard animal that wanted nothing more than to run away someplace and hide.

"This is our new bookkeeper," Rick told the young man gently.

Her eyes full of compassion, Elise rose from the stool and reached out her hand. "Hello," she said at once. "My name is Elise."

Tentatively, the young man reached out, taking her hand in his grip for barely a moment before releasing it and pulling away. Then he bowed his head and looked down as if ashamed of himself and unwilling to let her look upon him anymore. At last he managed to gather himself, take a deep breath, and with apparent excruciating effort, reluctantly opened his mouth to speak.

"Hello," he finally said in a low, raspy voice. "I am Fabio."

The Gather

CHAPTER EIGHT

They all did the best they could for him.

Liliana tried to remind herself of that as she walked across the piazza toward the church that evening. After the accident, the doctors had tried as best they could to mend Fabio's shattered body: the fractured pelvis and hip, his mangled knee, the shattered facial bones, and the burns, *caro Signore*, the burns. All of it and much, much more, the wounds so deep and enduring, too much to take in. The mere thought of that August night, the most passing recollection of that horrifying moment after she had fled like a mad woman to the surreal scene at *il muro* and beheld for the first time what had become of her beautiful boy as they pulled him up from the rocks below and loaded him into the ambulance, after four years it still brought her to tears. And yet, for all the horror, she could not deny that it had been a miracle, a truly joyous one, that Fabio had survived at all. For that she had been thankful, for his two friends had not been as fortunate.

Of Caterina, Liliana would only come to know of her through the words of the priest who said her funeral Mass. She had driven to Pescara that day to attend the ceremony with Maria and Giovanni, Enzo's parents—only one day removed from having buried their son. What a time of anguish it had been for them. The mind-numbing grief that came with losing Enzo was burden enough without the added weight of knowing that he had been the one behind the steering wheel and thus in their minds, and perhaps of others, ultimately responsible for the tragedy. After the service, Liliana had felt her heart break as she watched the two approach Caterina's mother and father, inconsolable in their own grief, to express their sorrow. To her relief there had been no accusations, no words of recrimination, only the shared agony of their loss. They were all strangers united by their tears and the crying need to know how it all had happened, how Caterina had come to be in the car, how Enzo had missed the turn that was so familiar to him. All of it a mystery.

Fabio, barely conscious in his hospital bed, was the only one who knew the true story, but he would never speak of it in the days to come. The days would turn into weeks, the weeks to months, and suddenly three years would pass without his ever offering a single word of explanation as to what had happened that night. And so the only consolation for the grieving parents would be their fervent hope that the two youths had died instantly in the horrendous wreck, that God, while sparing Fabio, had already taken them into His arms by the time the car finished tumbling over the rocks and exploded into flames.

For the townspeople of Mont' Oliva, the shock of that terrible night was matched only by the sight of Fabio weeks later when, still bandaged and bedridden, he was finally brought home to recuperate. At first, friends and relatives had come almost non-stop to the house, intending to do their best to cheer him up and offer support to Liliana. Their visits, though, were as often as not more a source of agitation than comfort to mother and son. One could not help but look upon Fabio and feel compassion, but try as they might it was all but impossible for his friends to hide the distress in their eyes at seeing the broken young man. It was a relief in many ways when the flood of visitors inevitably slowed to a trickle until at last only Pasqualina came every day.

Many more days would pass before Fabio was able to muster

the strength to finally raise himself out of the bed for the first time. That afternoon Liliana had tried in vain to caution him to wait a day or two more before trying, but Fabio was determined. With his mother at his side, he struggled to his feet and remained upright for but a moment—just long enough to see his reflection in the mirror on the bedroom door. His own shock at what he saw caused his weak and fragile legs to buckle, and he crumpled at once to the floor. It was only with the help of Emiglio, an elderly neighbor who happened to have been passing by the house when he heard the commotion inside, that Liliana was able to get him back onto the bed.

Later, after Emiglio had left them, Liliana stood in the bedroom doorway, watching over her son as he lay in brooding silence, his blank gaze fixed on the ceiling, his eyes eerily vacant like lamps after the flames have been extinguished. It was not until that moment when she finally understood the true extent of what had happened to him—and that realization overwhelmed her, just as it had Fabio. The bruises and the broken bones, the horrible burns across his neck and shoulders, the shattered nose and cheek, all these were nothing compared to what had happened inside. That much was plain to see, and she understood why. Even when one day he was able to stand on his own and walk, Fabio would never dance again. That fact in and of itself mattered little to her, but she knew how much it meant to him, and that, she was certain, was what had brought the black emptiness to his eyes. Something deep within him, that beautiful thing that Liliana had always known was there, had died.

Sometime after, when he was finally able to leave the confines of the house, Fabio took to hobbling aimlessly about the village, always after nightfall, always keeping to the shadows like a specter. Perpetually sullen and irascible, he greeted no one he might happen to pass, and accepted no greeting in return no matter how sincerely offered. It was not long before others made as much a point of avoiding him as he did them. Sympathy for

Fabio eventually gave way to contempt, so much so that a day finally came when even the lovelorn Bettina would shutter her window at his approach.

On and on it went that way for months. What was to be done with him, Liliana had lamented. How long could she let it go on? If something were not done soon to help him find his way out of the darkness, she feared it might become too late, that her son's life would end in destruction. He was dying before her eyes, and there seemed to be nothing she or anyone else could do to stop it.

It was Pasqualina who first voiced the idea of contacting their uncle, Zio Enrico, to see if there might be a place for him there in his glassmaking shop, perhaps a chance for Fabio to learn a trade, to get away and do something with his life. Letters were written and calls were made, and when all was finally arranged, Fabio at last made his long dreamed of voyage to America.

Liliana climbed the steps to the church door and paused before going in. Clutching her shawl more tightly about her neck, she turned and looked back across the dark and deserted piazza. It had been over a year now, she reflected, since she had sent Fabio away, over a year of waiting and hoping in vain for some word from him, some glimmer of light to show her that he had found his way to a new life. The painful separation had given her ample time to ponder over and over again the tragic accident, to ask why it had been allowed to happen, and why Fabio had been singled out by fate for such cruel treatment. In time, the answer had become very clear to Liliana. The fault, she came to believe, was her own, not Enzo's nor that of anyone else. She herself had brought it all about, of that much she was certain, and by now she understood how. Liliana had fallen away from the Church and the Mass after Franco had died and left her a widow with a young child. Mired in her own bitterness she had chosen to ignore God, as she felt that He had chosen to ignore her— and this, she was certain, was the result.

Liliana let her thoughts drift back across the ocean to America, hoping they might find Fabio. She stood there, wondering about where he was at that moment and what he might be doing, until high above her a gust of chill wind moaned through the bell tower. The mournful sound broke her reverie and brought her back at once to the church steps. Liliana felt a shiver run up her spine, and she was instantly tormented by the thought that perhaps she had made a terrible mistake in sending Fabio away. There was no way for her to know, and there would be none until one day when, God-willing, she finally heard from him again. Till then there was nothing else for her to do but to pray and ask for forgiveness, as she had done every day and night since that sad afternoon when she had struggled to lift her son from the floor. And so, with rosary beads in hand, she turned quickly back to the church door and went inside to light a candle and pray for Fabio.

CHAPTER NINE

Fabio turned away from the searing heat of the furnace and placed the glass bowl he had just fashioned within it atop the stainless steel table. When it had sufficiently cooled, and the glass hardened, he took the bowl in his hands, held it up to the light, and considered it for a time. He examined every detail: the contours of its exterior, the swirling, twisting patterns of color within, and the curious asymmetry of its overall form, a characteristic that had already become something of a hallmark of his work. Behind Fabio the door opened and someone entered. Somewhere in the back of his mind he knew that it was Zio Rick, who was by now no doubt watching over his shoulder from a discreet distance. The greater part of his consciousness being far removed from that spot, lost in some remote and isolated place, Fabio did not acknowledge his great uncle's presence, but instead continued his assessment of the bowl.

All with the object seemed to be as he had intended, but the more he pondered it, the more Fabio became convinced that there was something lacking in this latest work of his, some latent defect he had overlooked. Oblivious to his uncle's gaze and the heat breathing from the mouth of the furnace just to his side, he turned the bowl over and over, regarding it from every possible angle, methodically searching like a detective for the weakness, the missing element that made it unsatisfactory to his eye. Frustrated at his inability to discern it, he finally scowled in disgust and flung the bowl aside. It sailed out of his hand and across the work area, struck the wall, and shattered into a thousand bits.

Rick looked down at the shards of glass on the floor and shook his head. "May I ask what was wrong with that one?" he said after a long sigh. "From here it looked perfect."

Fabio mumbled something unintelligible.

"Hey, *solo l'inglese!*" Rick chided him. "No Italian. We speak only English in here, remember?"

Fabio grunted something else before giving a shrug. "I say that is why I no like," he at last replied in a defiant voice.

Rick gave a grunt of his own. Then he took a broom and metal dustpan from behind the door and handed them to Fabio. "And I say the only way your English is going to get any better is if you try speaking it a little more often," he said, " at least out of politeness, like after lunchtime when I introduced you to that nice young lady who is going to be working with us. You barely said a word to her before you went rushing back in here." He gestured for Fabio to sweep up his mess. Then, once more shaking his head in consternation at the smashed remains of the bowl, he added, "Why are you so careless with your work?"

"What difference makes it?" said Fabio. "It just sand, you always saying, right? I make another, this one only better."

"So says you," muttered his uncle.

When he had finished sweeping up the broken glass, Fabio emptied the dustpan into a cardboard box where rested the shattered final remains of several other of his creations. Having been found fatally flawed for reasons perceived only by their creator, they had met similar ends as the ill-fated bowl.

"You know, at the rate you're going, you're going to need a bigger box," noted Rick. "What are you saving all that broken glass for anyway?"

Fabio did not answer, but simply shrugged, as if to say that he himself was not completely certain. He gestured to the furnace.

"I done this day," he said. "You want I shut down."

"No, leave it burning," said Rick after a moment's contemplation. "I think maybe I'll do a little work myself for a while."

Fabio gave a nod and reached for the dark hooded sweatshirt hanging from a peg on the wall. He pulled it on and started for the door.

"See you tomorrow morning?" asked Rick.

"*Si*, Zio," replied Fabio. Before his uncle could correct him, he quickly added, "Yes," then he hurried out the door.

The late autumn sun had already dropped over the hill and darkness settled in on the town when Fabio stepped outside. Away from the warmth of the furnace, he felt cold, so he tugged the hood of his sweatshirt over his head and dug his hands down deep into the pocket. His head bowed as he started down the sidewalk, his face cloaked within the dark folds of the hood, he looked for all the world like a monk on his way to vespers.

He had taken but a few steps toward home when the sound of music playing nearby brought him to a halt. Reluctantly, Fabio forced himself to pull back the hood just enough so that he could look up at the row of windows glowing brightly on the second floor of the building across the street. Just below them across the building's facade ran a sign that read in elegant script "South County Dance Studio". As he often did when passing, Fabio gazed up at the studio with forlorn eyes, straining to hear the lively rhythm of the ballroom melody, watching to catch a glimpse of the couples inside twirling by in silhouette against the sheer curtains hanging in the windows. Now and then, he could hear the voice of the teacher calling out instructions over the music, and for a moment he was a young boy again back in Italy, listening to Signor Roberto, his own first dance instructor. A stern taskmaster, especially when he recognized true talent,

Roberto would bark out orders like a drill sergeant to Fabio and his fellow pupils, exhorting them to make every move with precision, every step perfect. Many, if not most of the children chafed at his method, but Fabio loved the hard work, the discipline, for even as a youngster he understood that without it he would never amount to anything as a dancer.

A passing truck rumbled by, startling Fabio, bringing him back once more to the sidewalk. As it sped off down the road and into the night, taking with it his memories, he turned and hurried on his way as fast as his hobbled legs could carry him. He passed the pub where the patrons inside were laughing and drinking, and limped by the pizza parlor a little further along where a group of teenagers was milling around outside. Quickening his gait, he kept his head bowed as he passed, trying to ignore the whispers and giggling of which he knew that he himself was the cause.

"Weirdo," he heard one of the boys say before he was out of earshot.

"Creepy," added one of the girls.

Someone else made another remark and the group burst into laughter.

Fabio paid them no heed, but continued along as fast as he could until he had rounded the corner and started down the side street. Relieved to be away from the lights on Main Street, he finally slowed and walked at a more moderate pace along the shadowy lane until at last he reached his uncle's house. There he went around the back and climbed the stairs to the apartment over the garage.

After he had let himself in, Fabio stood in the darkness for a time, hesitant to turn on the light. It was often this way for him when he came back to his little apartment after a long day at the furnace. Inside, a part of him wanted to believe that he had only been sleepwalking, that when the light came on he would suddenly awake to find himself back in his bedroom in Mont'Oliva, whole and healthy and vibrant once more, the tragedy at *il muro* nothing more than a vivid, harrowing nightmare. That vain, minuscule hope, preposterous as it might have been, was sometimes the only thing that sustained him when he was alone and night had descended, and so Fabio clung desperately to it for as long as he could until at last he took a deep breath and reached for the light switch.

The inevitability of the light, the sudden illumination of the confines of his drab little habitat, as always left him feeling empty and desolate. Resigned once more to reality, he looked about for a moment at his surroundings. The modest apartment boasted only one small bedroom and bath, a kitchenette, and a cramped combination living and dining room that accommodated one small couch and a round dining table and chair. In truth, had Fabio been inclined to expend even a modicum of effort to decorate it, the apartment could have been made into a passably pleasant dwelling place for someone living on his own. The walls, however, had remained barren, the entire space bereft of color like a prison cell. Fabio preferred it that way.

Deep in the pit of his stomach, Fabio felt the pang of hunger. He started toward the mini-fridge in the kitchenette, but then stopped short and turned to the table upon which rested a drawing pad and pencil. His inability to find the flaw in the bowl he had spent the afternoon making had gnawed at him the entire way home. He sat down at the table and began to draw, trying to recreate it on paper. He soon filled the page with a variety of renderings of it from different angles, all drawn quite accurately from recollection. Though he held it of no account, Fabio had discovered that he was surprisingly skilled in drawing. Before long he had filled up another page, and not long after that another still. Frustrated beyond words, he pushed away from the table and began pacing about, turning the bowl over and over again in his mind, desperately trying to understand what had gone wrong and how he might make it right the next time.

Beads of sweat now forming on his brow, Fabio went to the bathroom sink and turned on the faucet. He bent over and splashed some water on his face before glancing ever so briefly at his reflection in the mirror when he straightened up. That fleeting look was all that was required to set his head spinning. His pulse suddenly racing, his breath laboring, he backed out of the bathroom and took up pacing about the room once more, unable to keep his thoughts of the bowl from racing over and over through his mind until at last, spent from exhaustion, he turned off the light again and pressed himself into the corner. He crumpled to the floor and curled into a ball, slowly rocking back and forth until the panic passed and he felt safe again, enveloped in the darkness, like a child riding home in the back seat of a car.

CHAPTER TEN

Though there was a door from his apartment that opened to the upstairs corridor of his uncle's house, Fabio seldom used it. Instead he preferred to descend the steps to the back of the garage and walk around to enter by way of the front door as if he were any other visitor. He followed this circuitous route early the next morning, drawn along through the fog of his fatigue by the aroma of freshly brewed coffee wafting from Zio Rick's kitchen. Dark clouds had moved in across the sky overnight and a thin, cold drizzle was falling. The damp chill made the scent of the coffee all the more enticing.

When he came through the front door and stepped into the parlor, Fabio was greeted by the sound of a female singer and the band accompanying her coming from the CD player in the corner. He paused for a moment and cast his eye about as the music played. The room was modestly furnished with a couch, two upholstered chairs, a pair of bookcases, and a small upright piano. The walls, painted a plain off-white, bore two paintings, one a landscape of the Apennines the other a rendering of Saint Peter's Basilica in Rome. Over the fireplace, atop the center of the mantel, a crucifix presided over the room. The rest of the house was much the same in the simplicity of its decor; all in all, his uncle's living quarters were only slightly less austere than his own, but homey somehow.

Rick was at the table, perusing the morning newspaper when Fabio straggled into the kitchen. He lowered the paper to regard his nephew's bedraggled appearance and gave him a smug smile. "Ah, wake up, O sleeper," he intoned in a cheerful voice that Fabio found annoying at that early hour. "Rise from the dead!" Then he nodded to the counter where stood the coffee pot and an empty mug next to a bottle of anisette.

Fabio went and poured himself some coffee, but eschewed adding any of the liqueur. "What music you listen to?" he muttered over his shoulder.

Rick folded the paper and put it aside. "Tierney Sutton, a jazz singer I just discovered," he said enthusiastically. "Great, isn't she? You should try listening to her when you work—some real music—instead of that rap stuff you're always blasting in the shop."

"Jazz I no like," Fabio grumbled as he settled in at the table.

"Jazz I *don't* like," his uncle corrected him. "Or better yet, I don't like jazz."

"If you no like jazz, why you listen?" said Fabio, perfectly aware of his uncle's intention, but inclined at that particular moment to be contrary.

"Not me, you," said Rick. "*You* don't like jazz."

"I know, I just tell you."

"No, you said 'Jazz I no like'," Rick persisted. "In English you should say I *don't* like this, or I *don't* like that."

Fabio pretended to think things over for a time before taking a sip of his coffee. "I don't like this," he said at last, setting his mug down.

"Something wrong with the coffee?"

"No, coffee okay," said Fabio. "Jazz I no like."

"Oh, forget it!" exclaimed Rick, throwing his hands up. "You don't know what you're missing."

With that he snatched up the newspaper once more, snapped

it open, and went back to reading the morning's headlines. Fabio meantime went back to sipping his coffee, and for a time the two men sat in silence. At last Rick put down the paper and fixed his gaze on his nephew.

"You look tired," he said. "You should get to bed a little earlier."

Fabio gave an indifferent shrug. "I sleep plenty enough," he said, perfectly aware that the dark circle's beneath his eyes told a different story.

"Maybe," said his uncle thoughtfully. Then, pushing away from the table, he added, "But you should definitely try eating more. You're beginning to look like a walking skeleton."

That said, Rick went to the refrigerator and began to poke about inside it. Soon he withdrew a carton of eggs, a package of sliced salami, some cheese, and a small bunch of scallions. With the ingredients set out on the counter, he lined a frying pan with olive oil and placed it over the burner atop the stove. While the oil warmed, he chopped the scallions on the cutting board and shredded a few slices of the salami. Before long these were sizzling in the pan together, the savory smell of the scallions filling the kitchen. It would not be long before it would all cook to a crisp, so Rick quickly beat six eggs in a bowl, tossed in some salt and pepper along with a few broken pieces of cheese, and poured it all into the pan. Humming along to the music still playing in the parlor, he took a spatula and ran it with practiced skill in and around the outer edge of the solidifying eggs.

After a short while, when all had cooked to the desired consistency, Rick turned off the flame. He covered the pan with a large serving plate and expertly flipped over the entire contents onto it to display the golden brown frittata. Wasting no time, he placed his creation on the center of the table along with a loaf of bread, and turned back to the cabinet to retrieve some plates and utensils. Upon reinstalling himself at the table, he scooped out a slice of the frittata onto one of the plates and tore a hunk of bread from the end of the loaf. He passed both to Fabio before doing the same for himself. Then he made the sign of the cross and gestured for Fabio to eat.

Alone in his thoughts, Fabio had sat at the table the whole time, watching his uncle at work, not so much as lifting a finger to lend assistance. Accustomed his whole life to having someone else cook for him, it never occurred to him that perhaps it would have been a nice gesture to at least set the table or perhaps make some other offer of help in preparing the meal, simple as it might have been. But it had become something of a ritual with the two men, this Saturday morning repast, and Rick had never complained about his nephew's laziness, so Fabio took his fork in hand and without a word partook of the eggs.

"How's your frittata?" asked Rick after Fabio had swallowed a bite. "You want something to spice it up a little, a little Tabasco on it maybe? There's some in the fridge."

In truth, flavorful as it was, the taste of his food was a matter of indifference to Fabio. The only reason he ate at all was his inability to overcome his body's natural instincts insisting that he do so. He took no real pleasure in the act, and he never bothered, as he might have done for his uncle's sake, to at least make an attempt to show some.

Fabio shook his head. "Frittata fine," he said. Then, upon further consideration, he thought to add, "Thank you."

Rick sat up straight and smiled. "Ah, now there's a bit of progress," he said with apparent satisfaction before turning his attention to his own plate.

"Why you say that?" asked Fabio.

"Why *do* you say that," Rick corrected him, wagging a forkful of frittata at him for emphasis.

Fabio let out a grumble of impatience and rolled his eyes. "Why *do* you say that?" he said grudgingly.

Rick did not reply straight away, but instead settled back in his chair and hummed along to the music. Fabio did not yet realize it, but he had come far, literally and figuratively, since the day a year earlier when Rick had driven to Boston to meet him at Logan Airport. When he first beheld Fabio struggling to make his way out into the lobby after clearing customs, dragging his one suitcase along the floor, his first impression was that he had come across a wounded, cowering animal, one that would need very careful handling. For several days afterward Fabio barely spoke and rarely left the room Rick had prepared for him over the garage other than to accompany him to the shop. Along the way, Rick would invariably greet everyone they might pass while Fabio remained ever silent until they were safe within the confines of Vita Glassworks. In the beginning, Fabio had just sat in silence and watched him blowing the glass. In time, though, Rick gently coaxed his nephew into giving it a try. Fabio's first efforts were a bit comical; he always blew too hard into the pipe, making the bubble of glass too big. But he learned quickly. As the weeks went by and he started to get the hang of things, Fabio gradually began to open his mouth and speak, but only in Italian and to no one but Rick. It was then that Rick realized that his nephew would never be able to crawl out of his personal isolation if all he spoke was his native language, so it wasn't long before he began to insist that the two converse only in English.

"Because, my friend," Rick finally said pleasantly, "I believe that is the very first time that I've heard you say the words 'thank you' to anyone. You should use them more often, you know, those two little words. You'll be surprised at how far they'll take you." He paused and rubbed his chin thoughtfully. "Of course, I'm starting to get a little spoiled now," he went on. "When you first came to America, I was lucky if I heard you say anything at all. I hadn't been prepared for that when your mother told me that you would be coming."

At the mention of his mother, Fabio shifted uneasily in his chair and looked down at his plate. Despite the months of working side by side and living under the same roof, and his uncle's many attempts to draw him out, Fabio had never breathed a word about his mother, why she had sent him there, or anything at all about what had happened to him back in Italy. He had kept it all tightly locked within the confines of his heart, and he had no intention of letting it out.

"What she say about me?" he found himself murmuring just the same.

"Not much really," his uncle said cautiously, aware that they had unexpectedly stepped into terra incognita. "Mainly that you had been injured in a bad accident, that you were out of work and needed to learn a trade. I didn't need to know more, so I didn't ask."

"Why no?"

"Why *not*."

"Yes, yes, why not?" Fabio huffed.

Rick shrugged. "Everybody comes to this country for different reasons, Fabio," he explained. "Some come to find themselves or to be found. And others—well, sometimes they come to hide and lose themselves. There are lots of ways to do both of those things here." He gave a little sigh. "Anyway, I assumed you had to be one or the other. Do you understand?"

Fabio nodded that he did. He was inclined to let the subject go at that, for he was beginning to feel the first stirring of anxiety in the pit of his gut, but something made him press forward. Perhaps it was because, as reluctant as he was to speak about himself, he had always been curious about his uncle, who possessed his own brand of reticence.

"But why you—why do *you* come to America?" he asked.

Rick slowly placed his fork down and his expression grew sad in a contemplative way. He looked past Fabio with a vacant look, as if turning something over in his mind before answering. "What did they tell you about me back home?" he asked in reply.

"They say you going to be priest," said Fabio, "but you get, how you say—kicked out?"

"No," Rick said gently, shaking his head.

"You no want to be priest?"

"No, I didn't get kicked out, was what I meant," said Rick. "I walked out on my own."

"Why?' asked Fabio. "What happen?"

Rick took a deep breath and let it out. Then he forced a grin and gave a chuckle. "Maybe I'll tell you about it some other time," he said. He turned his ear to the parlor and fell silent for a few moments. "Anyway," he said, forcing another smile, "you really should try to develop a little better appreciation of jazz. It's one of the things I've always loved best about America."

"I no—I don't like jazz," Fabio reiterated, wearing a smirk as he enunciated each word with emphasis.

"Hah, well, what do you like then?" said his uncle, regaining his earlier light demeanor.

"I like to work," said Fabio.

"I've noticed that," said Rick. "You work a great deal. Why so much?"

The question caught Fabio off guard. He bowed his head for a moment, not sure if he wanted to answer.

"It make me forget," he found himself saying, barely above a whisper, before raising his head back up. Fearing that he had made a mistake in revealing even that minuscule glimpse of his inner self, he cast a quick glance across the table at his uncle and went back to eating his breakfast in silence.

For his part, Rick said no more, but simply nodded.

Later, after he had finished eating, Fabio pulled on his sweatshirt and started off to the shop. He knew that Rick would be joining him there before very long, so he was anxious to take advantage of whatever time he would have to work alone. Unfazed by the damp wind that buffeted him, he hurried down the sidewalk and turned the corner onto Main Street, all the while berating himself for having said so much. What if his uncle had pressed him to speak further of what it was that he was trying to forget? What if he had revealed the truth about what had happened that night at *il muro?* What if he had told him that Enzo and Caterina had not died instantly in the crash as everyone had prayed they had, that the two had been very much alive when the car burst into flames just as Fabio was trying desperately to reach them?

The questions swirling in his head, his heart suddenly pounding in his chest, Fabio pressed on, quickening his gait until he was limping along as fast as his legs would allow him. At last at the shop, his hands trembling, he fumbled with the key until he managed to turn the lock and fling open the door. Then he fled to the back room. Before long he was standing at the furnace, working the glass, letting the searing heat of the flames consume his thoughts while the radio blared the mindless music he craved, drowning out the voices in his head, those of his dying friends crying out to him over and over without cease.

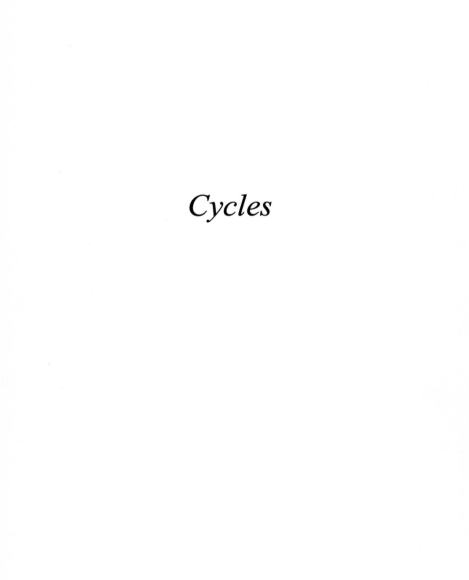

Cycles

CHAPTER ELEVEN

"If I can help you in any way, please let me know," said Elise.

At the sound of her voice, Fabio stopped what he was doing. It was late morning, almost noon one day the first week of December, and he had been in the back room, sweeping up the shattered remains of another ill-starred creation. With Rick off helping Eddie lay out the course for the upcoming cyclocross race that weekend, he had spent the entire morning there alone by the furnace, working away with the glass in silence, never once venturing out into the front of the shop. Having been enjoined (for the benefit of the shoppers) not to turn on the radio while he worked unless it was to listen to Christmas carols or something reasonably festive, Fabio had passed the time in a state of nervous agitation. All the same, despite the absence of the loud, angry music from which he normally derived comfort, he still preferred to confine himself to the back room where he could remain hidden from the world outside and lose himself in his work. It was the one place he felt safe, a feeling that had only deepened since the day Elise first came to work at the shop.

It had been nearly two weeks now since Elise started, but Fabio had yet to adapt to the disruption. Though there was nothing in particular to which he could point, no quirks in her personality or behavior that annoyed him, he found Elise's mere presence decidedly unsettling and he avoided her at all costs. After all, he had only just become accustomed to working and living with Zio Rick, and to life so far away from Mont'Oliva. How long had it taken him just to muster the nerve to leave the house and follow his uncle to the shop? Days? Weeks? He could not even remember. Those early days after he came from Italy were spent in a seemingly endless swirl of anxiety and despair that warped his notion of time, and the relentless merger of days into weeks and weeks to months all passed in a blur like in a troubling dream. It was only when he finally put his mind and hands to work making the glass that Fabio finally began to awaken from it. Now that he had, he dreaded the intrusion of strangers—be they customers or co-workers—into what he had come to consider his private sanctuary. It had not yet occurred to him of course that this was precisely the reason Rick had felt the need to hire Elise in the first place.

His misgivings about her notwithstanding, Fabio could not suppress a modicum of curiosity about the newcomer. Somehow, in the brief time that she had worked there, she seemed to have acquired a rather detailed understanding of glassmaking in general and the history of Vita Glassworks in particular. Of the latter, she seemed to know more than he, a state of affairs that vaguely confounded him. That she seemed rather adept at her position was another source of annoyance. Perhaps it was her quiet, easy manner with people, her Caribbean accent, or the charming lilt of her voice, but people seemed to like her right away and rare was the customer who left the shop without buying at least some small item or another. How she accomplished both was something of a puzzle to him. And so, at hearing her greet a pair of customers who had just come into the shop, he unceremoniously dumped the shards of glass he had just swept up into the ever-burgeoning cardboard box on the floor and went to the door. After a moment's hesitation he leaned his head close to listen. Then, nudging the door open just a crack, he peered inside.

Gazing through the narrow gap between door and frame, Fabio could see the display shelf on the far wall. Behind it the sun beamed in through the window panes, setting the vases and goblets and other glassware aglow while sending colorful streams of fragmented light down onto the floor like pieces of candy spilling from a bowl. Just then Elise unexpectedly crossed his line of vision, prompting Fabio to jump back. Leaning closer once more, he watched the young woman walk back to the counter. There she took up her perch on the stool behind it and proceeded to busy herself with some paperwork while keeping careful watch on the customers—all the while unaware that she herself was under observation.

"Yes, they are all handmade right here on the premises," Elise suddenly said in reply to some question Fabio had not been able to quite make out. When she rose from the stool and walked back out of sight. Fabio nudged the door open a bit wider until he could see her again.

"The owner is from Italy where he learned glassmaking from his father," he watched her say to her customers, an elderly man and woman Fabio had never before seen in the shop. "So, you see, it is a family business here, handed down from many generations. As a matter of fact, his nephew has come from Italy to take up the trade now. His work is quite intriguing."

"How nice," said the woman.

"Nice and expensive, I bet," muttered her husband, looking about with a skeptical eye.

"Oh, pay no attention to him," huffed the wife to Elise. "He doesn't know anything." Then, with a slightly pained expression, she added, "But we're not looking for anything too big, if you know what I mean."

Elise smiled. "Yes, of course, I know just what you mean," she said easily. "Come, I'll show you some things that I think you will like very much to give as Christmas gifts."

While recounting some of the history of the shop, Elise guided the couple out of sight to the other side of the store where, from what Fabio could discern, she showed them the Christmas tree ornaments and Nativity figurines as well as some of the other smaller pieces Rick had made. The foray apparently met with success for the couple soon reappeared at the counter where Elise wrapped up two items they had selected. Not long after, she walked the couple to the door and sent them on their way, wishing them a pleasant Christmas season. Then, to Fabio's chagrin, she turned and began to walk straight towards him.

Contrary to appearances, Elise had of course been perfectly cognizant all along that a pair of eyes was scrutinizing her every move. It had been the same way every day since she first came to work. Whenever the front door opened and a customer walked in, the door to the back room inevitably opened ever so slightly as well. At first Elise assumed that the strange young man in the back was merely curious to see what reaction customers might have to the glasswork he had made. In time, however, she realized that it was herself that he was watching. That this should be so puzzled her. To date, their brief, awkward encounters with one another had been less than heartwarming. Distant and brusque in his manner toward her, Fabio seemed perpetually ill at ease despite her every attempt at cordiality. Had he not behaved the same way towards everyone else, at least from what she had observed, she might have taken offense. That not being the case, she chose to simply accept his unpleasant demeanor as an artist's eccentricity. She wondered, though, about what had happened to him. How had he come to acquire the scars on his neck and shoulders, and what had caused his cheek to be misshapen as it was? To hide the former, she had noticed, he had taken to wearing long sleeve shirts, even while working at the furnace. As to the latter, short of wearing a hood there was nothing to be done to hide his face, so he simply turned and looked the other way whenever they crossed paths, almost as if he were pretending that she was not there. But since she *was* there, and would be for the foreseeable future, Elise felt compelled to do her best to put him at ease if she could without playing along and pretending that *he* was not. And so, after her customers had gone on their way, she walked straight to the back room, gave a knock on the door, and entered.

By this time Fabio had already whirled away from the door, scurried to the furnace, and hastily grabbed a blowpipe to give the appearance that he had been occupied all the while with his craft instead of spying on his co-worker. There he remained, refusing to look her way when she came in.

"I'm going out to get a sandwich for lunch," Elise announced pleasantly. "Would you like for me to pick up something for you too?"

Fabio gave a glance over his shoulder then continued to do his best to appear busy. "I no eat lunch when I work," he said ungraciously.

"Oh, okay," replied Elise, unperturbed by his gruff tone. "Then how about Mister Rick? Will he back soon? Do you think he would like something?"

Fabio grunted and shook his head. "No," he said. "He out helping with cyclo-cross all rest of day."

"Cyclo-cross?" said Elise. "What is that?'

Fabio gave a sigh of impatience, as if to indicate that she was disrupting his work with her questions. "A race on the bicycle," he told her, feigning weariness. "A race through the woods." Then, anticipating her next question, he quickly added, "They do each year to make money for the kids."

"What a nice thing to do!" Elise gushed. "And Mister Rick helps them. Will you go and help them too?"

Fabio shook his head. "Zio go," he replied uneasily. "I stay to work."

"That word, zio, what does that mean?" said Elise. "I've heard you call him that before."

"It mean 'uncle'," said Fabio with another sigh.

Elise smiled. "Hah, I should have guessed," she said, laughing at herself. "Thank you for telling me. Maybe you could teach me some more Italian words someday."

"We speak only English here," Fabio snapped in reply. Then he moved farther away to the other side of the room.

The smile drained away from Elise's face. "All right then," she said softly. "Just watch the shop for me, if you would. I'll be gone just a few minutes."

With that she turned and left him.

Alone, Fabio immediately regretted the way he had spoken to her. He knew that she was just being polite by asking if he wanted something for lunch. The least he might have done would have been to thank her for the offer. He hadn't, though, and there was nothing for him to do about it now, so in spite of Rick's orders to the contrary, he turned on the radio full blast and set himself back to work.

CHAPTER TWELVE

Saturday morning found a shivering and yawning Fabio behind the steering wheel of his uncle's ramshackle pickup truck. Rick had already arisen well before dawn and gone off with his cycling cohorts to help finish setting up the course for the cyclocross race before competition commenced later that morning. Before leaving he had roused Fabio and given him instructions to drive into Narragansett, the seaside town adjacent to Wakefield, where he was to stop by the local bike shop there and pick up two sets of spare wheels being lent for the race. It was a rather undemanding mission, but the bitter cold of that morning made his eyebrows ache and the early hour weighed heavily on him, making the journey feel acutely burdensome. Groggy and grumpy with fatigue, he drove past the town beach and glanced out over the bay. The sun had just crept over the horizon, sending flecks of orange light skipping across the tops of the waves as they tumbled onto the shore. Too drowsy to appreciate the lovely sight, Fabio turned his attention back to the road, gave his head a shake to rid himself of the cobwebs, and motored on until he reached the shop on the north end of town.

A trio of cars with bicycles affixed to their roofs were parked in the lot when Fabio pulled up to the shop. His shoulders hunched up against the cold, he stepped out of the truck and walked to the front door. Entering, he found a small group of men standing by the counter, chatting and laughing. Some looked to be of his own age, others a bit older. All had the lean, athletic look of cyclists, and he guessed rightly that they were all planning to compete that day.

"The course will be hard as a rock this morning," one of them was saying.

"I like it that way," replied another. "Makes it faster."

"Yeah, so long as you stay up on your bike," added a third, drawing a laugh from the others.

At seeing Fabio approach, one of them smiled, nodding to the window. "That's Rick truck I saw you drive up in," he said affably, "so I'm guessing you're Fabio."

"Yes," said Fabio through a yawn. "I've come for wheels for race. Rick say I should ask for shop owner Will."

The other man smiled again. "That's me," he said. "Rick told me you'd be coming. Hold on a minute while I go grab 'em for you."

While Will went off to the back of the shop, Fabio kept a discreet distance from the other young men who were continuing their discussion of the race course. They were obviously good friends, and there was an air of excitement and anticipation in their voices that Fabio envied. It reminded him of how he once felt when he was with his own friends on the piazza or at *il muro*, planning a night out or looking forward to an upcoming dance competition. The memory brought a feeling of shame and he felt the back of his neck go hot, for he no longer had such friends anymore, or even the camaraderie of rivals for that matter. He had lost them all along with the easy self-confidence he once possessed. He had forgotten how to be part of a group, how to join in the talk and the laughter and the spirit of a shared adventure. Indeed a taunting voice inside Fabio warned him away, telling him that he no longer even deserved these things, that he was meant to be alone, and so he began to edge toward the door, intending to wait outside for Will to return with the wheels. It was just then when one of the younger men unexpectedly turned to him.

"Hey, are you racing today?" he asked Fabio pleasantly.

Fabio stopped dead in his tracks, the back of his neck growing hotter still, for the others had turned to look at him as well. "No, I no ride the bike," he said awkwardly.

"Oh," said the young man. "Just helping out?"

Ashamed to admit that he had no intention of taking part in the event other than to drop off the wheels before returning at once to bed or the safe confines of the shop, Fabio replied with a noncommittal shrug.

"That's cool," said the other man. "It's for a good cause." Then he turned back to the others just as Will emerged from the back with the wheel sets.

"Here you go, one Shimano, one Campy," he said, handing the two pairs of wheels over to Fabio. "Thanks for taking these over for me. Tell Rick I'll come by this afternoon if I can get out of here for a while to help him out in the wheel pit."

Taking the wheels in hand, Fabio mumbled that he would do so and hurried out the door to the parking lot.

"And tell Eddie to give me a call if he needs anything else," Will called after him.

Fabio deposited the wheels in the back of the truck and answered with a wave before climbing back behind the wheel. He hastily started the engine and got back on the road.

Unfamiliar with the location of the race venue, Fabio glanced down at every opportunity at the passenger seat where he had left the directions Rick had written for him. They guided him down a wooded lane running parallel to a river flowing out toward the bay. Before long he arrived at a stretch of stone wall where he was to turn away from the river and up onto Prospect Road, itself a wall of sorts that climbed virtually straight up to the highway crossing a half mile away. When he made the turn, the abrupt steepness of the hill caught Fabio by surprise. Muttering a curse, he quickly stepped on the clutch and fumbled with the stick to downshift the engine. The grinding gears clamored in protest before they caught and the sputtering old truck reluctantly started up the climb.

The road ascended in long steep sections punctuated by several flattened steps where once, in a bygone era when the road was unpaved, travelers ascending the hill would stop to rest their horses. Atop the hill, two stately residences with great sprawling lawns stood guard on opposite sides of the road, looking out to the distant bay. Fabio glanced in his rearview mirror but once halfway up the hill and was astonished to see how precipitously the road dropped off behind him back down to the stone wall and the river beyond. The sight unnerved him and he felt a stab of fear in the pit of this gut. He quickly focused his gaze straight ahead until he reached the crest of the hill and the road mercifully dipped down to the crossing. Once there Fabio breathed a sigh of relief and at the turning of the stoplight sped across the highway to the adjoining road. At last, a few miles later, he came to a school where he turned in and steered the truck down the drive to the playing fields in the back where the day's races were set to be held.

When he stepped out of the truck, Fabio stood at the edge of the parking lot for a moment and cast his gaze about at the scene. Everywhere he looked was alive with frenetic and seemingly disconnected activity, and the air of that frigid morning full of sound. He heard the lively banter of people working together, voices shouting out instructions, the banging of hammers, and from somewhere off in the nearby woods the wail of a chainsaw. Just ahead of Fabio, up a short but steep section of road, a half-appended banner marking what he surmised would be the start/finish line for the race dangled from a telephone pole. Just below it, across the road, a crew of workers was busy assembling the scaffolding for the stage from which the race announcer would call the races—and to which presumably the other end of the banner would be attached. Meantime along a chainlink fence lining the road up to the stage, someone was hanging the company banners of all the race sponsors. Fabio saw that of Vita Glassworks already prominently displayed among those closest to the finish line. Further on, beneath a wooden shelter, a pair of women was running a set of electrical lines to power the computers at the registration table while down on the nearby athletic fields that extended for hundreds of yards, another crew was marking a zigzag race course over the hardened turf with long stretches of wide yellow tape tied to plastic stakes pounded into the ground. Here and there, all around in different locations, others were tying the tape around trees and signposts and whatever else might be at hand to mark the mile-long course which seemed to twist and turn every which way across the fields, along the road, around some nearby tennis courts, in and out of the surrounding woods, and who could tell where else. Out in the distance at the base of a steep embankment bordering the far side of the fields, up which the course apparently ran, Fabio saw yet another group hammering down stakes to secure a set of low wooden barriers. There were people everywhere, volunteers all, hurrying about at a near-frenzied pace to ready the course in time for the first race, not a soul standing idle save he.

Fabio felt no great urge to take part in the goings on, but simply the desire to deliver the spare wheels to his uncle as instructed and get on his way as quickly as he could. He scanned the fields until he spotted Rick over in one corner talking with Eddie. Wasting no time, he took the wheels from the back of the truck and, mindful of his gimpy legs, carefully negotiated the little grass hill down to them.

"There you are!" said Rick jovially at seeing him approach. "Where have you been, the day is half gone."

"I get wheels like you ask," Fabio muttered.

"Like I *asked*," Rick corrected him.

At that he took the wheels, set them aside, and before Fabio could protest, handed him the end of a roll of the same yellow tape being used to mark the course. "Stand over there and hold this, will you," he told his nephew.

Fabio reluctantly walked to the indicated spot some ten yards away while Rick let out the tape. "Stop right there," he said. Then, laying down the roll of tape, turned back to Eddie. "What do you think?" he said. "We make a separate lane here to enter the pit?"

Eddie, who had the fatigued but focused look of a man on a mission, scratched his chin and considered the proposition. "I just want to make sure there's enough room, Rick," he said. "I don't want anybody squeezing in and causing a crash when they try to get back on the course." Rick agreed and the two men briefly took to discussing the situation before the cell phone on Eddie's hip rang. Eddie put the phone to his ear.

"Be right there," was all he said before snapping the phone shut.

"Places to go, Mister Race Organizer?" said Rick.

"And people to see," sighed Eddie with a wry smile. "You know what you're doing, Rick. Just use your best judgment and it will work out fine." Then he was off to tend to the preparation of some other part of the course.

Rick looked over the immediate vicinity and scratched his own chin in silent thought for a moment before turning to Fabio who, with tape in hand, was still dutifully if impatiently awaiting further orders.

"What I do now?" said Fabio with undisguised ill humor.

Rick tossed a wooden stake over at Fabio's feet then lobbed a hammer his way. "Bang that stake down right there and tie the tape to it," said his uncle. "Then throw back the hammer so I can do the same over here."

Fabio stooped down and picked up the hammer. "What this

place for?" he asked as he pounded down the stake.

"This is going to be the wheel pit," said Rick. "It's where the riders can take a free lap during the race."

The cold air stinging his hands now, Fabio tossed the hammer back to Rick and began with fumbling fingers to tie the tape around the stake. "What is free lap?" he asked absentmindedly.

"If a rider gets a flat or has mechanical trouble with his bike, he can pull out of the race for a lap and get a new wheel, sort of like in auto racing," his uncle explained. "That's my job today, to help riders change wheels before the race comes round again so they can jump back in."

"Hmm," Fabio grunted skeptically. "Sound to me like easy way to cheat just to get rest. Not very fair to others."

"Nah," said Rick with a chuckle, taking the hammer in hand. "It's a rugged course out there and breakdowns can happen to anybody. It's only fair that racers take a free lap to get fixed up and back in the race. And besides, that lap goes by very quickly. Believe me, they don't get much rest. Everyone understands. It's not cheating at all, it's just part of racing. Everybody needs a free lap now and then."

Fabio shrugged indifferently and dug his hands down deep into his pockets. "Are you not cold?" he asked with a shiver, noting that his uncle wore a cap, but no gloves and only a long sleeve shirt and fleece vest over his upper body.

Rick smiled. "The best way to stay warm on days like this is to stay busy," he said.

"I think maybe better to just stay inside," said Fabio, unconvinced. "I go to work now."

"Elise is going to be watching the shop today," said Rick quickly. "She can handle things. Why don't you hang around here for a while longer and lend a hand setting things up if you can? They could use the help, you know. *I* could use the help. Besides it would do you good to stay out in the fresh air away from that furnace for a day. Who knows, you might even enjoy watching the races. The first one is going to start at nine."

Fabio looked away with doubtful eyes back toward the stage where the banner over the starting line still dangled helplessly by one end. There was a gentle pleading in his uncle's voice that gave him pause and made him consider staying. In spite of it, Fabio shook his head. "I must go, Zio," he said. "I must work." Before Rick could try to convince him to change his mind, Fabio abruptly turned heel and with a perfunctory *ciao* hurried back up the hill.

Installed once more by the steering wheel in the relative warmth of the truck, Fabio quickly reached for the key to start the engine, but found that he could not bring himself to turn it. A great wave of guilt and anxiety had suddenly overwhelmed him and he sat there in turmoil, berating himself for not staying to help while at the same time arguing with himself that he must leave at once. Unable to decide whether he should stay or go, too weakened in spirit to quell the now warring factions within his mind, he closed his eyes as he often did in these situations and simply surrendered himself to both sides in the hope that hostilities would somehow cease of their own accord. With a sigh of resignation, he let himself slump sideways against the door and waited.

CHAPTER THIRTEEN

It was not until much later, when he heard the ringing of cowbells, that Fabio finally reopened his eyes. The sound jolted him out of a deep sleep and, in a moment of panic at not knowing where he was, he jerked upright, striking his knee hard against the bottom of the steering wheel. The blow sent a spasm of sharp pain through his leg and Fabio let out a groan as he tried to find his bearings. At first he could see nothing of the outside world, for his breath had completely fogged upped the inside of the truck's windows. It was not until he rubbed clear a spot on the windshield and saw a line of cyclists pedal by that he came to himself and remembered that he was at the race.

The sky overhead had turned a slate gray, and here and there snow flurries were drifting down through the air when Fabio pulled himself out of the truck. Once more on his feet, he looked about the parking lot and rubbed his eyes. He was astonished at how long he had slept. It was already afternoon and round about in the parking lot cyclists who had competed in the earlier races, of which he had no recollection whatsoever, were changing out of their cycling uniforms and stowing their bicycles in or atop their cars. Back on the course another line of racers zipped close by in a blur of colorful jerseys. The group careened up the hill past the stage at the start/finish line while onlookers lining the finishing straight cheered and rang cowbells.

"Prime lap! Prime lap!" screamed the race announcer over the public address system as they whizzed by and disappeared over the top of the hill.

A "prime" was a prize awarded at different points in a race to the first rider across the finish line on a given lap. That the announcer had called one as the group passed by gave Fabio to assume that it must have been the lead group of the race. He looked down below to the fields where another group was giving chase, twisting and turning like a snake across the still hardened turf. Further back on the far side of the fields, other riders were dismounting their bikes and carrying them on their shoulders over the wooden barriers before struggling up to the top of the embankment where they hopped back on and pedaled off into the woods. Where they went and what obstacles they encountered there Fabio could not tell, but it wasn't long before they streamed out of the woods once more and plunged back down another part of the embankment where they turned abruptly back onto the fields. It was obviously the latter stages of the race for there were riders dispersed everywhere out on the course, pedaling up and down the hills, in and out of the woods, this way and that, all the action as frenetic and seemingly disconnected as things had appeared in the morning.

"Oh my word, who invented this sport, Escher?"

The melodic, laughing voice took Fabio by surprise, for he had not seen the young woman to whom it belonged approach from behind and stand just a few feet off to his side. Looking out with him across the fields, she pushed back the hood of her coat so that as he turned towards her he saw her lovely face in profile. Something stirred deep inside Fabio, something long ago forgotten, and at once he found himself straightening up, trying to stand a little taller despite his still aching knee. It was just then that, quite unexpectedly, she turned to him and smiled, and for a moment it was as if the cold dark clouds of that December afternoon had parted ever so slightly to let through a single hopeful ray of sunlight.

"Do you know how many laps there are to go in the race?" she asked, her blue eyes radiant against her fair skin and auburn hair.

Fabio swallowed hard and self-consciously raised a hand to cover his cheek.

"I think—"

As he was speaking, another man came and stood opposite him at the young woman's side. "Come on, Laura," he said before Fabio could finish. "Let's go up and watch the rest of the race from the start line."

At the sight of the other man, Fabio instantly fell silent and lowered his head. Shrinking back, he did not look up again until the pair turned and walked away arm in arm. By then the gray clouds had converged once more, snuffing out the fragile sliver of light that had beguiled him for a fleeting moment. Once more Fabio became aware of the throbbing pain in his knee. Brought back to reality by the relentless discomfort, he hobbled down to the wheel pit where Zio Rick was busy replacing a wheel for one of the racers who had flatted out on the course. Fabio stood just outside the taped area watching, his uncle unaware of his presence until after the pack had come round again and he had given the rider a healthy shove to send him back into the fray.

"Hah! Just in the nick of time!" exclaimed Rick, decidedly if inexplicably pleased to see his nephew at just that moment. "Come in and stay here. I have to go get ready."

Fabio looked wide-eyed at his uncle and then back toward the finish line stage where the announcer was shouting, "Four laps to go in the race! Four laps to go!" as the lead group whizzed by, urged on by the crowd and the inevitable cowbells.

"*Me?*" said Fabio, turning back to him in alarm. "But I no know how to make the wheel change!"

"Don't worry about it," Rick assured him. "There are no

more free laps after four laps to go. Just stay here and watch the rest of the wheels until I get back." With that he hurried away up the hill.

"But where go you!" Fabio called after him.

"But where are you *going*?" Rick shouted back over his shoulder.

Scowling, Fabio spoke no more, but simply brought an end to the exchange with a rather vigorous gesture that only one of Italian heritage might appreciate. Then, cold and miserable, he sat down on the ground, brought his knees as close to his chest as he could to stay warm, and waited.

As the announcer had promised, the competition came to its conclusion four laps later when, amidst great cheering and evermore ringing of cowbells, two riders who had managed to break away from the lead pack in the waning moments of the race sprinted up the final straight and crossed the line, one but a whisker's breadth in front of the other. Over the next few minutes the remainder of the shattered field pedaled up to the finish in dribs and drabs where the riders were greeted by appreciative applause. When the last of them came in, Eddie took to the stage and addressed the gathering.

"What a day of racing!" he enthused, his voice echoing across the field. "How about a hand for this elite group that just put on such a great show for us!" The crowd dutifully applauded. "And how about another for all the sponsors and volunteers who helped out in so many ways, and helped us raise over ten thousand dollars today!" Another great cheer went up. Soon after, the top three finishers of the race were called to the podium where Eddie presented them with their medals.

Assuming that this was the end of the day's events, Fabio got to his feet and looked around for Zio Rick, at the same time hoping he might catch another glimpse of the young woman, Laura. Neither was anywhere in sight. "And now, everyone," he heard Eddie saying over the public address system, "I'd ask that you please stay with us for just a few minutes more to watch our final race of the day, a special three lap event. We scheduled this race last so that some of our...let's say experienced athletes, many of whom have been helping out today, could have a chance to get on their bicycles and show us what they can do. And so at this time I'll ask all those competing in the age sixty and over category to please come to the starting line now!"

Fabio at first ignored the modest group of twenty or so riders at the starting line while he continued to scan the crowd for his uncle. Then he paused and looked harder at one late-coming entry just then rolling up to join the others. Fabio's jaw dropped open.

It was Zio Rick.

"Gentlemen, you have three laps to race," Eddie's voice boomed a moment later. "Unless there are any questions about the course..." He paused and chuckled when none were forthcoming. "I didn't think there would be since most of you helped set it up. All right then, you all know the rules: pedal hard and stay upright. You'll start when I count you down from three. Three...two...one...off you go!"

The group, with Rick nestled somewhere in the middle, pedaled away to a round of enthusiastic cheers from those who had remained to watch. When they disappeared into the woods, Fabio sank back down to the ground and sulked. Though he had done virtually nothing all day he was tired and he wanted to go home. At the same time, he could not suppress an inexplicable feeling of excitement churning in his stomach; he was eager to see how his old uncle would fare in the race.

And so Fabio watched with interest when the group passed by all together on the first lap. He picked out Zio Rick right away in his familiar red cycling jacket, the jacket already unzipped down to his mid-section as he chatted away with his fellow riders. All the riders in fact were talking and laughing amongst themselves as they rolled along at a moderate clip, and it seemed to Fabio that the race was little more than a bunch of friends out together for a spirited ride.

By the time the group passed on the second lap, however, the pleasant chatter had ceased and the riders, though still more or less together, were now stretched out in single file. Leaning forward in as aerodynamic a position as nature would allow their aging bodies, they pedaled with discernible purpose, smiles gone, their faces stoic. Before long they were passing through the start/finish area where Eddie rang the bell signaling the start of the race's final lap. With cowbells clanging, the crowd whooped it up for the older riders.

Suddenly it became a real race.

Belying their years, the riders in unison stood up on their pedals and careened off into the woods at a remarkable clip. A short time later four racers re-emerged in tandem, the beneficiaries of an "attack", a sharp acceleration by the more fit riders that had left the rest of the shattered field giving chase a few seconds back. To Fabio's astonishment, Zio Rick was one of the leaders!

"It looks like we've got a breakaway group trying to escape the pack!" exclaimed Eddie. "We'll see if they can stay away till the finish!"

Round the course the leaders went, into the woods and out again, past the wheel pit where Fabio sat, back down onto the fields, and up to the wooden barriers, all the while Zio Rick visibly struggling to keep pace with the other three, but still there.

"*Andiamo, imbecile,*" Fabio found himself murmuring, inwardly urging his uncle on. "*Forza!*"

Just then the leader of the escape group caught a foot while stepping over the last of the wooden barriers. He stumbled briefly and came to an abrupt halt, causing the two riders close behind to collide with him. The three became briefly entangled, just long enough for Rick to pass them all. With his bike slung over his shoulder, he lumbered up to the top of the embankment, remounted, and pedaled off into the woods a few seconds ahead of the others.

"It looks like none other than Rick Vitale in the lead!" cried Eddie when Rick reappeared a few moments later and started the plunge back down the embankment. "Let's give a big cheer to bring him home!"

The cheers however turned to gasps when, halfway down the embankment, Rick's front wheel struck something, perhaps a rock or root, in its path. It instantly began to wobble in a rather disconcerting way that gave everyone watching to know that Rick was about to lose control of his bicycle. Sure enough, the wheel twisted almost completely perpendicular to the frame just as rider and bicycle bottomed out onto the field and jolted to an awkward stop. Physics took over and, a split second later, Rick went over the handlebars and landed flat on his back.

Zio Rick was dead, Fabio was certain of it. Oblivious to his aching knee, he sprang to his feet and dashed out across the field, limping along towards his uncle as fast as his damaged legs would carry him until he himself stepped in a rut, tripped, and fell headlong onto the gnarly turf. A raucous cheer went up from the crowd, and Fabio wanted for all the world to crawl beneath the earth to hide. Humiliated that he had made a spectacle of himself in front of everyone, but otherwise uninjured as far as he could discern, he quickly gathered himself and got to all fours. It was then, as he raised his head, that Fabio realized that the crowd had not been applauding his unfortunate tumble after all. Instead they were cheering on Zio Rick, who had somehow managed to rise from the dirt and remount his bicycle. By this time, of course, the rest of the field had already passed him by, but that no longer mattered. Wearing a great grin, he pedaled gamely on to the finish line where he received a hero's welcome despite finishing dead last. He was greeted with handshakes and pats on the back, and compliments from Eddie, who praised him for having the bravado and good sportsmanship to get up after such a hard crash so near the finish of the race.

Meanwhile, alone and unnoticed at the center of the field, Fabio got to his feet, dusted off his clothes, and cast a desultory look up at the stage where the applause had yet to die away. He stood there knowing that there was no way for him to do the same, to somehow turn disgrace into triumph, and so he turned away from the celebration and trudged with head bowed back to the wheel pit to guard the spare wheels and await his uncle's return.

Chapter Fourteen

The night before Christmas, a few weeks later, Fabio rode with Rick to the home of Carmine, an American-born cousin whose exact relationship to both men, regardless of how many times his uncle tried to explain it, was lost to Fabio somewhere in the distance amongst the far branches of the family tree. Carmine and his wife, Angie, lived in Cranston, less than an hour's drive north of Wakefield. It was an easy ride. Still, having yet to venture outside of South County, Fabio perceived the journey as taking much longer, and he inquired more than once along the way as to how much farther they had to travel. Rick chuckled each time for he realized that his nephew had unwittingly already acquired a Rhode Islander's somewhat skewed sensibility about distances. This mindset was no doubt reinforced when at last they arrived at the house early in the evening and Angie herself, a born and bred Rhode Islander, greeted the two as if they had just completed a trek across the Yukon.

"Come in, come in!" she cried happily, if fretfully, when they came to the door. "*Dio mio*, what a ride to come up all the way here from Wakefield—so dark and cold out, and it's supposed to snow tonight!"

Fabio swallowed hard when he stepped inside, the seemingly endless car ride instantly forgotten. The warm little house was crammed full of people, so much so that he and his uncle could barely move away from the front door. They were all strangers to Fabio save for Carmine and Angie who he had met but once earlier in the year when they stopped in Wakefield to visit the shop. Zio Rick, perhaps cognizant of his nephew's growing panic, gave him a playful nudge with his elbow and began at once to introduce him to his American relatives. There were third and fourth and fifth cousins in attendance, old and young, most of whom he had no idea even existed. Everyone, however, seemed to know of Fabio, and they all took turns asking him about Italy or what he thought of America and how long he planned to stay. It was as convivial a gathering as he could have hoped for. Be that as it may, Fabio felt as though he were suffocating, that their cordiality was squeezing the very breath out of him. To his relief, Angie soon intervened, announcing to everyone that it was time to eat. The attention mercifully deflected away from him, Fabio lingered for a time in the front hall, letting Rick and the others precede him into the dining room.

The food was laid out buffet style on the dining room table. Angie had of course prepared the requisite seven fishes. There were fried smelts and snail salad, baccala and shrimp, baked eel and stuffed calamari, and a big bowl of linguine tossed with garlic, olive oil, tuna, and olives. Carmine's contribution to the cornucopia of *frutti di mare* was a single boiled lobster that presided over the center of the table. It was a beautiful, bountiful feast, and at the sight of it there was more than one exclamation of *"Abbondanza!"*.

Fabio waited until everyone else had filled their plates before venturing into the dining room. Not particularly hungry, he chose just a few of the shrimp and a spoonful of snail salad to put on his own plate. Then he grabbed a slice of bread and ducked his head into the living room, looking about for some quiet spot where he might hide himself and eat while Rick socialized with his cousins. He spied a small den off the living room and made his way there, doing his best en route to wear a smile while at the same time covering his cheek as he squeezed past everyone.

When he stepped into the den, Fabio saw that it held a small love seat and a leather recliner. Carmine was sitting in the latter with his granddaughter on his lap, reading to her from a book. That his plate of food was going cold on the side table next to him seemed not to bother him in the least. At seeing Fabio standing awkwardly in the doorway, Carmine smiled and gestured to the love seat. "Come, Fabio, sit down and eat!" he said jovially.

Fabio nodded and sat down across from the pair.

Carmine glanced at Fabio's plate and gave him an incredulous look. "Is that all you're having!"he exclaimed. "What's the matter, you don't like fish?"

"No no, fish very good," said Fabio, forcing a smile. "I just no like to eat so much all at once some of the times."

"Read, Papa Carmine, read!" said the little girl impatiently.

"Okay, okay, Giuliana!" laughed Carmine, turning his attention back to his granddaughter. "Be patient. Hmm, let's see, where were we? Ah yes, here we are. The children were nestled all snug in their beds..."

While Carmine read the story, Fabio picked at his food, his thoughts drifting back to earlier in the day at the shop. Though Rick had insisted that she need not bother to come to work— it was the day before Christmas after all, and he planned to stay open just a few hours for the benefit of any last minute shoppers—Elise arrived at the shop that morning promptly at nine as always.

"You never know," she had explained brightly. "You might get a rush of customers and need the help."

As things would turn out, the only person to walk through the door was a rather lovely older lady, elegantly dressed against the cold in a full length camel hair coat and stylish fur hat. At seeing her enter the store late that morning, Rick immediately dropped what he was doing and hurried over to greet her. They were soon ambling about the shop together, Rick pointing out some newer pieces here and there in his collection, all the while exchanging pleasantries in a way that suggested the two knew each other well. Indeed, it was clear to see from the looks on their faces that they quite enjoyed one another's company. After he had guided her around the store, helping her pick out one of the decanters—a gift for a friend, the woman had explained—Rick had lingered with her by the counter, chatting about the weather, while Elise rang up the purchase and gift-wrapped the box. Shortly after, it seemed that it was only with great reluctance that the pair bid each other a Merry Christmas and parted company. When the woman had gone on her way, Rick stood by the window, watching until she had disappeared around the corner.

Fabio could not suppress his curiosity, for he had never seen the woman before. "Who was she?" he asked.

"Yes," said Elise, sounding equally intrigued. "She was quite lovely."

Rick gave a shrug. "I don't know," he admitted. "Just a customer. She just comes into the shop every now and then."

"*Just* a customer?" said Fabio, He arched an eyebrow and exchanged glances with Elise who wore a somewhat skeptical expression of her own.

Rick looked back and forth between the two. "What?" he said, puffing himself up in a display of indignation.

"Oh, nothing," said Elise.

"*Niente*," added Fabio sotto voce, and no more on the matter was said.

Shortly after lunchtime, Rick announced that it was time to close up the shop and went straightaway to his office. He soon returned bearing two envelopes. Without ceremony he handed the first of these to Elise. "Your wages for the week, Miss Celestin," he said with mock formality.

"Thank you, Mister Rick," she replied with equal gravitas.

"And this is also for you," said Rick, this time with true

geniality as he handed over the second envelope. "Just a little something from me and Fabio in appreciation for all your nice work this season."

Fabio of course had no notion whatsoever as to what Rick had given her until Elise had opened the Christmas card the envelope held and found the bonus check folded inside. His uncle had apparently been generous for the young woman's eyes opened wide in surprise when she saw the amount written on it.

"Thank you so much, Mister Rick," she gushed. "I don't know what to say."

"Well, there's a lot less inventory on the shelves this year than there normally is," said Rick warmly. "And we have you to thank for that, so you don't have to say anything."

"Well I have something for both of you, too," said Elise, hurrying behind the counter. She soon produced a paper shopping bag, reached inside, and withdrew two round bow-tied tins. "These are cookies I baked at home," she said modestly, handing one to each man. "Just a little thought."

"A very nice thought," said Rick. "Thank you, Elise. Merry Christmas, or as we say in Italy, *Buon Natale!*"

"*Buon Natale*, how nice that sounds," said Elise. Then, turning mischievous eyes to Fabio, she added, "And I thought we spoke only English here."

"Carmine!"

The voice jolted Fabio back to the present.

"Carmine!" Angie called again.

Carmine leaned his head toward the door and looked out into the living room. "Yes, dearest?" he called patiently in reply.

"Come and set up the portable crib in the bedroom so Stacy can put the baby down for a while," said his wife.

Carmine grinned and gave Fabio a wink. "No rest for the weary," he chuckled. With a sigh of resignation he helped Giuliana off his lap and got to his feet.

"Where are you going, Papa?" his granddaughter protested.

Carmine smiled down at her and patted her head. "Orders are orders, my little darling. But don't worry, I'll be right back." With that he passed the book over to Fabio. "Try to hold down the fort for me while I'm gone, will you?" he said. Then he dutifully hurried off to the bedroom to attend to the portable crib.

Giuliana, wearing a green velvet dress and white stockings, stood watching her Papa walk away before turning her inquisitive brown eyes to Fabio. She regarded him for a long moment then looked down at the floor and stuck a foot out towards him. "Do you like my shoes?" she asked sweetly.

Fabio looked at her little patent leather shoes and for the first time all night gave a genuine smile. "Yes," he said with a nod.

"They have bows, did you see?" she said.

"They are very pretty," Fabio told her.

The response seemed to please the little girl and a moment later she was sitting by Fabio's side. She took the book from his hands and began to flip through the pages. "Tell me the story?" she said, looking up at him hopefully.

Fabio gave a little shrug and shook his head. "I sorry," he said, "but I no read so good yet."

"Why not?" she asked innocently.

Before Fabio could formulate an appropriate reply, Giuliana unexpectedly stood up on the couch, leaned over against him, and unabashedly began to inspect his facial features. She took his chin in her hands and turned his face from one side to the other, her eyes studying every detail with that mesmerizing curiosity that only little children have. Fabio was completely captivated by it and made no move to disturb her deliberations. Her assessment of him went on for a few moments more before Giuliana finally paused and reached out to touch his misshapen cheek. Her eyes showing concern, she ran her fingertips across its contours, now and then gently applying pressure.

"Does it hurt?" she asked in the tiniest of voices.

"Sometimes," said Fabio. "Just a little."

At that Giuliana pulled herself closer and kissed his cheek. "All better now?" she asked.

"Much better," said Fabio, a tear coming to his eye. "Thank you."

Giuliana smiled and sat back down at his side. "Good," she said, opening the book once more. "Now tell me the story."

*

Rick and Fabio did not stay very late at the party. Rick had imbibed one or two glasses of wine and thought it best to get on the road back to South County before he was tempted to have one or two more. For his part, Fabio had been prepared to go home before they even entered the house, so there were no complaints from him when his uncle gave him a nod, letting him know that they would soon be getting on their way. When it came time to go, the two bid everyone a Merry Christmas and took their leave at the front door amidst a great flurry of hugs and kisses and promises to get together again soon after the new year. Once more in the car, they drove straight to Wakefield, but not directly home as Fabio had hoped. Instead they stopped first at the house of Joe, the submarine sandwich man, who was hosting a Hanukkah party that very same evening. Had it not been for Rick's assurance that they would not be staying long there either, Fabio would have remained in the car. Reluctantly, he got out and trudged with his uncle up the front walk.

Joe, who apparently had that evening imbibed one or two glasses of wine himself, greeted the pair at the front door and with great joviality ushered them in. Like Angie and Carmine's house, his home was full of friends and family, loud talk and laughter. Joe led them directly to the center of the boisterous gathering in the living room where the children were sitting on the floor, playing dreidels for chocolate coins wrapped in gold foil while the adults all around were busy kibitzing among themselves. There he held up his hand for quiet.

"Everybody, listen to me, this is my friend, Enrico, and his nephew, Fabio," he told them all. A chorus of hellos and welcomes ensued before Joe held up his hand once again. "Enrico is his real name, by the way, but everybody calls him Rick." He put his arm over Rick's shoulder and gave a sly wink to the others. "And Rick, tell them what you call me," he said.

Rick gave a smile and shrugged. "Giuseppe," he answered.

"Ah, now did you hear what he called me?" said Joe, looking about with wide-eyed incredulity. "*Jew*-seppe!"

The observation prompted a second chorus, this time of feigned indignation, expressions of dismay, admonitions, and wagging fingers despite Rick's protestations of innocence.

"But that's all right, that's all right," cried Joe to quell the comic uproar, "Rick's a Catholic, so he and I are what you might call spiritual *paesans*. It's an important night for him too, you know, so I'll let him get away with it just for tonight!"

With that he beckoned for someone to bring Rick a glass of wine and the two sat down to talk with the others. For a moment Fabio stood all alone amidst the gathering. It was the second time his uncle had abandoned him that night. It was the sort of thing that he did with increasing frequency of late, and Fabio suspected that it was his way of tossing him into the social waters, so to speak, and leaving him there to sink or swim. Holding his breath, Fabio drifted over toward the dining room where the candles on the menorah cast a pleasant glow across the table festooned in blue, white, and silver ribbons. Just then an older, curmudgeonly gentleman, whose name he would later learn was Saul, came and stood next to Fabio, gazing with him at the table.

"Too bad," Saul lamented with a heavy sigh, gesturing at the empty platter to one side of the table. "It's a beautiful table, but the latkes are all gone."

"The what?" said Fabio.

"The latkes," repeated Saul. "The potato pancakes. Ooh, they were so good. You should have had some, but they're all gone now. But what are you going to do? That's what happens when you come so late!"

"Sorry, but we come from other party tonight," explained Fabio somewhat sheepishly, a hand over his cheek.

"Ah," said the old man with another heavy sigh that belied the mischievous twinkle in his eye. "That's right, I forgot, it's that *other* holiday tomorrow. Tonight you people eat fish, right? What's that all about anyway? What's with all the seafood?"

Fabio himself was not quite sure of the reason, but there was something disarming about the old gent, and he felt compelled to hazard a guess. "Because Gesu feed the peoples with the fishes and the bread," he offered, lowering his hand.

The explanation must have seemed plausible to Saul, for he rubbed his chin and nodded thoughtfully. "Eh, I heard that story too," he said, "so I guess it does all makes sense in its own way. But us? We eat the latkes and the sufganiyots, those things that look like donuts there on the other plate. You should try one before they're all gone too, they're delicious. And then of course we light the menorah."

"And what mean all that for you?" asked Fabio, for some reason strangely at ease with this perfect stranger.

The old man held up a finger and his face took on a most solemn expression. "Ah, now there's a very very good story, my friend," he said. "It's one you should hear." With that he gave Fabio a pat on the shoulder and nodded to the table. "Why don't you get a sufganiyot for yourself then come sit, and I'll tell you all about it...."

*

The snow Angie had foretold earlier in the evening had started to come down by the time they left the party. Though it was a good deal later than Rick had assured him they would stay, Fabio was not terribly put out. The sufganiyots were indeed sweet and delicious, and Saul had kept him relatively entertained with his recitation of the historical origins of Hanukkah. In truth, Fabio had attended little to the particulars of the dissertation; Saul for all intents and purposes lost him completely not long after commencing his rather detailed narration of the exploits of Judas Maccabeus. There was, however, something about the obvious pleasure that the old man took in the telling that the younger man found curiously soothing. And so, while his uncle talked and drank with Joe and the others, Fabio had sat there quite silent, respectfully listening in a sort of dream state somewhat akin to meditative. Thus the time passed quickly and when Rick finally beckoned for him to take his leave, it was almost as if he had been abruptly awakened from a light, very pleasant nap. Getting to his feet, it had not been without a modicum of regret that Fabio bid Saul a polite but inevitably brief goodnight before going off to find his coat.

"He's a little quiet," Fabio heard the old man saying behind him as he made his way to the door, "but he seems like a good boy."

Joe walked out to the car to see them off, he and Rick both in exceedingly good spirits. Suspecting that this was at least as much due to having ingested more liquids than latkes as it was to each man's inherent good nature, Fabio saw fit to coax the keys from his uncle before letting him get behind the wheel. Rick did not protest and, after promising Joe that next year they would arrive in time to pray the Halle with him, he settled into the passenger seat to let Fabio drive home.

Somewhere along the way on the short ride back to the house, Rick's apparent good spirits left him. Fabio did not notice it until he pulled into the driveway and went to hand the keys to him. Rick did not take them right away, but instead gazed blankly out the window for a moment, wearing a look of what seemed to Fabio distant regret. It was something he had never before seen in his uncle's eyes, perhaps because he had always been far too preoccupied with regrets of his own to make note of them in someone else. In any case, he was anxious to get inside, so he gave the keys a jangle.

"You go in to bed now?" said Fabio.

Coming back to himself, Rick gave a half smile and took the keys. "No," he said simply with a shake of his head. Then he opened the door and stepped out of the car. Fabio got out as well and stood there watching him.

The snow was coming down in earnest now, the ground already covered in a thin shroud of white. All was quiet save for an occasional passing car and the chiming of church bells coming from the other side of the village.

"What you do now?" asked Fabio, concerned that he might be contemplating getting back into the car and driving off someplace on his own.

"What do you think?" said Rick with a harrumph. "I'm going to Mass." He paused and looked intently at his nephew. "Why don't you come with me," he said.

"Maybe better you not drive," Fabio suggested. "You drink the wine tonight."

Rick gave a rather loud belch. "Who said anything about driving?" he said. "The church is just across the bridge and over the hill. It's an easy walk. Are you coming?"

"No," said Fabio.

"Why not?"

Fabio had not been to Mass in eons and even though it was Christmas Eve he felt no particular urge to go at that moment, so he answered with the only plausible excuse that sprang to mind. "The knees," he said, looking down. "They make me to hurt in cold. Too far to walk."

"Don't worry," replied his uncle, "your knees will feel better after you spend a little time kneeling on them. It's a good night for it."

Fabio had no ready reply for that particular observation, so he stood there in silence, his hands dug deep into his pockets to keep warm, before breaking into a wry grin. "For man who no want to be priest, you like to do the preaching," he said.

Rick gave a shrug and started to walk away.

"How about I make the driving?" Fabio called after him, but by then Rick had deposited the keys into his coat pocket and was crossing the road.

Fabio looked up at the snowflakes streaming down from the darkened heavens and grumbled in consternation. His uncle was in no condition to drive, but he was not in prime condition to walk alone all across town in the snow, either. There were a thousand places along the way where he might slip and fall and hurt himself. Fabio did not need the guilt of knowing that he had just let it happen, so he gave another grumble, tugged his coat collar tighter about his neck, and hurried off to catch up.

*

By the time Mass ended and the two had returned home through the snow, Fabio was near ready to collapse, though not because of his knees. The church had been packed to capacity and, squeezed into the pew as he had been amongst his fellow sinners, he had spent the better part of the Mass trying gamely not to hyperventilate instead of attending to the liturgy. It was the third time his uncle had dragged into a crowded place that evening, and now he was exhausted and all but frantic to find himself ensconced once more in the safe solitude of his apartment. Just the same, when the two men finally came to the house, Fabio did not immediately go up to his own quarters, but instead followed Zio Rick inside into the downstairs living room. Something was puzzling him. He had wanted to ask his uncle about it ever since they filed out of the church with the rest of the congregation, but he had been hesitant to ask. And so he had waited.

Once inside, Zio Rick, who himself looked quite bedraggled, apologized for having nothing to offer him before slouching into a chair in front of the television. There he picked up the remote control, turned on the television, and scrolled through the channels until he came to a replay of the Pope saying Mass earlier that evening at the Vatican. Despite having just come from church, Rick settled back and watched intently, softly humming *Adeste Fideles* along with the choir. Fabio meantime took a seat at the end of the couch and watched with his uncle for a time before his curiosity to know the answer to the question that had been puzzling him so finally overcame him.

"Zio," he asked, "I no never go to church since I was very little boy, so tonight I no go up to take the Communion. But you, why do you no go?"

"You mean, why *didn't* I go?" said his uncle with a yawn.

"Yes, yes," huffed Fabio impatiently. "Why *didn't* you go?"

Rick gave him a faint, but sad smile and turned back to the television. "Because I've not been to confession," came the simple reply. "It would not have been proper."

In all the month's since he first came to America, Fabio had not known Zio Rick to have missed daily or Sunday Mass even once. He was as friendly and charitable, as good a man as he had ever known, and the mere notion that he might have anything at all to confess that might keep him from taking Communion struck Fabio as somehow vaguely preposterous.

"But why no, Zio?" he said, unable to suppress a grin. "Since when you need the confession?"

Rick turned and looked at him with that same expression of distant regret that Fabio had seen earlier in his eyes. "I've not been in forty-two years," he said.

Certain that he must have not heard his uncle properly, Fabio asked him to repeat himself. When the query elicited the same response, Fabio gaped at him, dumbfounded, a thousand questions suddenly swirling in his head.

Rick turned away and breathed a weary sigh, as if he knew it was inevitable that some of these would soon be posed. "It was a woman," he said in a faraway voice before Fabio could speak.

"Who, what woman?' said Fabio, now totally bewildered.

"Just before I was to be ordained, I fell in love with a woman," said Rick. "Her name was Adriana. That was why I left seminary. I was going to marry her."

"But, but where she go?"stammered Fabio, scratching his head, trying to process it all. "What happen?"

"Not long after I made my decision, she got sick and died," Rick replied without emotion. "And that's all anyone needs to know."

Even so, Fabio wanted to know more. "But all the time," he said, "still to now you don't—"

"I love the Church," said Rick, anticipating the question, "and I wanted to serve her, but I broke my vows, or at least the ones I was going to take, and I've always felt sorry about that. I know it was wrong, and I *knew* it was wrong then, but at the same time I've never been sorry that I fell in love with Adriana—except that maybe what happened to her was my fault, that God was angry with me." He paused and shook his head sadly. "I don't know," he sighed, looking down at his hands. "Anyway, I've always felt terribly that I walked away from my calling, but I still love Adriana, even now. So, you see, as much as I love the Church, I cannot rightly go to God and ask for forgiveness for something about which I don't feel true regret. And so, when I go to Mass, out of respect, I can't take Communion. Do you understand?"

"No," said Fabio. "You are good man."

"Hmm," said his uncle with a grunt. "Sometimes more than that is asked of us." With that he turned away, settled back in the chair once more, and closed his eyes.

Fabio looked away to the window and outside to where the snowflakes were drifting down in relentless streams through the pale yellow glow of the streetlight across the road. "I no understand," he said as he watched them fall. "First you give up being the priest to be husband for the woman, but then you give up the woman forever and live all alone like the priest? Where is the sense?"

Fabio turned back, expecting a reply, but he saw that Rick had already fallen asleep and was now snoring softly in the chair. Not wanting to wake him, for he well understood the peace that one could only find in sleep, Fabio took a blanket from the couch and gently laid it over him. Satisfied that his uncle would be all right, he quietly went on his way to bed, but not before breaking the standing rules of speech in the house.

"*Buon Natale, Zio*," he whispered.

February

CHAPTER FIFTEEN

February—and there was no end in sight.

Fabio yawned and stared out his bedroom window at the front yard. It was just after dawn, the sun barely a smudge of orange hanging low behind the veil of a dark gray sky, all about outdoors still agloom, the cold night not yet completely chased away. A thin glaze of hard, crusty snow lay across the yard and the bony branches of the trees were swaying in the wind, scratching at the frigid air.

His feet cold against the hardwood floor, Fabio stood there shivering. Where, he wondered with almost desperate yearning, was the mid-winter thaw he had heard about, the one that was to have arrived by now and spelled the end of the hard cold weather? Instead of moderating, the winds had seemed to have grown only more fierce, the cold more biting as the days wore on. Growing up in Mont' Oliva at the foot of the mountains, Fabio had seen his share of chilly winters, but nothing to match this interminably bleak season. For weeks on end he had struggled to survive it, his spirits plummeting with the setting of the sun each day, and climbing not much higher than the mercury when it came round again to rise. This morning, as with so many of the mornings preceding it, he had struggled just to pull himself from beneath the bedcovers. Now, looking out at the frozen landscape with forlorn eyes, facing the prospect of another frigid day, he felt a dull ache of despair in the pit of his gut.

How long would it go on?

From down below came the sound of the front door being pulled shut and the crunch of snow beneath boots. Soon after, he saw Zio Rick come into view, the hood of his coat pulled up over his head as he trudged down the driveway and across the street on his way to morning Mass. Fabio watched in weary fascination. How did his uncle do it day after day? Did he never sleep in? He shook his head and turned from the window. Then he gave another yawn and slouched to the kitchenette to make coffee.

Later, after he had practically sleepwalked to the shop, Fabio found his uncle in the back, already preparing to light the furnace while he hummed along to the march from Aida playing on the little cassette player he had used for who knew how many years. Like his nephew, Rick liked to listen to music while working, but his tastes, as one might expect, were decidedly different. At seeing Fabio walk in, he turned down the volume a bit and waved him over.

"Come here," he said brightly, "I want to show you something."

Fabio gave a little groan for he was not yet nearly ready to start work, and of no mind to listen to one of his uncle's occasional dissertations on glassblowing technique. It was still much too early; he needed a little more time to adequately rouse himself. More to the point, Fabio was not at all anxious to start regardless of his state of consciousness. Perhaps it was the incessant winter taking its toll on him, but his glassmaking efforts of late had been decidedly lackluster. He hated everything he started, so much so that his cardboard box of glass scraps had grown near to overflowing. Just the same he obeyed his master and drew closer.

"Let's go, Virgilio, light!" muttered Rick, fiddling with the mechanism to ignite the old furnace. "Don't give me a hard time this morning, I've got a lot to do." Virgilio, perhaps feeling as averse as Fabio to starting work that chilly morning, was disinclined to light right away. "Come on, my friend," Rick gently prodded it as he adjusted the gas valve, "it's time for us to get to work. Don't be stubborn."

As his uncle often spoke this way to the furnace, Fabio paid no particular heed. Zio Rick, he had observed over the months, had something of a love hate relationship with the appliance. There were times, while working, when he talked to it like an old friend, but then others when he bickered with it like they were an old married couple. And then were times, like this one, when he took to patiently cajoling it like one might a contrary old horse that was in no mind to get galloping no matter how much it was spurred. His uncle's patience, however, quickly began to run thin.

"Don't think I won't get rid of you and buy a new furnace," threatened Rick, giving it a knock on the side. "I can get another loan if I need it, you know, and then you'll be out on the street. So come on now and light, *stunato!*"

"Ayy, *solo l'inglese qui!*" Fabio reminded him. "English only."

"Watch yourself, young man," said his uncle in a distinctly menacing tone, but then the furnace ignited and the burners roared to life. "Ah, there we are," he said, brightening once more. "I knew all it needed was a little convincing."

Rick let the furnace burn for a few minutes before adding the silica, the raw material used to make the glass. Generating nearly two thousand degrees of heat within, the furnace melted the granular substance in a matter of seconds, turning it into a pool of liquid fire, one that could now be gathered and reformed into something new and beautiful. By then both men had already peeled off their jackets and sweaters. There was no need for them what with the heat blasting from the furnace's mouth.

Satisfied that all was ready for them to get started, Rick reached over to the tape deck and turned the volume higher.

"Must we have?" groused Fabio, who was not particularly fond of Verdi.

"Yes, now watch and listen to what I tell you," said Rick, taking one of the blowing pipes from the wall. "I've been thinking about your work, how you're always looking for something wrong in your new pieces, some defect that you can't ever find."

Fabio squirreled up the side of his mouth in a look of stoic resignation, gave a nod upwards, and shrugged. "God like to punish me that way," he said, only partly joking.

Rick paused and looked at him for a moment. "Why would he bother," he replied, "when you already do such a good job of it yourself? Now pay attention." He took the blowing pipe and, humming along to the music, rested it on the lip of the furnace. "The problem," he went on, "is that sometimes you—all of us really—sometimes we just get a bad idea stuck in our heads that makes us look at things the wrong way, and no matter how hard you try, you can't shake it out. In your case, you're sure you're doing everything right when you start out, but you end up certain that you've done something wrong."

"Maybe," said Fabio, at the moment only mildly interested. "So what I do?

"First," said Rick, "you must see that the flaw is not in the glass, it's in your head."

Fabio made a queer expression and looked down at his feet. "The floor—is in my head?" he said a bit confused.

"Not the floor, the flaw," replied Rick. Then, suddenly cognizant of the misunderstanding, he laughed and said, "The defect, the thing that you think is wrong in the glass. That's what's in your head. It's just in your imagination, and the harder you look for it, the harder it is to find, because it's not really there, and that's what makes you mad."

"So," Fabio asked once more, "what I do?"

"It starts with the gather," said Rick, setting the pipe on the furnace's sill. "The gather is everything."

"This you already tell me many times," noted Fabio.

"That's because it always bears repeating," said his uncle patiently. "Now watch, please."

Fabio dutifully obeyed and leaned closer.

"You have to make sure that you do everything properly right from the start," said Rick rolling the pipe a little to the right. "You have to be certain that you set the pipe just right and then you lower it just enough until you can see the reflection of the glass on the tip. And then..."

Rick dipped the pipe ever so slightly, just barely enough for it to touch the pool of molten glass. Then he turned the pipe two full rotations to let it gather up just the right amount of the red-hot liquid before bringing it back to level.

"You see?" he said, casting a look over his shoulder to make sure that Fabio was still watching. "Now that we've gathered the glass properly, we can start to work."

With the practiced efficiency that only comes from years of patient toil and discipline, Rick blew a puff off air into the pipe, breathing life into the glowing bulb on its tip so that it expanded like a small balloon. Before long he fashioned it into a simple goblet, rather nondescript but adequate to his purpose.

"Now, what do you see?" he said, holding it up for Fabio after it had cooled. "What did I do wrong? Where is the flaw?"

"Nothing that I see," answered his nephew.

"That's right," said Rick, nodding. "You see nothing wrong with it because there *is* nothing wrong with it, at least nothing that really matters. Only God could make it perfect, of course. We know that there is at least some little flaw in it somewhere, even if it's too small to see. It's like that with anything we do. We accept that there will always be some sort of defect, some little shortcoming in whatever we do. The idea is to simply do your best, and to try to keep getting better without worrying about being perfect, otherwise you'll end up stuck on one thing and never move on to something new. Do you understand?"

Fabio nodded yes, even though he was not quite certain of what his uncle was trying to teach him.

"And it's the same with your work," Rick went on, "but your mind won't let you believe it. Even when you make something that is as perfectly imperfect as you can make it, it keeps tricking you into thinking that there's something there hiding from you, something important you shouldn't have overlooked. It's not there, but you drive yourself crazy looking for it anyway. It's like there's a beast inside your brain, and it's always hungry."

"So, how do I stop it?" asked Fabio, for the first time feeling a spark of true interest.

Rick gave him a wink. "You just have feed it," he said.

"Feed? How?"

"Just watch," said his uncle, laying a finger aside of his nose.

Fabio leaned closer and looked over his shoulder as he took the goblet and heated it once more in the fire for a brief time. When it was ready, Rick drew it out of the furnace and inspected it for a moment before taking a scoring knife in hand. This he carefully inserted into the goblet and made some modification within that Fabio could not readily observe. When he was done, he smiled and passed the goblet to Fabio.

"Now, do you see?" he said with an air of satisfaction.

Fabio gazed hard into the goblet. "No," he said, shaking his head. "For what do I look?'"

"The flaw," Rick explained, still grinning. "The one I put there myself."

"I no find nothing," said Fabio.

"I can't find anything," Rick corrected him. "That's because you don't know where to look, but I do, and that's the point. You see, instead of looking for some flaw that's not really there, I put in one of my own, one that only I can find. You could do the same. Put in some little imperfection on purpose that no one else but you can see and then you don't have to worry about finding it anymore because it will always be right there where you put it."

"And that way the beast no more hungry?" said Fabio thoughtfully.

"That's how you feed it," said Rick with a wink. "I'm guessing that all you need to do is give it a little crumb and that alone might just be enough to do the trick."

Not completely convinced, yet intrigued by the concept, Fabio turned the goblet in his hand, still gazing inside before turning inquisitive eyes to his uncle. "And what if someone else find this crumb?" he asked pointedly. "Like the one you make."

"Then he'll know the whole thing was made by a human," said Rick simply. "It wouldn't be the end of the world, you know." At that he shrugged and reached for his sweater. "Anyway, it was just an idea," he said, pulling it over his head. "I thought it might help. Give it a try if you like, but that's up to you."

Fabio mulled it over a moment. "Okay, maybe I give a try," he said, "but need I do with Aida still?" This he said while casting a baleful look at the tape player.

'No," chuckled Rick. "I guess you can do without that if you want. Now, if you'll excuse me, I have to go upstairs to see what our associate is up to on the second floor." With that he gestured to the furnace, indicating that Fabio now had it all to himself, and went on his way.

Left alone, Fabio waited until the door had closed before turning off the cassette player. The strains of Aida now but a memory, he reached into his sweatshirt pocket and pulled out his new iPod—a Christmas gift from his uncle which from Rick's point of view was as much a gift to himself as to Fabio—and inserted the ear buds into his ears.

"Floors and flaws," Fabio muttered to himself while he scrolled through his play list until he found a tune suited to his disposition. The music now thumping in his ears, he reached for the blowing pipe and rested it on the furnace sill. With the searing heat from within bristling the hairs on his arm, he lingered there for a time, nodding his head to the rhythm of the music, staring blankly into the flames. When the moment felt right, he lowered the pipe to the glass, wondering all the while what sort of crumb he might possibly conjure up to keep the beast in his brain finally at bay.

CHAPTER SIXTEEN

Forbidden by his uncle to smoke inside, Fabio stepped out the back door and into the alleyway on the side of the building that led out to the street. He had been at work for some time, trying with only a modicum of success to take Rick's advice to heart, and now he felt the need for a break. Situated as it was between the shop and the building next door, the narrow alley rarely saw direct sunlight most days, and virtually never at this time of year when the sun traversed such a low arc through the sky. The area, as a result, was perpetually in shadows, a state of affairs Fabio ordinarily found to his liking, but less so now with the wintry chill.

His shoulders hunched up against the cold, he tugged a cigarette from the pack in his pocket, stuck it in his mouth, and with hands trembling fumbled with the lighter. The cigarette lit, he drew in a deep breath from it and exhaled a long lazy plume of gray. Despite the dim light and the cold, Fabio liked the close confines of the alley and often sought refuge there, as evidenced by the collection of cigarette butts strewn everywhere at his feet. When he wasn't working, this was one of the few places in which he felt at ease. Perhaps it was because this vantage point, hidden away as it was in the shadows, allowed him to observe people going in and out of the coffee shop across the street and the motorists and pedestrians passing by without he himself being readily observed. The tiny sliver of a view offered him but a mere glimpse of life away from the flames of the furnace, but more often than not, that was all he craved.

The music from his iPod still thumping in his ears, Fabio stared absentmindedly down the alley and blew out another puff from his cigarette. His eyes followed the smoke as it drifted upward and quickly vanished into the chill air, but not before drawing his line of sight to the windows above on the second floor. Though Zio Rick often went up there to store one thing or another, Fabio had never so much as set foot on the stairs. For whatever strange reason, the mere idea of ascending to the second floor had always filled him with an odd sense of foreboding, and so he rarely looked at the door behind the front desk that led to the staircase, never mind consider stepping through it. Just the same, he felt vaguely annoyed at knowing that Elise was up there right now with his uncle, sifting through whatever it was that he kept there, discovering who knew what about the business while she helped him sort things out.

Though he would have been loath to admit it, especially to himself, Fabio felt a distinct if inexplicable pang of jealousy. The feeling was complicated by another, that of guilt, that had gnawed at the back of his mind ever since that afternoon in the shop when Elise had offered to buy him a sandwich for lunch. That he had responded with such unwarranted rudeness had weighed on him ever since, and he had kept his distance from her as much as possible just to avoid being reminded of the incident. That she, for her part, continued to treat him with relentless civility—a state of affairs he found mildly irksome— only served to heighten his discomfiture.

Intent on ignoring the goings-on above him, Fabio began to look away, but just then the motion of a figure passing by the window caught his eye. He fixed his sight anew on the window, waiting for a time to see if whichever of the two it had been, his uncle or Elise, would reappear. When neither came into view, he turned off his iPod and tugged out the ear buds. Standing quite still in the cold, his ear inclined to the second floor, he strained to listen. At first Fabio heard only the whisper of the breeze through the alley, but then, after a moment or two, he could clearly discern the sound of voices coming from inside. Muffled as they were by the interior walls and windows, he could make out nothing of what was being said, or by whom. Standing there shivering, wondering what was being discussed up there above him, that lingering sense of foreboding he felt about the second floor very quickly gave way to a different feeling: curiosity. Fabio stayed there, struggling in vain to resist its pull as he gazed up at the window, till at last he took one last puff from his cigarette, flicked the butt to the ground, and promptly went inside.

"Shouldn't we keep those?" Fabio heard Rick saying when he began to quietly ascend the stairs to the second floor.

"No, Mister Rick," came Elise's reply. There was in her voice a distinct air of impatience, indicating perhaps that this was a question that had been posed more than once.

"You're certain."

"Yes, Mister Rick. These bank statements are from twenty years ago. Please trust me, the whole box should go."

Fabio paused a few steps from the top of the staircase. The floor above now at eye level, he stood on tiptoe and peered through the open door and into the room. There, not far inside, Elise was kneeling before a cardboard box—one of many from what he could see—sifting through a handful of papers while his uncle stood behind her, looking over her shoulder. Their backs to him, they did not notice Fabio standing in the stairwell, watching them, until the creak of one of the old wooden steps beneath his feet betrayed his presence. Both turned at once and looked at him.

Fabio's first instinct was to scurry back down the stairs, and he was about to do so, but a smile of reassurance from his uncle gave him to know that he had nothing to dread.

"Well, hello there," said Zio Rick. "Come on up, if you like."

Meek as a mouse, Fabio climbed the remaining stairs, but hesitated when he reached the top.

"Don't be afraid to come in," Rick told him with a chuckle. "There are no monsters up here—at least none that we've discovered yet."

"But watch your step anyway," Elise advised him. "And you might want to go back for your hat and gloves, it's freezing up here."

Fabio walked in and looked around.

It was a large, unpartitioned room he found himself in. Its ceiling open to the rafters above, the room spanned the entire length and breadth of the old building. It might have been an airy place had it not been for the astounding mass of clutter filling virtually every inch of the floor. Fabio looked slowly about at it all. Everywhere there were bags and cardboard boxes full of papers—old financial records and the like, he assumed—heaped upon one another willy-nilly. Along with them there were stacks of old books and magazines, out of date telephone directories, and bundles of newspaper. Off in the corner lay a pile of old blowing pipes and other tools, and nearby a collection of old wooden chairs and a small table with a broken leg. Roundabout everywhere else lay boxes of goblets, decanters, vases, and all manner of forgotten glassworks found, he could only surmise, unworthy for sale and abandoned for who knew how long to collect dust like the rest of the paraphernalia in the room.

It was a mess.

The whole sight struck Fabio as exceedingly strange, for it was so much at odds with the Spartan, uncluttered order of his uncle's house. He said nothing at first, but cast his gaze about, unable to conceal a look of mild surprise.

"You no like to throw away much," he opined at last.

Rick gave a wistful sigh and shrugged. "I've been putting stuff up here for forty years," he said by way of explanation. "You'd be amazed at how quickly it adds up without your even knowing it." He gave another shrug and nodded at him. "So, what brings you up here, Master Fabio, to help, or have you decided already to call it a day?"

His hands tucked under his armpits, his shoulders scrunched up close to his ears, Fabio gave a nervous cough to clear his throat and looked down at the floor, his brain feverishly working to concoct some plausible reason other than mere curiosity for his deciding to join them. "No," he replied at last in a hesitant voice. "I take break and go to shop across street now for coffee." He paused and cleared his throat again before adding, "I just want to see who want coffee too."

Now it was Rick's turn to wear a look of mild surprise. He exchanged glances with Elise, who bore much the same expression, and gave a chuckle of pleasure. "Well, that's very nice of you to ask," said Rick, exchanging another glance with her. "I don't want anything for myself right now, thank you, but perhaps El—"

"I would love one," said Elise right away with a laugh before he could finish. "I think I'm getting frostbite up here!"

"Okay, I go then," said Fabio softly without looking up as he began to back away.

"But let me give you some money first," offered Elise.

"No no, " said Fabio at once. "I pay."

With that he abruptly turned heel and started back down the stairs. He had not gone far when from behind him he heard his uncle give a grunt. "Hmm," he heard him saying before he was out of earshot. "Now there's even more progress..."

When Fabio returned a short while later, the bag holding the two cups of coffee in hand, he found Elise sitting at the counter, sifting through a box of papers she evidently had brought down with her from the second floor. At seeing him come through the door, she stopped what she was doing and looked up at him with a kind smile. Fabio did not return the smile as he timidly approached her, but instead cast a quick eye about for his uncle, who was nowhere to be seen at the moment.

"Zio in back?" he asked, setting the bag on the counter.

"No," Elise replied pleasantly. "He said he had some errands to run and that he would be back later on." Then, with a mischievous sparkle in her eye, she added, "He also said to tell you that you were in charge while he was gone."

"He alway say that," Fabio mumbled. "It just his joke."

"I'm sorry, what did you say?" Elise asked innocently, pretending that she had not heard him.

"Not the thing," replied Fabio.

"You mean nothing."

Slightly taken aback, Fabio cocked his head sideways and looked at her with raised eyebrows. "I mean nothing?" he said, confused.

"No," said Elise, shaking her head. "What I meant is that you *should* have said nothing."

Fabio was even more confused now, and growing a bit annoyed. After all who was she to tell him that he should not speak? Suddenly aware of the misunderstanding, Elise covered her mouth, as if she were trying not to laugh, which only added to his pique.

"I'm sorry," she said sweetly to put him at ease. "All I meant to say is that instead of 'not the thing' you should say *noth-ing*."

She pronounced the word again with enough emphasis that Fabio at last understood and his cheeks flushed from embarrassment. "Just like Zio," he grumbled, reverting once more to speaking under his breath.

Elise chose to ignore the remark and instead turned her gaze to the paper bag and eyed it with a questioning look. Without being asked, Fabio opened the bag and handed her one of the cups. The other he took for himself. Then, not sure of what to say or do next, he tossed the bag into the trash can and stood there awkwardly staring at his cup.

Elise wasted no time in opening hers and took a sip. "Ooh, this is so good after being upstairs in that ice box," she cooed. "Thank you."

Fabio simply nodded in reply and turned to go. Something, though, made him stop. He slowly turned back and, swallowing hard, looked at her with an expression of, if not contriteness, something close to resignation.

"In Italy," he told her, "we say *grazie*."

Elise's face instantly lit up.

"Well then," she said, her eyes gleaming with delight. "*Grazie!*"

"*Niente*," Fabio replied, looking quickly away.

Then, without another word, he left her and hurried off back to work.

CHAPTER SEVENTEEN

Early Saturday morning a few days later, Fabio took his uncle's truck and went for a ride. He had no particular destination in mind. He had awoken that day in horrendous spirits, his insides churning with anxiety. The usual solace he found in glassmaking eluding him, fleeing for a time seemed the only remedy for his foul mood.

He had slept only fitfully the night before, his sleep troubled by a dream of Enzo and Caterina. It was a recurring nightmare, variations of which had first begun plaguing his nights not long after he left Italy and came to America. In this most recent rendition, the dream began pleasantly enough with the three of them all together once more in the car, Fabio and Caterina in the back while Enzo drove, all of them laughing and singing along to the music on the radio. Then somehow, in that way that can only happen in a dream, Caterina was suddenly sitting in the front next to Enzo, leaving Fabio alone in the darkness of the back seat. Looking past his two friends and through the windshield, Fabio could see *il muro* coming into view at the bottom of the hill, and he was instantly gripped by that terrible ponderous feeling of dread and despair at knowing what awaited them. He tried with all his being to scream out to warn his friends, who seemed blissfully oblivious to the danger, but somehow he could not find the breath to speak. It was just then, an instant before impact, when Caterina, smiling seductively, turned around and, crooking a finger at him, softly said, "Come here, *bello*, I want to tell you something." Then came darkness and panic and the sensation of falling until at last he awoke in a cold sweat, his heart pounding in his chest. Fabio began a great many mornings in that fashion.

The dream still fresh in his mind, Fabio drove out of town into Narragansett and turned south. He had never before ventured into that part of the town, so now seemed as good a time as any to explore it. It was a nondescript stretch of road he found himself following for some time before at last he came to a stoplight. There he turned off the main road onto a long causeway that brought him into the center of the little fishing village of Galilee on Narragansett's southernmost tip.

Fabio pulled into an empty parking space on the side of the principal street through the village and climbed out of the truck. A sharp, bitingly cold wind whipping off the gray green waters of the nearby channel greeted him. Above, the clouds in the darkened sky were twisted and gnarled like bread dough being kneaded. A shiver running up his back, Fabio pulled the hood of his sweatshirt up over his head, dug his hands deep into the pocket, and began to walk over to the wharf where the ferry for Block Island was just pulling out. There were, from what Fabio could see, few passengers on board, and those were safe and snug in the warm confines of the vessel's interior. Fabio stood at the wharf's edge and watched the ferry churn away down the channel and out toward the open sea that lay between the village and the island some seven miles off the coast.

After the ferry had cleared the breakwater, Fabio took to meandering along the docks, breathing in the salt air and the smell of fish, and observing the gritty fishing boats moored one after the other. There was hardly another soul about, indeed the place was all but deserted, something he found to his liking.

When he came to the final dock, and had seen all he cared to see, Fabio walked out to the road and began to head back toward the truck.

It was just then that he looked up and saw an enormous mass of gray clouds barreling out of the sky straight at him. Stunned by the sight of it, Fabio stood there gaping in awe. In the next instant, before he even had a chance to brace himself, a furious snow squall blew in like a tornado, the wind whipping so hard that he could scarce look up into it. Leaning hard into the gale, Fabio struggled just to take a step into the blinding swirl of white. Harder and harder the snow came down; harder and harder the wind whipped all around him in a dizzying frenzy.

Fabio had never seen anything like it.

Then, just as suddenly as the storm had appeared, the winds ceased and the snow disappeared, and for a moment or two the clouds parted just long enough to let pass through a few hopeful rays of sunlight. The frenetic change in weather was so dramatic that it felt surreal to Fabio, but then again he had not been raised in New England.

"Yeeeeee-haaa!" came a voice up ahead of him.

Fabio looked up and saw a man, rather short and stout, walking a dog in his direction. Somehow he had not seen him before the squall had hit. As the man drew nearer, Fabio could see that he was an old salt, his pleasant round face weathered by many years on the water. The old man gave Fabio a nod and a wink, his bright blue eyes beneath his bushy eyebrows twinkling with delight.

"How did you like that, son? Can't beat Mother Nature when she wants to put on a show," the man laughed. "Let's see 'em match that down in Disney!"

"No, I guess," said Fabio, brushing the snowflakes from his shoulder.

His expression turning serious, the old man leaned closer and eyed Fabio with obvious concern. "Say, you all right there, my friend? It was just a little snow squall, but they can still knock the stuffin' out of you when they catch you unawares. You need a ride home or somethin'?"

"No, no thank you," said Fabio, forcing a feeble smile. "I have truck just up road."

"Okay, if you're sure, " said the man, "but just take care of yourself. Winters can be a little rough around here, you know."

"Yes," said Fabio, giving a rare ironic laugh. "I know."

Then he trudged back to the truck.

"You all right?" said Rick, peeking over the top of the newspaper after Fabio had returned home a short while later.

Fabio gave a shrug and fidgeted disconsolately with a paper napkin which he was slowly pulling apart shred by shred and rolling into little balls. "Winter is long here," he finally said.

"Ha, you noticed," replied his uncle. "I suppose it's true, our winters can be long, but if you stay here long enough you kind of get used to them, almost get to like them."

"Like?" said Fabio, incredulous.

"Maybe not like," said Rick, "but you find them more tolerable. Even when you don't, spring always comes sooner or later. It's like that with everything in life. You just have to be patient."

The two were at the kitchen table, drinking coffee—Rick with his usual splash of anisette—and nibbling on Italian toast with Nutella. For whatever reason, Rick had not bothered to make a frittata or anything else for them to eat that morning. Fabio never cooked at all, so the two men had gone without a proper breakfast other than the coffee and toast. The pantry looking bare, prospects for lunch, as far as Fabio could perceive, were equally bleak, so he consumed as much of the toast as he could hold. As he did so, Rick gazed thoughtfully at him.

"You look tired," said his uncle after a time. "Have you been sleeping?"

Fabio gave another shrug. "Usually yes, okay," he said, "but not so much last night, so I no feel so good today. I feel like the capellini in the water too long."

Rick gave a grunt and chuckled. "Funny, isn't it? " he said. "Give a man a good night's sleep and he can stand up to anything the world might throw at him. Deprive him of it, though, and you can knock him down with just the touch of a feather."

"It no funny when you the man," Fabio observed.

"Hmm, no, I suppose not," said Rick. He rubbed his chin for a moment and gazed past his nephew, his eyes someplace else for a brief time before he came back to himself with an harrumph. "You know, I think what you might need—and myself, I might add—is to get out of Dodge for a little while. That might put a different spin on things for you."

"Out of Dodge?" asked Fabio, his face showing confusion.

"It's an old expression," chuckled Rick. Then suddenly mindful of a potential play on words, he added, "Why don't we get out of the house and *into* the Dodge, and I'll explain it to you while we're on the way."

"*Into* the Dodge?" said Fabio, even more puzzled.

Rick gave a sigh and shook his head before downing the rest of his coffee. Then he pushed away from the table and stood. Giving Fabio a nudge as he passed, he headed off to the living room, whistling a tune.

"Come on, Hoss," he said over his shoulder. "Just put a coat on and saddle up the truck."

*

When they arrived in Providence some forty-five minutes later, Rick pulled off the highway and drove up the street and under an archway from which was suspended an enormous pine cone, a symbol of welcome to those entering the Federal Hill neighborhood in the center of the city. Atwells Avenue, the main thoroughfare through that part of town, was bumper to bumper with traffic as it often was on Saturday afternoons when people flocked there for lunch or an early dinner at one of the many Italian American restaurants lining the street. From there they could hurry downtown afterwards to catch a basketball game at the Dunkin' Donuts Center, a concert at the Providence Performing Arts Center, or perhaps a play at the renowned Trinity Repertory Company. Rick rolled slowly along, searching for a place to park, until Fortune smiled on him when he spied someone up ahead getting into his car. A few moments later the pickup truck was safely parked on the side of the street. The two men stepped out and began to walk down the bustling sidewalk. Fabio looked about with curious eyes. He found the place so different from Main Street back home in Wakefield. It wasn't just the restaurants and bakeries and the hustle and bustle. It was something else he felt in the cars passing and the people coming and going, a different energy that, despite the cold, he found somehow appealing.

"Where we go now?" he asked as they went along. "We out of Dodge yet?"

"I think we're as far out of Dodge as we need to get," laughed Rick in reply. "I thought we would get something to eat, if that's okay with you."

"Okay very much," said Fabio, nodding.

"Good," said Rick, "because I'm hungry." He looked ahead to Angelo's Civita Farnese Restaurant just up the block. "How about Angelo's?"

"If you think good, then fine with me," said Fabio. "I hungry too."

"Don't worry," Rick told him. "They serve fast—if we can get a seat. This place has been here forever. You'll like it. I used to come here all the time when I lived in Providence."

The restaurant was quite busy when the two walked in. All of the booths were taken; the only available places to sit were two seats across from one another at the center of one of the large communal tables where people sat and dined with perfect strangers. Fabio's hunger greater than his reluctance to sit with people he did not know, he dutifully followed his uncle and took a seat at the table.

The two ordered wine and shared a plate of fried calamari, rings of fried squid tossed with oil and hot peppers, for an appetizer. Then Fabio ordered a plate of veal and peppers while Rick selected the tripe, the lining of the cow's stomach served in a zesty, aromatic tomato sauce, explaining that he had not had that particular delicacy in ages. Fabio found the food much to his liking and ate, as did his uncle, with much gusto, the crowded table about him but a minor distraction. Afterwards the two men strolled over to DePasquale Square, a rather nice piazza in the center of things that Fabio imagined would be a rather pleasant place to visit in warmer weather. There Rick led him into a café on the opposite side of the piazza where they each had coffee and a cannoli to top off lunch.

Zio Rick was in fine spirits when they left the café and began to amble back across the square. He took to recounting for Fabio his experiences living in that very same neighborhood long ago when he first came to America. Two years he had stayed there before deciding to move his glassblowing operation to South County.

"I loved it here in the city," he explained as they walked along, "but something about South County put a spell on me. I couldn't resist it." He suddenly took on a wistful air. "It was hard, though," he said, "and still is in a way. I made many friends while I was living here. They were good to me and I miss them. I don't visit as often as I should."

"Do they visit you?" Fabio ask pointedly.

"Ha! No, they don't," laughed Rick. "That's because this is Rhode Island and people who live in Providence think that Wakefield is somewhere on the far side of the moon."

Rick suddenly stopped in his tracks and looked across the

street at a small hardware store. "Speaking of old friends, let's stop in and say hi." Then he gave Fabio a gentle swat on the arm and beckoned for him to follow him across the street.

Rick led Fabio straight up to the counter when they walked into the store. Ahead of them a man several years older than Fabio, but still very much young, was talking to a man closer to his own age behind the register. Fabio felt a pang of shame in his gut for the two looked strong and confident and in control of their little corners of the world, the way he once felt about himself.

"So Ray, how's married life and being a daddy treatin' you, huh?" said the younger man as he rang up the other's purchases.

"It's pretty nice, Johnny," replied the other man. "You should give it a try."

"Yeah, right," snickered the one called Johnny. "Get back to me on that if you get a chance when you're not changing diapers." He paused to scrutinize a pack of light bulbs the other man was buying. "These are forty watt," he observed. "Going for a little low-light ambiance at your place?"

"Yeah," said the one called Ray. "That and a little low-light electric bill, if you know what I mean."

"Oh yeah, I guess I can see that," said Johnny as he continued to ring up the other items. "So anyway, what's the deal with your brother. I haven't seen him in a dog's age. Doesn't he go out anymore."

"Ayy, he's been busy," said Ray. "He scored a job with the state at the department of economic development."

"Hey, good for him," said Johnny.

"And besides that he's got a girl," added Ray. "Actually, they're pretty serious."

"Oh, great," groaned Johnny. "Another one bites the dust."

"Don't knock it till you've tried it," said Ray with a smile.

All the items finally tallied, Johnny bagged it all and handed it over the counter. Ray gave a nervous cough.

"That's...um...on our account?" he asked sheepishly. "I know we're a little behind."

"Don't worry about it," said Johnny easily. "You always catch up. Just give my regards to everyone at the Villa, okay?"

"Thanks," said Ray. The two shook hands and he went on his way.

When Rick stepped up to the counter, Johnny took a moment before he recognized him.

"Ayyy, Ricky V, the master of glass disaster!" he exclaimed. "Talk about a blast from the past! How long has it been?"

"A long time, Johnny," laughed Rick.

"Too long," said Johnny.

Rick nodded in agreement and turned to Fabio. "Johnny, this is my nephew, Fabio. He came over from Italy last year to work with me."

"Hey, how you doin'," said Johnny affably as he shook Fabio's hand. "What happened, did you get stuck workin' in the family business, too?"

"Like that, maybe yes," replied Fabio shyly.

"Yeah, well don't worry too much about it," joked Johnny. "It's not so bad after several miserable years or so. You get numb after a while, if you know what I mean."

"What's all the commotion out there?" boomed a voice from the office behind the counter.

"Oh, no, now it starts," muttered Johnny, rolling his eyes.

That said an older woman, but one Fabio would not think to call old for she was still beautiful and vibrant, came out of the office and stood there with hands on hips, gaping with a big smile at his uncle.

"Enrico Vitale!" she exclaimed with much the same surprise as Johnny. "How long has it been?"

"I just asked him that same question, Ma," Johnny pointed out.

"So I'm asking him again!" his mother screamed.

With that she hurried around to the other side of the counter.

"Hello, Teresa," said Rick, smiling warmly as the two embraced.

"Where have you been all this time, how come we haven't seen you in so long?" asked the woman. "We thought maybe you went back to Italy."

Rick smiled and gave a little sigh. "You know how it is, Teresa. It's hard for me to get out of South County."

"I know, I know," sighed Teresa wistfully. "It's hard for me to leave Providence. My whole life is here." She paused and gave him a gentle poke in the chest. "So, are you still making that beautiful glass like you used to?"

"I'm still trying," laughed Rick.

"What try?" said Teresa, turning to Johnny. "You've seen that decanter and set of wine glasses he made for us that time. They're the most beautiful things I own."

"Yeah, they're nice, Ma," opined Johnny.

"And he just gave it to us as a gift for no reason," Teresa went on.

"Oh no, I wouldn't say that," said Rick with a grin. "You and Nick were always very good to me when I first came here. You were some of my first friends in America. I've never forgotten that."

"Nice," said Teresa, evidently please by the remark. Then she turned to Fabio. "And who is this?"

"I am Fabio," he said right away, for once introducing himself instead of waiting for his uncle to do it for him. "I work for Zio Rick."

"Ah, Rick's your Zio, that's nice." She stepped closer and regarded him with mother hen eyes. Then, much like Giuliana had done on Christmas eve, she unabashedly reached up and took his chin in her hand the way mothers do. She gave him a searching look, one from which Fabio found it impossible to look away. At last she let him go and gave his face a little pat.

Then, shaking her head, she clicked her tongue.

"Fabio, you need to eat," she told him with great conviction in her voice.

"Well, we just had lunch," Rick offered.

"Well, he needs to eat some more!" Teresa blustered. "You think I can't recognize these things?" Then, in a gentler voice, she said to Fabio, "Tell your uncle that you want to come to my house tomorrow, or any Sunday you want, and I'll make sure you eat right."

"Yes, maybe someday that be nice," said Fabio.

"No maybes!" declared Teresa, her authority now firmly established.

Fabio nodded and, for perhaps the first time since he set foot in Rhode Island, gave a genuine smile. Then he shrunk back and listened in silence once more while Rick caught up with the others.

Later, after they had said their goodbyes—Rick having promised to bring Fabio up for Sunday dinner one day soon—the two climbed into the truck and got on their way back to Wakefield.

"Back to Dodge?" said Fabio as they drove down the ramp onto the highway south.

"That's right," chuckled Rick, still very much in high spirits. "Let's hope it's still there."

For a long while, Rick hummed along to the radio while Fabio rode in silence. He had found himself thinking about the woman, Teresa, and how much she reminded him of his own mother, Liliana. Closing his eyes, he let his thoughts drift home to Mont' Oliva, a place he rarely let them venture. Fabio knew that his uncle kept in touch with his mother, letting her know, from time to time, how he was doing. For his part, though, Fabio had yet to call or write or try in any way to contact his mother, or anyone in Italy. Why he had yet to do so was as much a mystery to himself as it was to everyone else. Fabio loved his mother, and he well understood why she had sent him away to America; she had done it out of love for him. All the same, the mere thought of speaking with his mother or Zia Pasqualina or anyone in Mont'Oliva released inside him a cascade of shame and anguish and guilt, and so he took great pains to avoid doing it.

"So, what did you think of Federal Hill?" said Rick after a time, shaking him from his reveries. "Not a bad place, eh?"

"No, not bad," said Fabio, nodding in agreement. "I like very much. And I glad you get to see old friends."

"They're good people, the Catinis," said Rick. "I've known them for a very long time."

"I think the mother like you a little bit," said Fabio, giving his uncle a sideways glance.

Rick cleared his throat. "Well, like I said, we've been friends a long time."

"That not the kind of like I mean," said Fabio with a rare mischievous gleam in his eye. "It seem like lots of the women like you. You know, I am thinking maybe Dio just not mean for you to be priest."

Fabio had made the remark in jest, but he regretted it right away for it had obviously struck a nerve in his uncle, who looked vaguely stunned by it. Rick made a queer expression, as if he were trying to see something far down the road, and he promptly fell silent, his former high spirits instantly evaporated. His lips pursed, he said nothing further the remainder of the ride home.

By the time they pulled into the drive way, Fabio's own spirits had plummeted. The thought that he had somehow hurt his uncle was more than he could bear.

"Zio," he said after they had gotten out of the car, "you know I only make the joke."

"Yes, yes," his uncle reassured him. "Don't give it another thought. We'll talk later."

With that he gave Fabio a pat on the shoulder and went

inside.

Fabio did not go straight up to his apartment, but instead watched his uncle go into the house. He stood for a time in the driveway, staring at the front door until he heard a murmuring coming from inside. Curious, he crept up the stairs onto the porch and closer to the door, listening intently all the while. Rick, he found, had left the front door slightly ajar. Unable to resist, Fabio peeked through the storm door and inside where, to his dismay, he saw his uncle on his knees, sobbing uncontrollably. It was heartbreaking, and Fabio's first inclination was to rush in and help his uncle to his feet. But then he decided that perhaps he had done enough damage for one day, that perhaps it would be better to let his uncle have his privacy. And so Fabio turned away and headed back down the porch steps. He stopped in the driveway and, with a sigh, considered for a few moments the snow crusted yard and the frigid air. Then he trudged around the garage to his apartment, wondering all the while as he went if February would ever end.

Drifting

CHAPTER EIGHTEEN

"So, what do you think," Joe was saying to no one in particular as he was putting the finishing touches on a chicken cutlet sub, "why do good things happen to bad people?"

When—as was usually the case—no one in particular responded to the query he had set forth, Joe stopped working for a moment. He turned from the cutting board and, with arms crossed, surveyed the room crowded with lunchtime patrons. To all appearances, no one had even heard his question; everyone seemed to be quite contentedly munching away on their sandwiches or chatting while they waited for theirs to be prepared, and so Joe turned his gaze to the Wall of Truth and scanned it, searching for some philosophical tidbit that might fit the bill. Finding none, he turned his attention back to his customers.

"So, anyone?" he said aloud.

"Anyone what?" someone shouted back over the din of conversation.

"Anyone want to explain to me why good things happen to bad people?" Joe asked.

A state of relative quiet fell over the assemblage.

"I think you've got the question wrong," suggested Tommy, who was one of the regulars on hand.

"Yeah," someone else spoke up. "Shouldn't it be the other way around, why do bad things happen to good people?"

"Nah, I already know the answer to that question," said Joe with a dismissive wave of his hand. "It's the other one that's got me stumped."

A spirited discussion ensued, one in which, as usual, no particular rules of order were observed. It was just the sort of rambling, rambunctious discourse that Joe liked best, and so he encouraged everyone to keep it going while he carried the bag with the chicken cutlet sub and other sandwiches he had just prepared to a customer waiting outdoors.

When he stepped outside, Joe stopped and turned his face to the sun. March had been almost as brutal as February, April as cruel as advertised, but now May had arrived in all its miraculous splendor, and suddenly it was if they had skipped spring entirely and gone straight to summer. Joe breathed deep of the warm pleasant air and watched a flock of geese pass overhead on their way north. Then he turned to deliver the bag of sandwiches to his customer who, at the moment, was hidden behind the pages of the newspaper at one of the tables on the sidewalk.

"I don't blame you for sitting out here," said Joe, setting the bag on the table. "It's too nice to stay inside. Then again, I wish you had sat inside. I would have really liked to get your input."

"On why good things happen to bad people?" said Rick, folding the newspaper.

"Exactly," said Joe. He sat down at the table with him and pulled out the sports section from the newspaper.

"Well, I of course know the answer to that one," said Rick with a dismissive wave of his own and a sly look in his eye.

"Ha! I'm sure you do," laughed Joe. "And will you tell me?"

"Sure," replied Rick. "When you tell me the answer to the other question, the one about bad things happening to good people. That's the one that's got *me* stumped."

"Hmm," muttered Joe as he quickly surveyed the front page

of the sports section. With a sigh he folded the paper and stood back up. "You drive a hard bargain, my friend," he said at last. "I'll have to give it some thought over my next few subs. Then maybe I'll tell you."

"Fair enough," said Rick getting to his feet as well. "Philosophers have been wondering about these things for what, thousands of years, right? I guess I can wait through the making of a few more sandwiches before I get an answer."

"Ah," said Joe, raising a finger sagely, "but don't be surprised if the answer you get isn't the most palatable one."

"Yes," Rick replied with equal sagacity, "but will the sandwiches you make while you're thinking things over still be just as palatable regardless?"

Joe broke out in a great smile. "Of course, my friend," he laughed. "That is simply one of the great truths of Wakefield."

With the bag of sandwiches in hand, Rick soon ambled away down the sidewalk and around the bend to Vita Glassworks where the front door was wide open and the "Open" flag swayed back and forth in the gentle breeze. He cast a glance up at the second floor where the windows were also wide open, wondering what Elise had accomplished there that morning. To his astonishment, she had made enormous progress over the winter in sorting out the old papers and records, tossing out what was no longer worth keeping and organizing whatever was. To be sure, the second floor was still very much a disaster area, but at least someone had come to its rescue. There was still hope.

"*Mangiamo!*" Rick called up the stairs after he went inside.

Elise came to the top of the stairs and gave him a curious look. "I'm sorry, Mister Rick," she said, "what did you say?"

"I said 'let's eat', my dear," he told her. "The sandwiches are in the bag on the counter."

"Thank God," she laughed. "I'm starving."

With that, Elise came down the stairs and went behind the counter for her purse. When she opened it and took out her wallet so that she might pay for her sandwich, Rick waved her money away. "No," he told her firmly. "Today I'm treating everyone. It's the least I can do, especially for you since I haven't been much help to you up there." This last remark he made while casting a rueful look upwards at the ceiling.

"Oh, I don't mind," said Elise sweetly. "It's what you're paying me for after all."

"Yes, perhaps," admitted Rick. "But working conditions on the second floor probably aren't what you expected them to be when you took the job."

"That is true," Elise teased him. "As cold as it was up there in the winter, it's already just as hot as summer—and so musty! Perhaps I should go on strike."

"How about I just get you a fan," Rick suggested, "and that way we'll avert any possible work stoppages."

"I think I could live with that," she said, smiling ear to ear. "So, let's eat...or what was it you said?"

"*Mangiamo*," Rick told her, pulling her paper-wrapped sandwich out of the bag. "Or more correctly, *mangia*, which is me telling just you to eat."

"Just me?" said Elise.

"Yes," Rick told her. "It's too nice to eat indoors. I'm taking my sandwich with me down to the park. I hope you don't mind." He pulled another sandwich from the bag. "First, though, I just have to deliver this to my nephew."

"Oh, let me," said Elise right away.

"Are you sure?" asked Rick. "He was in one of his moods this morning when he was blowing glass. You know how he gets."

"Don't worry," Elise assured him. "I'll manage."

"Well, all right, I'll let you," said Rick reluctantly. "Just please keep an eye out for flying glass, if you know what I mean."

"I will," Elise laughed. "I know exactly what you mean, so

don't worry, I know how to duck."

When she walked into the work area, Elise found Fabio standing off to the side of Virgilio where he was considering, with a jaundice eye, his latest creation. It was a rather unusual bowl of deep red hue with an exaggerated uneven rim that curled over the side in a way reminiscent of lava pouring forth from a volcano's mouth. Unaware, due to the music playing in his ears, that he was being watched, he turned the bowl over and over in his hands, examining every inch of it, growing ever more visibly agitated. To Elise, the bowl was a marvelous piece, as strangely twisted and tortured and beautiful as anything she had seen him create. All the same, its creator had evidently found it somehow lacking for with a great cry of exasperation he raised it over his head, ready to hurl it against the wall.

"Wait, please don't!" screamed Elise in alarm. Springing forward, she reached out to stay his arm, dropping their sandwiches in the process.

Stunned at the intrusion into what he considered a private affair, Fabio shook the ear buds from his head and gaped at her in indignation. At the sight of his face wide-eyed with outrage, Elise immediately sprang back.

"I'm sorry," she blurted out, her own indignation rising, "but I couldn't just let you destroy it. It's so beautiful! What is wrong with you?"

Beads of sweat rolling off his head and shoulders, panting as if he had just finished a brisk run, Fabio lowered the bowl, but continued to glare at her with outrage. "You no see?" he seethed. "It all wrong!"

"No, I don't see," said Elise, not backing down. "*No one* sees, and that's the point, you idiot. Don't you understand? That bowl is perfect just the way you made it. We could sell it for a good price."

"I no care about the selling of the work," grumbled Fabio, taken aback by the young woman's audacity.

"I *don't* care about selling *my* work," snipped Elise, unable for some reason at that moment to resist correcting him.

Fabio looked at her in confusion. "*You* don't care about selling the work?" he asked.

"No, *you*," cried Elise, she herself now very much agitated. "Never mind, learn how to speak English! How long have you been here? Whatever! Meantime, while you may not care about selling your work, I'll bet that Mister Rick does. After all, he has to pay for the building and the lights and the gas for the furnace and everything else. Running this place isn't just a hobby for him, you know, have you ever thought about that? And, by the way, I happen to make my living here, too. Every piece that you break is one that I can't sell."

"You no understand," murmured Fabio, heaving a sigh, his shoulders slouching as if the energy had suddenly drained out of him.

"You *don't* understand," said Elise, once again unable to resist correcting him, but softening her tone at the same time. She gave a sigh of her own and reached out toward the bowl. "Come on," she gently pleaded, "give it to me and let me put it out front. I promise you, someone is going to buy it and then you won't see it ever again. Won't that be much better than just smashing it to bits and then all your work would have been for nothing?"

With great hesitation, Fabio relinquished the bowl. Elise took it from his hands and cradled it as one might a child rescued from a hostage scenario. She did not take it out front right away, but instead put it safe aside on a nearby shelf. She left it there and turned to retrieve the sandwiches which still lay on the floor where she had dropped them. Thankfully, they had stayed wrapped and appeared unsullied.

"Come on," she said gently, nodding toward the back door. "*Mongolamo*."

Fabio's face scrunched up into an expression of acute

bewilderment. "What is it you say?" he asked, clearly befuddled.

"*Mongolamo*," repeated Elise. "You know, let's eat."

"Ah, *mangiamo*, you want to say!" exclaimed Fabio.

"How do you say it?" replied Elise.

"*Man-gia-mo*," Fabio sounded out the word. Then he gave a grunt of smug satisfaction and as close to a chuckle as Elise had yet to hear him utter. "*Mongolamo*," he scoffed, shaking his head. "Maybe I need to talk the English better, but you no talk the Italian so good."

"Well maybe if someone took the time to teach me a little better," she said, eyeing him sharply, "I might speak it a little better, you know."

"Maybe yes," said Fabio with a shrug. "But you know you call me idiot."

"Sorry," said Elise. "I didn't mean it." With that she beckoned for him to follow and started for the door.

"Hmm," Fabio grunted. "And maybe you no mean it when you say you can sell bowl for big price?"

"Oh no," she said over her shoulder with a laugh. "*That* I meant."

"We see," muttered Fabio. Then he followed her outside to have his lunch.

CHAPTER NINETEEN

The days of May passed, the weather growing ever warmer and more pleasant. Fabio's disposition, however, warmed only very little along with it. Winter or summer, it seemed he remained cool inside, or at best lukewarm, no more or less happy or sad while he worked away at the furnace day after day; hot or cold it was all the same to him. Still there was one great advantage to the approach of summer that he had come to appreciate. And so, late one particularly warm and breezy afternoon, Fabio decided to drive to the beach.

When he arrived there, he was not surprised to find the parking lot quite near to full. He suspected it had been that way for most of the day. How could one have expected otherwise at a seaside community such as this? He parked as close as he could to the beach, stepped out of the truck, and stood there for a time, surveying the shore.

All about, even though the sun had nearly set, people were still sitting on the sand, enjoying the pleasant weather of that early evening. Down at the water's edge little children were frolicking with delight, running back and forth to stay ahead of the broken waves as they rushed up onto the sand. Out further the water was dotted with a sizable contingent of surfers taking turns riding the great swell of waves that had been kicked up by the balmy wind blowing out of the southwest. It was there to which his attention was most drawn.

Fabio had taken an interest in surfing toward the end of the previous summer. It was perhaps the only thing in which he had taken an interest since he came to America, other than blowing glass. He was, of course, not at all proficient at the sport, in fact he rarely even stood up on the used surfboard he had picked up cheap at a local surf shop that was going out of business. His knees could not handle it for more than a few moments at a time. For all that, he loved simply being out on the water. There was something inexplicably soothing about it, and he had missed it dearly, waiting through the cold winter months for the warm weather to return.

Despite the warm air of that afternoon, the water would still be chilly, so Fabio wrapped a towel around his mid-section, peeled off his clothes, and discreetly pulled on his black neoprene wetsuit as quickly as he could lest anyone see the scars on his back and shoulders. With a glance around to make sure that no one had been watching, he pulled up the zipper and lifted his surfboard out of the back of the truck. Wasting no time, he took the board under his arm and started down across the sand to the water.

Fabio loved the anonymity of the beach. He knew that no one would pay him any great heed as he waded into the surf and slipped onto his board. Out on the water he would not have to worry about his limp, or his damaged shoulder; he wouldn't need to speak; and no one, not even his fellow surfers, would take much note of his face, nor would they be able to see the scars covered by his wetsuit. To the eyes of all on the beach or anyone who might happen to look his way, he was just another black form bobbing atop the waves. It was just the thing that he most preferred, to be hidden in plain sight.

It required a few strong strokes for him to paddle through the churning surf and out beyond where the waves were crashing down, but soon Fabio made it beyond the break line and joined the rest of the cohort of surfers there. For his part, Fabio did not even attempt to ride in on a wave, though there was a steady stream of promising swells upon which he might have done so. Instead he sat up on the board, his legs dangling off the sides, and let the waves roll by beneath him while he watched the other surfers try their luck. After a few minutes, he gave a sigh of relief and breathed deep of the salty air. Then he swung a leg over to the opposite side of the board and let himself slip into the water.

Laying flat atop the water, buoyed by his wetsuit, his surfboard tethered to his ankle, Fabio surrendered himself to the sea's embrace and let the waves lift him gently up and down so that he felt like a child being rocked in his mother's arms. Perfectly relaxed now, he floated that way for some time, staring straight up into the deep blue of the darkening sky directly above then over at the splashes of orange and purple still dabbing the clouds to the west. Behind him a full moon had crept over the horizon like a giant silver dollar, tossing its shimmering light like innumerable shiny coins across the ocean. It would not be long before the stars, one by one, would start to appear. It was perfect, and Fabio remained there simply drifting, oblivious to the rest of the world, content to contemplate nothing.

As much of an escape as it might be from the present, however, his time floating on the water was never enough to let him escape the past where the tides of his brain invariably seemed to carry him. And so, after a time, as inevitably happened on the rare occasions like this when he was able to quiet his mind, Fabio found his thoughts drifting back to Mont'Oliva, to his childhood and his mother, to his exploits on the dance floor, and to his friends, especially Enzo. As the motion of the waves turned him round about, he gazed into the face of the moon and recalled a Saturday night in what felt to him a lifetime ago when he and Enzo were teenagers. The two had been sitting by the fountain on the piazza, staring up at the stars, trying to make plans to go somewhere, anywhere that evening. They were bored, like all teenagers, and desperate to get out of their little village for a time, but neither had a car nor any money. It was maddening. Fabio recalled the acute feeling of suffocation he felt at that moment, the oppressive fear that he was stuck forever, that he would never get out of Mont'Oliva. There was, of course, nothing to be done for it, and so the two ended up wandering down to *il muro* to join the rest of the town's teenagers on that dreary Saturday night.

The memory was still oddly fresh in Fabio's mind, and as he continued to float in the water he tried without success to think of the reason he happened to recall that particular night. He could think of none. One notion, though, did occur to him. He was as stuck in Wakefield as ever he might have been in Mont'Oliva. Just the same, looking back on that long ago night, one thing was certain. As bored and desperate to get out of his little hometown as he might have been, Fabio would have given anything to be right back there once more with his friend alive and at his side. The thought that he could not was a source of deep pain, and it brought back the memory of their final night together when everything in his world changed irrevocably in an instant. Fabio could not bear thinking about it any further, so he climbed back on his board and began paddling back toward the shore, and so back to the furnace.

There really was no reason to return to Vita Glassworks that evening. Rick and Elise had already long gone home. Fabio, however, could not resist the urge to work. Several ideas for some new glass creations had recently taken up residence in his imagination and they were pestering him to breathe life into them. And so before long he was back at the furnace, blowing odd shapes of glass, stretching and twisting and contorting them every which way, content to be alone and occupied with his endeavors.

Fabio kept at it for quite some time, working away without stop, lost as always in his music till at last he decided to give himself a little break. Mindful of Zio Rick's still-standing edict forbidding smoking indoors, he stepped out into the side alleyway where he lit a cigarette and blew a puff of smoke into the night air. It was still comfortably warm, so Fabio ambled up toward the front of the building. There he sat down on the pavement and leaned back against the side of the building. With the full moon now shining directly overhead like a spotlight, he cast his gaze across the street to the dance studio on the second floor. He could hear the music playing and now and then caught a glimpse of a couple twirling by the window.

Fabio listened to the music and dreamed.

It was a tango they were playing, of that he was certain. He tapped his finger to the beat against the pavement, imagining the dancers in the class, the precise movements of their feet and arms, the way the partners looked past one another, their bodies coming close then moving away, every part of them in synchronized motion, all to the tempo of the music. Just then, though, as he was losing himself in a memory of his own days in dance class, the countless hours he had spent training, the music abruptly ended.

The class apparently over, Fabio took a last draw from his cigarette and flicked the butt to the ground. He was about to go back inside when he looked across the street and saw the dance students, all of them adults, starting to emerge from the building and out onto the sidewalk. There was much talk and laughter between them, that joyful buzz of people who have spent time together working toward a common goal.

Fabio envied them.

Giving a sigh, he got to his feet and started back inside to the furnace, but stopped when, from among the several voices, he caught the sound of a young woman's laugh. There was something vaguely familiar about it, yet Fabio could not quite place it. Careful to stay confined to the shadows, he turned back to the street, crept closer to the sidewalk, and peered out from the corner of the building just in time to see a young man and woman crossing the street in his direction. The two were in silhouette as they approached, and Fabio could distinguish nothing of them. It was not until they stepped up onto the sidewalk and into the glow of the streetlight above that at last he saw them clearly.

At the sight of the young woman, her auburn hair and blue eyes, Fabio knew her at once. Dumbfounded to see her, he stood there gaping, his heart suddenly pounding in his chest, all thoughts of glasswork that night dispelled.

"That was so much fun tonight!" he heard her enthuse.

"Yeah, I think we did a pretty good job cuttin' up that rug," joked the young man with her. Then he put his arm around her waist and the two started down the sidewalk together.

Something once again stirred deep inside Fabio, something long ago forgotten, just as it had that cold afternoon in December when he had first seen her. Now, as he had then, he found himself straightening up, trying to stand a little taller despite his achy knee. But it was, of course, pointless. Alone, hidden in the shadows of the alley, Fabio could only watch them go. He felt a terrible desperation at not being able to follow the woman, to take her where she was going instead of the other man. At the same time, a thrill of wonder surged through him at having seen her again at all. And so he stayed there, watching her go until she and her friend rounded the corner. When the two were out of sight, Fabio fell back against the building, breathless with excitement.

"Laura," he whispered to himself.

Then he hurried back inside to shut down the furnace.

CHAPTER TWENTY

It was Elise who first noticed a difference in Fabio.

She first spoke of it to Rick near the end of the day some weeks later when the two were on the second floor, surveying the state of affairs there. While Rick and Fabio had been working overtime to prepare for an upcoming art festival, Elise had been diligently poring over the contents of each and every box of old bank records and sales receipts and all the rest, assessing their contents and, more often than not, tossing everything out. Her youthful spirit, the one that allowed her to dispose of the old useless clutter without giving it a second thought, was exactly what Rick lacked and one of the reasons he had come to value her so much. It was also the reason why she had succeeded in clearing so much space, although now much of it had been refilled with pieces of new glasswork spread on the floor, waiting to be boxed.

"You've done so much, and it's all very beautiful," noted Elise, looking over the collection of new work. Rick had created some truly lovely pieces. It was Fabio's work, however, that had caught Elise's attention. She took a moment to kneel down to consider some of his new pieces. "Fabio's work has changed a little, I think," she said softly.

"How so?" replied Rick.

"Well, take this one," said Elise. She picked up a piece of amber-colored glasswork, a sort of fanciful abstract statuette Fabio had blown, and ran a finger over it's cool smooth surface. "I don't know exactly how to explain it," she said, "but it's different from the things he used to make when I first came to work for you. So is everything, if you look at what's here. It's all so much more delicate and pretty. Everything he made before used to seem...I don't know...so twisted and tormented."

"Ah, you picked up on that too," said Rick with a chuckle. "All along I thought I was the only one."

"Don't get me wrong, it was all fantastic," Elise hastened to add, "and I think all these new things are fantastic, too. I guess I'm just curious about why it happened, about what changed his work."

"Quite honestly," said Rick, considering the pieces on the floor with a thoughtful gaze, "I've been so preoccupied with my own work, that I haven't paid much attention to his. But I can see now exactly what you're talking about. How interesting. Why has his work changed this way? Well, the only answer I can offer is that something changed with him, something inside. You see, I've always thought that what's inside you is what gets blown out when you're a glass blower. It can't help but show up in the work. I think it's that way with artists in any art form, but I think it's particularly true with Fabio. If there's less torment in his work, if it's a little more gentle, then maybe that means what's inside him is a little more gentle. As you know by now with my nephew, that can only be a good sign."

That said, Rick smiled and brushed his hands quickly together as if to indicate that his business there was finished. "I think, Miss Celestin," he told her, "that now might be a good time to call it a day and go home."

"Oh no, not yet," said Elise. "I have some things to do downstairs before I can go home."

"I would argue with you, but I know it would do no good," chuckled Rick. "Fabio's still down at the furnace, of course. He'll probably be there for a while. So just lock up and go whenever you're ready."

With that he bid her a goodnight and went on his way.

Later, after Elise had gone down to the first floor, she spent some time filing sales receipts and getting the month's bills together. It was early evening now and all this work could have waited for another day, but she decided to use it as an excuse to linger for a time. At last, when it was time to close up the shop, she went back to the work room where Fabio was stationed as always by the furnace. As usual, the ear buds for his IPod player were stuck in his ears and he was lost in the music, oblivious to the outside world. There was, however, one great difference about Fabio that she noted right away, something she had not known him ever to do since they first met.

He was humming along to the music, his body swaying to the rhythm as he worked.

Elise was so charmed by the sight that she stood there smiling, afraid to disturb him. She was about to back away without telling him that she was locking up for the night when Fabio turned her way. He tugged out one of the ear buds and gave her a questioning look.

"I'm sorry, I didn't want to bother you," she said. "It's just that I'm getting ready to lock up."

"Okay," said Fabio. "What is time now?"

"It's almost seven."

Fabio looked mildly panicked. "Seven?" he gasped.

"What's the matter," said Elise with a smile. "Someplace you have to be?"

"Just time to take break, that's all," he replied uneasily.

"Well, it's time for me to go home," she told him. "I'm going to stop across the street for an iced coffee before I do. Would you like one?"

"No," said Fabio. He paused. "I mean to say, no thank you. I just need to take break now."

"Have it your way," said Elise brightly. Then she left him and, after locking the door, crossed over to coffee shop on the other side of the street. After ordering her iced coffee she did not leave the shop right away, but instead took a seat at the bar by the window. From that vantage point she could observe the front of Vita Glassworks across the street as well as the alleyway on the side where she saw the door open and Fabio step outside. Elise watched him closely as he moved very quickly up toward the front of the building, but held himself back from the sidewalk. There he stood, clearly agitated, looking back and forth, up and down the street. What in the world, Elise wondered, was he looking for?

Very soon, people began to walk up the sidewalk and into the door that led to the dance studio above the coffee shop. Elise could see that Fabio was watching them all, but for what reason she could not discern. At last, though, a young woman came up the sidewalk right past the alleyway where Fabio stood unnoticed. At the sight of her, he sprang back, almost cowering. As she stood there waiting to cross the street, Fabio clung to the side of the building as if stricken and he did not straighten up again until the woman had walked away and was out of sight.

Elise sat there, taking in the scene, perceiving at once what it was that had wrought the change she had noticed in Fabio's work. One look at his face as he watched the other woman before he turned and went back inside was enough for her to suspect the answer. It was not, however, an answer she particularly relished, and so while Fabio went back to work and the young woman, whoever she was, to dancing, Elise took a last sip of her coffee and went home.

CHAPTER TWENTY-ONE

Fabio waited.

The weeks had passed—first one then two then three and four—and every Wednesday night would find him in the alleyway, waiting to catch a glimpse of Laura, who he had first beheld at the cyclo-cross race. How impatient he would be to see her! Back and forth he would pace like a caged beast, lighting one cigarette after the other until the time for her dance class would draw near and he would see her coming up the sidewalk with her boyfriend. It was of course always a keen disappointment to see the young gentleman accompanying her, but that detracted little from the pleasure he took in seeing her. It was like a dream. But alas the moment would pass too quickly when she rushed on by the top of the alleyway and crossed the street to the school. Fabio would stay hidden in the shadows, watching and noting every detail about the young woman: her hair, her eyes, what she was wearing, whether she seemed happy or sad, all the while hoping just to hear her speak. For a few fleeting seconds she would be close enough for him to reach out and touch, and then an instant later be distant as the stars. Then would come the endless hour he would spend waiting for her class to finish, waiting for the chance to see her again.

It was, Fabio well understood in the back of his mind,

pathetic and completely pointless to pine for Laura, but it was just far enough in the back for him to ignore. How could he resist? Since encountering her that second time, everything in his world suddenly looked different to him, brighter in some way, as if he had been wearing dark glasses all along and not known it until the sight of her removed them. More than that, she gave him something he had yet to find since he came to America. Hope. Fragile as it might be, it was like finding an oasis after crawling through the desert, and Fabio could not help but gulp down its water.

And so, as he did each week, Fabio dutifully, if anxiously, waited inside that evening for the dance class to end, the seconds seeming to drip by with the slow, maddeningly deliberate pace of a leaky faucet. When at last the hour drew near, he hurried outside to the alleyway and took up his position against the building near the sidewalk. There, away from the streetlight, sufficiently obscured in the shadows, he stood and waited, listening as always to the music, watching the shadows of the dancers as they twirled by the windows, wishing for all the world that he could be up there with them.

When the class ended and the students began leaving the building, Fabio craned his neck to see them until at last Laura and her boyfriend appeared. The two were all smiles, laughing and joking about something, it seemed to Fabio, that had happened in class. As they came closer and stepped up onto the sidewalk the young man took Laura's hand, pulled her close, and placed his other arm around her waist.

"What do you say we give that move another try?" he laughed.

"Oh no, Mark, please not again," Laura kidded him. "You almost killed me the last time in there."

"This time for sure," he promised. "Ready? And one and two..."

Mark proceeded to attempt a cross-body lead, a common

enough dance move in which the man firmly leads the woman across his body in such a way that the two partners eventually exchange positions when it is completed. That at least is what Fabio surmised Mark was attempting, for his execution of the move only vaguely resembled the proper technique. To make matters worse, he attempted to spin Laura when it was done and dip her for effect. Unfortunately he botched that as well and nearly dropped the young woman onto the sidewalk, which prompted more laughter from the pair.

"Bah, *imbecile*," Fabio found himself snickering in spite of himself.

"What?" said Laura unexpectedly, turning in his direction.

Appalled that either had heard him, Fabio froze.

"What's that?" she called again into the darkened alleyway, this time more insistent. "You know, I can see you over there."

Keeping to the shadows, wanting for all the world to flee, Fabio gave a nervous cough. Then, very tentatively, he stepped out into the glow of the streetlight beaming overhead. He cringed for a moment, covering his cheek, fearful that his appearance might repulse her.

Eyeing cautiously this stranger from the shadows, Mark took Laura by the arm. "Come on," he told her. "Let's get going."

"No wait," she said. She took a step closer to Fabio and regarded him for a moment with a look of curiosity. "You look familiar," she told him. "Have we met?"

Fabio nodded yes. "At cyclo-cross race," he said in a timid voice. "We talk for just the minute."

"That's right!" exclaimed Laura. "I remember. It was freezing that day!" Then, over her shoulder to Mark, she added in a playfully rueful tone, "*You* dragged me out there that day and made me stand outside in the cold."

Mark replied with a roll of his eyes and gave a sideways nod of the head, indicating that he wanted them to be on their way. Laura, however, turned back to Fabio and gave him a smile.

"What's your name?" she asked.

"I am Fabio," he answered, his legs quivering.

"I'm Laura and this is Mark," she said.

"What are you doing hanging around in the alley, Fabio," said Mark, still watching him with suspicious eyes.

"I work here," explained Fabio, gesturing to the shop. "I come out into alley to take break."

"Where are you from?" asked Laura. "You have an accent."

"I am from Italy," he told her.

"Ooh, I would love to go to Italy someday," Laura sighed. "Wouldn't you?"

"Right now I'd like to go home," said Mark.

"Don't listen to him, Fabio," she said. "He's just grumpy because you laughed at him."

"I sorry, I no mean to laugh," said Fabio earnestly. "It just that he do move all wrong."

Mark folded his arms. "Oh really," he said with an air of disdain. "And I suppose that you could do it better?"

The question hung in the air for a very long time, so long that the couple was about to go on their way when Fabio finally forced himself to answer.

"Maybe," he replied, swallowing hard.

"Is that right?" said Mark. "And what would you know about it?"

"I dance once...a little," Fabio told them.

"Oh, let him show us," said Laura breezily, taking a step toward Fabio. She reached out her hand. "Come on, Fabio," she said. "Show us how it's done, if you can."

"Laura—" Mark began to protest.

"What are you worried about?" she told him. "He can't possibly be any worse at it than you are."

"Thanks a lot," he grumbled.

Laura turned back to Fabio with her hand still extended.

"Well?" she said.

Fabio gave Mark a questioning look by way of asking for his consent.

"Whatever," grumbled Mark with a roll of his eyes.

Turning to Laura, Fabio swallowed hard again and took her hand in his. At her touch he felt life flowing back into him. He stepped up to her and slipped his arm about her waist, exhilarated to feel her body so close to his, to breathe in the scent of her hair, and for a moment he was back at Seven Up with Caterina in his arms. He would have been content to stay that way forever, but he knew that the moment would be fleeting, and so he went straight to work.

"It done like this," he began. "One, two, three..."

At that Fabio danced with her but a few steps before making a series of turns during which he deftly guided her across his body. The moves completed, he let her spin and dipped her just as her boyfriend had attempted, except Fabio executed the move with easy precision, before quickly pulling her upright.

"Wow, that was perfect!" gushed Laura.

Even Mark was impressed. "Well, I guess that shuts me up," he chuckled. "I think I'm jealous."

Fabio might have been exultant were it not for the searing pain shooting up through his knee. The dance movements, modest as they had been, were terribly stressful and it felt for all the world as if someone were attempting to saw off his leg. With beads of sweat forming across his forehead, he quickly said thank you, bid them a *buona sera*, and retreated back through the alleyway to the shop.

"Hey, thank you, Fabio!" Laura called after him, but by then Fabio had hurried inside and closed the door.

Wednesdays

CHAPTER TWENTY-TWO

Every summer, the Town of Narragansett hosted a two-day art festival drawing artists from all around. It had been several years since Rick had taken part in it, but with Fabio's glasswork growing more intriguing by the day it seemed as good a time as any to show off some of it—not to mention some of his own. The exposure at the always well-attended event might help the shop, he reasoned, but even if it didn't, the entry fee was not exorbitant. All things considered, he decided to reserve a spot.

The festival was idyllically situated directly across the road from the ocean in a little park next to The Towers, a lovely turn-of-century stone building that arched over the road like a medieval bridge. Once it served as the gateway to the famed Narragansett Pier Casino before the posh resort was destroyed by fire in the early 1900's.

By mid-morning on the first day of the festival that following Saturday morning, the park had sprouted dozens of neatly-aligned open-sided tents, their square white tops gleaming in the bright June sun like low-lying clouds beneath the crystal blue sky. Under them sat the artists with their works: paintings of all sorts, drawings, graphics, photography, wood and bronze sculpture, and, of course, glass.

"What a glorious day!" proclaimed Rick once their work

was properly arranged and they could settle down and sit in the shade.

Zio Rick, Fabio observed, was clearly in his element. All that morning, while they were setting up the tent and the displays, Rick had exchanged greetings with the other artists. There seemed to be no one he did not know, or did not know him. It was like a big reunion and his uncle was thoroughly enjoying it.

"It is a gorgeous day," agreed Elise, who had come to help set up. For her part, she seemed equally taken with the goings on.

Even Fabio to this point had been reasonably animated, almost cheerful by his standards. However, after having diligently assisted with transporting the glasswork from the shop and setting up of the tent and displays, he had immediately grown restless and bored with the affair. The reason, of course, was that his thoughts were elsewhere. For three days running he had done little else but dwell on his brief dance with Laura. In his mind he dissected over and over again every second of the experience, reliving every detail: the feel of his arms around her, the touch of her hand in his, the light of the moon on her hair. All of it overwhelmed his thoughts. Until Wednesday came round again, and he had the chance to see her once more, little else seemed to matter.

"Why we must be here?" he groused with a yawn.

"Why?" laughed Rick. "How can you ask such a question? You've been working hard, haven't you? And you've produced some fine glass that is quite unique. It deserves to be seen, don't you think? After all, getting a chance to show off what you can do is half the fun of making your living in our business. You can't just work all the time, you know. Sometimes you have to play a little."

Assuming a contemplative pose, Rick took a deep breath and puffed himself up in a certain way that always let Fabio know that he was about to impart to him some tidbit of wisdom or sage advice.

"Having fun," he went on in a professorial tone, "is as important in life as breathing, you know. It's food for your spirit, and your spirit always needs to be fed. That's why you have to learn how to put an element of fun, at least a little bit, into everything you do. It's like putting seasoning on your food. Without it your food is bland and you won't want to eat it. It's the same with your work. If it's not fun, at least every now and then, then it becomes pointless drudgery, and what good is that? The thing is that you have to make time for fun just like you do for other things in your life, like eating dinner or putting gas in your car or brushing your teeth. "

"Blowing the glass is no like brushing the teeth," Fabio pointed out.

"No, it's not, but I know you get the idea," replied Rick, aware that his nephew was just in one of his contrary moods.

"But what we do all day here, just sit?" Fabio griped.

"Well, that's up to you," said Rick with a grin. "You can always stand if you prefer."

"Ha ha, the funny joke," sulked Fabio. Then he sunk down into his chair, wearing a sour expression.

It wasn't long before the crowd showed up and people began coming and going through the tent to ogle the glasswork that Rick had selected for display. More often than not the three of them simply sat and politely nodded, but occasionally someone would ask a question about one piece or another. That's when Rick would spring into action and describe for them the glassblowing process and how a particular piece might have been fashioned, never forgetting of course to mention that they might enjoy a visit to the shop where there was much more to see. Elise would do her part by discreetly offering them a brochure.

From what Fabio could observe, the two actually seemed to be enjoying themselves. As for himself, he was reluctant to speak no matter how often others showed interest in his work or

Rick tried to prod him into it. This, naturally, would always have been the case regardless of where they might have been.

"There are so many people, Mister Rick," said Elise later in the day when there was a lull of visitors coming to their tent. "This is a wonderful show to be in."

"I think it's worth it," said Rick with a nod of agreement.

"But nobody buy a thing," noted Fabio dryly. He could not guess at how many people had looked at their work, but for all those who had expressed interest, particularly in his own work, few had inquired as to prices and no one had bought a single piece. It all seemed like a waste of time to him.

"No one has bought anything *yet*," Rick replied. "But plenty of people have seen our work and they'll remember. Someday they'll come to the shop, or they'll see something we made in someone else's gift store. That's just the way it works. Today is not just about today, it's about tomorrow too."

"Tomorrow is another day of festival," Fabio pointed out.

"Not *tomorrow* tomorrow," Rick started to explain.

"Don't explain," said Elise, covering her mouth to hide a grin. "He knows."

"Hmm, maybe," grunted Fabio, annoyed that his ruse had been found out. He turned and looked out across the park to the beach. The surf was up and a large contingent of surfers were out riding the waves. He closed his eyes for a moment, losing himself in a daydream of being out there on the water with them. It was just then, when out of the blue, like a song drifting to him on the pleasant summer breeze, he heard the sound of a familiar voice calling his name.

"Fabio, is that you?"

Fabio, his eyes instantly wide open, sat upright and whirled around in time to see the voice's owner walking toward their tent.

It was Laura.

"See, it is him," she said over her shoulder to her boyfriend who was following close behind. "I told you so."

Before Fabio could utter a word of greeting, Laura walked straight over to the tent and stood before him, her face aglow in a radiant smile.

"I'm Laura," she said sweetly. "Remember me from the other night?"

"Yes, yes," replied Fabio at once, completely flustered. "Of course I remember."

He jumped to his feet, in the process bumping into one of the glass displays and knocking a stack of brochures from the little table next to him onto the grass. He stooped to pick them up, but thankfully Elise got there first for him.

"And this is my boyfriend, Mark," said Laura.

"Hey, Fabio," said Mark affably, reaching out his hand. "Good to see you again."

"Yes, it is good," said Fabio as they shook hands.

By now he was aware that Zio Rick and Elise were looking on, the former with obvious curiosity, the latter with something of a more inscrutable look. In any case, Fabio felt compelled to introduce them.

"This my uncle, Rick, who I work for," Fabio told them nervously. "And this Elise, who work with us too."

"Hello, Laura," said Rick with a great smile.

"Hello," said Elise.

"So, all of you make these beautiful things?" said Laura, gesturing to the glasswork.

"Not all," Elise told her. "Just those two. I only help run the shop."

"And we make lots more than these," said Rick. "This is just a little sampling of what we do."

"It's all so beautiful," said Laura as she and Mark began to walk about the tent, admiring the glass. "And you make it all at your shop?"

"Oh, yes," said Rick. "For many years."

"How nice," she said.

Fabio was desperate to say something to her, but nothing would come to mind, so all he could do was stand there in silence and watch until he heard Laura give a little coo of delight.

"Look at this one, Mark," she said, pointing out a piece of glass, orange and yellow in hue, that vaguely resembled a snail, but was twisted and contorted around itself.

"Wow, that's pretty cool," he said with a nod.

"And this other one too," said Laura. "Aren't all of these on this shelf so different." She turned to Rick. "I really love these."

"Ah, those are the work of my protégé," said Rick, feigning a look of jealousy.

Laura turned the other way to Fabio and smiled.

"I see you're a man of many talents," she told him. "How did you make all these?"

Bashfully, Fabio described for her, as best he could, a little of the glassblowing process and the techniques he had used to fashion the particular pieces she had pointed out. To his delight, she listened to every word. It was the first time Fabio had ever spoken at length to anyone, other than Rick, about his glassblowing. As it was, he rarely spoke at length about anything at all. His newfound verbosity did not escape the notice of his uncle and Elise.

"Well, I love all your work," said Laura when he had finished. "Now I know where to go the next time I need to buy a gift."

At that remark, Rick gave Fabio a look as if to say, "See what I mean? It's not just about today."

"Yes, you must come," Fabio told her. "Anytime at all."

"Meantime we'll look for you next time for another dance lesson out on the sidewalk," joked Mark. "I can use the help."

"Yes! That was so amazing the other night," laughed Laura. "I wished you had shown us some more. Why did you disappear so quickly?"

Fabio felt his cheeks flush hot. "Well, you know, the furnace need to be shut down," he said awkwardly. "I just in hurry."

"Well, maybe we'll see you again like Mark says," she told him. "Thank you for letting me see your work. It's amazing."

With that she and Mark went on their way.

"You are welcome," said Fabio dreamily as he watched her go. Anyone with eyes could see that he was clearly smitten.

"In Italian you would say *prego*," said Elise with a certain acerbic air.

"That's true," said Rick, giving her a sideways glance. "But what is all this about dance lessons on the sidewalk?"

Fabio did not reply right away but instead kept watching until Laura disappeared into the crowd. A thousand ideas were suddenly dancing in his head and for the first time since he could remember, he felt lighter than air.

"It just about the fun," he said, turning at last to his uncle. "Maybe you right, maybe it time to feed the soul."

Then Fabio did the unexpected. He smiled.

CHAPTER TWENTY-THREE

Fabio held up the piece of glass upon which he had been working and regarded it with a dubious expression. He was alone at the furnace, Rick having gone off to the bank, and had been working most of the day on this single creation. He turned the piece over and over again, trying to determine where he was going wrong in attempting to fashion from the glass the vision he had in his mind. In the not too distant past, had he arrived at such a juncture as this, the shards of broken glass would already be scattered on the floor by the far wall. Patience and calm, however, had of late crept into his psyche, so much so that he no longer needed the loud, angry music he normally used to drown out the voices of regret and bitterness and self-doubt that normally clamored in his head. The voices had all mercifully gone silent and, despite all the odds against it, Fabio was becoming, if not quite happy, at least content in his work. It was no longer just an escape.

Fabio was, of course, aware of this change he was undergoing and what it was that had prompted it. He credited it all to Laura. Inside, though he had not realized it, it had begun that very first time he had seen her at the race, and started to grow when he saw her again that night when she was on her way to dance class. Had there been any doubt, it was all dispelled after seeing her in the park at the art festival. He was as drawn to her as ever he had been to a woman. The terrible voices in his head had fallen silent simply because Fabio had let them be overwhelmed by his dreams of Laura and the dreams he had of somehow winning her regardless of what *those* odds against him might be.

But that was all they were at this point, dreams. Happiness, of whatever sort he might find in his work, did not necessarily mean for him happiness in life, and Fabio knew that one could live on dreams for only so long. He had to find a way to turn his into reality. Until he did, Wednesdays would remain holy days of obligation. On those evenings, Fabio would make up some pretense—sweeping the sidewalk or washing the window, anything at all—for being out in front of the shop when Laura came along with Mark on her way to or from class. They all would exchange greetings and, now and then after class, Mark would demonstrate some dance move or other that they had learned and ask for Fabio's assessment. Fabio would inevitably nod approvingly and say, "*Bravo!*" It was all in fun, and all very fleeting, but just to hear Laura say, "Good night, Fabio, see you next week!" was enough to fill his lonely heart with hope.

Still, despite the change Laura had wrought in him, Fabio could not completely deny his fiery nature. And so it was only with a tremendous effort of self-control that he kept himself from flinging the piece of glass against the wall.

"*Mannaggia,*" he grumbled to himself.

"*Ma* what?"came a voice from behind him.

It was Elise. She had come in quietly and had been there for a short while, observing him as he worked. It was something she did with increasing frequency lately whenever she took a break from her labors to clear the second floor, or when things were slow in the shop.

Fabio looked at her and shook his head. "It just something we say when we mad or things no go right," he said, still assessing his handiwork.

"But what does it mean?" said Elise playfully, her curiosity piqued.

"Oh, no good thing," he said, but then paused and with an

impish expression told her, "I mean to say *nothing* good. Not very bad, but not very nice, really. Better you no know. I should no say it around you anymore."

Elise smiled.

"Well, now that you've told me *that*, you have to tell me what it means—or at least how to say it properly," she kidded him.

Fabio rolled his eyes, but relented without a fight.

"Okay," he told her, "like this. *Mahn-nah-gee-ah.*"

"*Man-nag-gia*," repeated Elise, more or less satisfactorily.

"And if you really mad you say *la miseria* after," added Fabio for good measure.

"*La miseria?*" she repeated, but with the accent incorrectly on the second i so that it sounded like la meez-air–EE-a.

"No," Fabio corrected her. "You say *mis-er-i-a,* no big accent."

"So it's *mannaggia la miseria?*" said Elise brightly, getting it right.

"*Brava*," said Fabio. "*Perfetto*. Just no say in front of Zio Rick, okay?"

"I won't," promised Elise, looking pleased with herself at having added another addition to the sizable Italian vocabulary she was beginning to acquire from her conversations with Fabio. "Someday I'll have to teach you a few words in Creole."

"Creole. What that?" said Fabio.

"It's a language we speak in Haiti," she told him.

Fabio cocked his head sideways as if he had not understood.

"I thought they speak there the French," he said.

"That too," said Elise with a laugh. "I'll teach you a little of both."

Fabio turned his attention back to his glasswork and gave a sigh of consternation. He was attempting without success to twist two tubes of glass around one another in a manner that only he could see in his imagination. How to do it in just the way that he envisioned had vexed him all that day. He stood there for a time, contemplating it in silence.

"It's very pretty, whatever it is," said Elise. "It reminds me a little of something Chihuly might do, just not as big of course."

"Who?" said Fabio

Elise looked at him wide-eyed. "Dale Chihuly?" she said, incredulous. "The glass sculptor? Don't tell me that you've never heard of him."

"I no never hear of him," said Fabio despite her request. "How *you* hear of him?"

"Um, I don't know, maybe because his work is really famous," she said with a hint of sarcasm in her voice. "Don't you ever study the work of other artists?"

Fabio gave a shrug of indifference and shook his head.

"So, where do you get your ideas?" said Elise, somewhat nonplused. She herself had made it a point to read whatever she could find about glassblowing when Rick first hired her, and so had gained a fair knowledge of the art and the industry. Had she mentioned it, Fabio would not have been surprised in the least. He had grown accustomed to her knowing more about his own craft than he himself.

In any case, Fabio once again did not reply right away to her query, but instead paused and looked toward the window through which the afternoon sun was beaming.

"The idea just come when it wants, like sun through window," he explained. "And all good till cloud come and take away light."

"And what do you do when the clouds come?" said Elise.

Fabio glanced at the box of broken glass he had been collecting and shrugged once more.

"Well, you can't break this one," said Elise, sounding a little alarmed. "It's too pretty. Somebody will definitely buy it."

"No, I no sell this one," said Fabio.

"Why not?"

Fabio did not give an answer, but instead put the piece of glass aside and nodded toward the door. "I think maybe I go outside, take little break. You come too?"

"*Un intervalo?*" said Elise with a sly gaze, waiting for confirmation that she had chosen the correct word.

"*Si, signorina,*" replied Fabio, nodding solemnly, "*un piccolo intervalo.*" With that he led the way outside.

The two sat for a time at the picnic table on the little patch of grass in the back. It was a sizzling hot day with but the slightest of breezes. Had they not been sitting in the shade cast by the building, it might have been unbearable. Fabio looked up at the sky. High above, a seagull held aloft by the breath of the hot breeze was gliding lazily along on its way back toward the ocean. He watched it for a few moments, wondering all the while if the surf might be up at the beach.

"It warm today," he noted after the gull had drifted out of sight, though he did not mind the heat.

"It's nice," said Elise. "I'm always afraid that the winter won't end and the warm weather will never get here." She paused and looked at him before asking, "What is the weather like where you come from in Italy?"

"Hot like this," answered Fabio. "Summer very very hot."

"Mm, in Haiti too," she said, nodding. "Except hotter and more humid. And everything goes very slow."

Fabio nodded in agreement. He thought back to all those scorching summer afternoons at home in Mont'Oliva when it would be too hot to breathe and taking a *siesta* was the only reasonable thing to do until the sun went down and the world came back to life again.

"If you no like the cold, why you come to here in America?" asked Fabio.

For a moment or two Elise said nothing, her face saddening a bit, but then she grinned and gave a little laugh.

"I really didn't have a choice," she finally replied.

"Why no?"

"Why *not*," she corrected.

"Okay, why *not*?" sighed Fabio, putting extra emphasis on the t.

That she had caused him some pique seemed to give her pleasure for she grinned again. Then she looked off into the distance and gave a little sigh.

"When I was just a little girl," she told him, "my father brought me to the orphanage and gave me to the nuns."

"Why?" said Fabio.

"I don't know," she said softly, "but I never saw him again. So I lived there until one day, when I was a thirteen, my aunt came for me and took me to America."

"And how you like America?" he asked.

"Oh, I thought I had died and gone to heaven," she said with a great smile. "In the orphanage we had next to nothing, which was at least better than what just about everybody else had. Here in this country, on the other hand, we have everything we could possibly want at our fingertips. Clothes, food, movies, cars, whatever we want. It's like paradise compared to where I was."

"It no seem like paradise to me," said Fabio with a grunt.

Elise leaned closer to him and studied his face intently for a moment with a curious expression.

"No?" she said. "And why not?"

Fabio swallowed hard, regretting having started this particular conversation, for he did not like to discuss his feelings about anything or anyone. In spite of that he felt obligated to follow her lead since she had revealed to him something about herself.

"When I come to America," he said uneasily, "I think maybe I die and go not to heaven, but to hell."

"You must have been going through a very bad time," said Elise gently.

Fabio looked away for a moment and nodded.

"Yes," he said. "A bad time. I thought all the while I am being punished, and for many days I afraid of everything and all the peoples I meet. All I want to do is hide in the room with blankets over the head. Then one day Zio Rick start to teach me how to work the glass, and so for long time I hide there at the furnace, still afraid of everything, but at least a little busy."

"And now?" she said.

Fabio let out a long breath and turned back to her. Then he jutted his chin out and held up his hands in an expression of what one might have interpreted as cautious satisfaction. "Now, things a little better," he admitted.

"Good," said Elise. Then, with a mischievous grin, she added teasingly, "Better enough to finish that piece you're working on instead of smashing it to bits?"

"Yes, ha ha," replied Fabio. "I no want you to call me idiot again."

"I would never dream of such a thing," she said sweetly. Then she nodded up at his head. "By the way, I notice that you've been letting your hair grow out a little," she said. "It looks nice."

Fabio acknowledged the compliment with a grunt before getting up from the table. Elise followed behind as he began to walk back into the shop. It was just then that Rick, back from the bank, appeared at the door.

"Ah, there you two are," he said with feigned displeasure. "I was beginning to think that there was no one working today."

"None of the worries," snickered Fabio. "We going back to job."

"Yes, he's actually working on something very beautiful, Mister Rick," said Elise. Then, giving Fabio a sideways glance, she said playfully, "I told him that it looks like something Chihuly might do."

Rick looked at her with a blank expression.

"Chi-who?" he said.

CHAPTER TWENTY-FOUR

Giorgiana Fiorelli was the first girl that Fabio ever kissed. It happened one spring day after school not long after he had turned thirteen.

Having grown up in the village together, Fabio and Giorgiana were friendly enough towards each other, though in that arm's length way of adolescent boys and girls. Giorgiana was a pretty girl, and Fabio liked her, but despite his growing prowess on the dance floor, he still lacked confidence with the opposite sex, and so he rarely spoke to her. That was why it caught him by surprise that afternoon when Giorgiana took it upon herself to sit next to him on the bus on the way back from school. All along the way home they talked—or more precisely Giorgiana talked and Fabio listened—about teachers and friends and school and the weather until at last they arrived at Mont'Oliva.

That, Fabio assumed, was the end of it, for the conversation came to an abrupt halt and the two immediately stood with the others to get off the bus. They had just descended the stairs and started on their way up the hill toward the village with the other children when Giorgiana surprised him again by unexpectedly slipping her hand into his.

Stunned by this development, Fabio looked straight ahead as if he had not noticed, but the touch of her hand sent tingles up his spine and suddenly he felt very weak, but in a wonderful way. Without a word between them, the two instinctively slowed their gait and soon fell well behind the other children. It was then that Giorgiana, squeezing his hand a little tighter, gently pulled him toward an apple tree by the side of the road where they would be out of sight, in so much as that was possible in a little place with so many watchful eyes as Mont' Oliva. Fabio could only let himself be pulled along.

It was a hot, sticky day that afternoon when Fabio and Giorgiana were standing together beneath the tree on the road up to Mont'Oliva. Across the valley, great towering thunderclouds were assembling over the mountaintops, blotting out the sun, and a wispy breeze was starting to kick up. A storm was heading their way, but the two youngsters were too distracted to notice. Instead, they dropped their book bags on the grass and stood facing each other with nervous eyes.

Giorgiana was, at this age, still slightly taller than Fabio, a circumstance he ordinarily found discomfiting, but at the present moment the matter of her greater stature did not enter his mind in the least. Given that it was she who had sat next to him on the bus, and she who had taken him by the hand and led him there beneath the tree, he was far too intrigued to see what would happen next to bother worrying about the disparity in their heights.

Wasting no time, Giorgiana stepped up close to Fabio and put her hand on his face. *"Tu sei bello,"* she told him, gazing deep into his eyes. Then, without another word, she kissed him.

It was the briefest of kisses, but in Fabio's mind it lasted an eternity. Giorgiana's lips were soft and moist and irresistible, and when she pulled away and smiled at him, Fabio reached out to pull her back, not noticing that the sky had suddenly gone black. It was just then, before he could try to kiss her in return, that they were startled by the crackle of lightning and a tremendous clap of thunder that made Fabio jump and Giorgiana screech. Before either could utter a word, the winds suddenly whipped up, the skies opened, and the rain came pouring down.

Instantly drenched, the two grabbed their book bags and, laughing and screaming the whole way, ran up the hill through the wild storm into the village to Giorgiana's house where her mother was waiting fretfully by the door. Fabio could only bid Giorgiana a quick *ciao!* as he sprinted by. He did not stop running until he came to his house where his own mother was waiting at the door for him. A few moments later he was standing by the window, drying his head with a towel as the amazing storm raged on. Just as the skies had opened, Fabio felt that his whole world had suddenly opened up in a new and wonderful way. As the rain threw itself against the window and the thunder boomed, he wondered all the while how he might find himself once more beneath the apple tree with Giorgiana.

Like that long ago day in Mont'Oliva, it was just such a hot, sticky afternoon in Wakefield, not unusual in July, the next day when Fabio was sitting in the shop alone. No one needed to consult a weather forecast to predict that sooner or later there would be a thunderstorm that day. One could sense it in the air, that is if one chose to go outside. It had been so warm that Rick, who ordinarily hated the expense, turned on the air conditioning first thing in the morning and left it running all afternoon despite the dearth of customers on that scorching day. Fabio, after finishing his glassblowing work at the furnace, had been all too content to sit in the cool of the shop and watch things for a little while Rick and Elise tended to one thing or another on the sweltering second floor. Just the same, with closing time approaching, he was growing anxious to leave, for thoughts of taking his surfboard to the beach had started to occupy his mind as he stared out the window. He had just settled back in the chair and lost himself in a daydream of being out on the waves when he heard the jingle of the bell attached to the front doorknob. The door swung open and to his astonishment in stepped Laura.

Judging by the conservative skirt and blouse she wore, she had just come from work.

"Laura?" Fabio gasped, jumping to his feet.

Laura walked directly up to the counter and stood there with arms folded. "Why do you look so surprised?" she said with a laugh in her voice. "I told you that I'd come to you the next time I needed a gift."

"It just that I no expect you today," offered a flustered Fabio in reply, beside himself with joy that she had come. "It good surprise. Very good."

Laura smiled and turned away from him. She cast an eye about at the glasswork on the shelves. "So this is all your work," she said, sounding impressed.

"Not all mine," said Fabio. "Just some. The rest my uncle."

"And you make it all here?"

"In back," said Fabio. "Furnace shut down now, but someday you come and I show you how we make the glass."

"That would be nice," said Laura. "I would love to see how it's done." With that she turned her attention to the shelves and gave a little sigh. "But for now I'm in a little bit of a hurry. I need a gift for someone." She gave him a sly gaze that made his knees go weak. "Whose work do you recommend I look at," she said teasingly, "yours or your uncle's?"

"Both very good," replied Fabio with a shrug.

Before he could say more, Zio Rick came clamoring down the stairs from the second floor, carrying a hefty cardboard box. Elise followed right behind him, a smaller box clutched in her arms. Looking hot and weary, the pair gaped in surprise at Fabio for it was a rare sight seeing him assisting a customer instead of hiding in the back by the furnace. It took but a moment though for both to recognize Laura, and everything became clear.

"Well, hello," said Rick with a smile setting his box down, "I do believe yours is a familiar face."

"Yes," said Laura pleasantly. "We met at the art show a few

weeks ago."

"I remember," said Rick.

"She come to buy gift," said Fabio, displeased at the interruption.

Rick gave her wink then looked at Fabio. "Well, don't let her waste her time looking at *your* work," he sniffed with an air of disdain. Then he gestured to the other shelves "The really good stuff is all over there."

Fabio snickered nervously in reply.

"Sorry," said Laura with that same laugh in her voice, "but Fabio was here first when I came in, so I guess anyone else's work will just have to wait until next time."

Rick gave a sigh of resignation. "Alas, the customer is always right," he said with a smile.

Fabio wasted no time, but guided Laura directly over to the shelves where his works were featured. There he followed her at a discreet distance, trying his best not to hover, but finding it all but impossible to resist watching her reaction as she held up each piece of glass. It was exciting beyond words just to have her near and he felt a flush of pride as she marveled aloud at his creations.

"I love this one," she finally said of a curiously formed figurine she had discovered that reminded one vaguely of a snail.

"I like too," said Fabio, nodding. "I remember day I make."

"Really?" said Laura intrigued. "What were you thinking about when you made it?"

Fabio scratched his chin for a moment or two before he held up his hands and shrugged. "That I no remember," he admitted. "I no think so much when I work. But I remember day because when I finish making Zio, my uncle, look at it and say it make him hungry for *scungilli*."

"Yes, I can see why he would," Laura laughed, touching his arm, making him go weak again. "Who could resist a recommendation like that? I guess I'll have to definitely take this one."

Elise, who to this point had remained silent, watching the goings on with a look of detachment mixed with mild distress, was nevertheless standing ready at the counter when Laura brought up her selection. While she tallied the sale and wrapped the glass in paper, Fabio excused himself for a moment and went into the back. He returned a short time later with a piece of glasswork in hand. It was two tubes of multi-colored glass whimsically twisted about each other and flared at the tops. Elise recognized it in an instant.

"This for you," said Fabio bashfully as he presented it to Laura.

"For me?" said Laura, stunned. "It's beautiful, but I can't let you just give it to me."

"No no," said Fabio. "None of the worries. I make just for you for present. I never sure when I see you, so now a good time as any to give."

Laura paused and ran her fingers over the glass. "It really is beautiful," she gushed. "It looks like two dancers."

"Like two dancers on the sidewalk," added Fabio.

"Yes," laughed Laura. "I can see that too."

"Then you like?" said Fabio.

"I love it," she said, clearly delighted. "Thank you so much."

With that she leaned close and gave him a kiss on the cheek. Rick and Elise could clearly see that Laura was no flirt, and that the kiss was merely a platonic gesture of gratitude. Judging by the look on his face, however, Fabio had interpreted it as meaning much more. And so he had. He was thrilled, and when it came time for her to leave, he followed Laura out the door like a puppy and stood on the sidewalk, watching her go until she was out of sight.

Back inside the shop, Elise exchanged a glance of concern with Rick and gave a little sigh. "*Mannaggia,*" she muttered.

Rick made no reply, but looked at her with eyebrows raised.

*

Later that afternoon, when he was done for the day, Fabio drove to the beach with his surfboard. Dark clouds were looming on the western horizon, but there were still plenty of people on the beach and in the water. A hot breeze was blowing, kicking up the spray on the tops of the waves. Despite the warm air, Fabio still pulled on his wetsuit and before long was paddling out through the surf.

Out past the breaking waves, Fabio sat up on his surfboard and drifted about for a time, idly letting the waves roll under him as he replayed over and over again in his mind Laura's visit to the shop. The thought of her kiss, simple and unromantic as it might have been, still sent shivers down his spine every bit as much as Giorgiana Fiorelli's had that day so long ago in Mont'Oliva. Giddy with delight—insofar as he was capable of giddiness—Fabio did not know what to do with himself. All he knew for certain was that he needed to find some way of getting Laura back in his arms again. Floating lazily on the water, watching the other surfers ride the waves in, Fabio suddenly felt inspired. And so, at spying the next great swell rolling in, he flopped down on the board and began to paddle. He caught his breath as the wave swept him up and he began to hurtle toward the shore. Gritting his teeth, he climbed to his feet and stood up on the board as down the wave it plummeted. The ride lasted for but a moment before Fabio's legs crumpled beneath him. Just the same, after he had finished tumbling over and over in the rushing surf and staggered back to his feet, Fabio did something he had not done in a very long time.

He laughed.

Excited by the escapade, Fabio began to paddle back out for more, but then the sky began to quickly darken and there came a great rumble of thunder. Reluctantly, he left the water along with everyone else and hurried with his surfboard back to the truck.

The sky was dark and twisted and angry, not unlike one of his glass creations, when Fabio arrived back home. It let loose the rain just as he was carrying his surfboard up the back stairs to his apartment. Instead of hurrying inside, though, Fabio stood on the back landing and watched the spectacle of the storm unfolding overhead. Great towering thunderheads were rolling through the skies like giant bowling balls while bolts of lightning crackled and darted around them. The rain came down in windswept torrents that lashed the trees and slammed against the houses, and it seemed to him that all of nature was convulsed with fury.

Fabio ought to have been frightened and hurried inside to safety. Instead he stayed there on the landing, a thrill of exhilaration surging through him as he watched the dazzling show. He opened his arms wide and breathed deep of the electric smell of the lightning, letting nature give him all the energy she would. Then he closed his eyes and let the bracing slap of the raindrops wash him clean of the bitterness and anxiety and guilt. Somehow, he felt certain, the world was opening up to him again in some inexplicable and wonderful way.

The storm passed as quickly as it had arrived. After he had gone inside, Fabio showered and put on some dry clothes. When he was dressed he stood for a time in front of the mirror, gazing at himself for the first time in many months, assessing his appearance as he tried to stand up straighter. There was no question, he did not like what he saw looking back at him, but perhaps there was some way he could work with it. He puzzled over it for some minutes. When he had finished this period of self-evaluation, he stepped out into the middle of the apartment and stood there, wondering what he should do next. He looked about the room. There were no trophies on display anywhere, no medals or ribbons, nor any posters hanging on the walls to give him inspiration. And yet, for all that, a plan was beginning to form in his head. The more he considered it, the greater it gripped him. He did not know if he could bring it to fruition, but he knew with certainty that he would have to try.

And so, resolved, he took a deep breath and slowly let it out. Then Fabio Terranova sat down on the floor and began to stretch.

Waltzing

CHAPTER TWENTY-FIVE

"So, what are your plans for today?" said Rick to Fabio.

It was a Saturday morning in August and the two were in the kitchen. Fabio was setting the table while his uncle tended to a potato frittata simmering on the stovetop. The requisite pot of coffee stood percolating on the counter. Meantime Vivaldi was playing on the stereo in the parlor.

"I go to work then to beach," said Fabio.

"Hmm," said his uncle as he poked around the edge of the frittata with a spatula, "going to do a little surfing?"

"No, I no go to do the surf today," he said.

"No? Why not?"

"I go to do the walking," said Fabio.

"Doesn't sound like much fun," opined Rick.

"Fun for me," said Fabio with a shrug.

He had told at least part of the truth. In addition to the regimen of stretching he had been following these last few weeks, Fabio had taken to walking at the beach to strengthen his legs. Up and down the shoreline, knee deep in the water he would go, pushing his legs a little harder each day through the bracing surf. It was low impact exercise that stressed his leg muscles just enough without overtaxing his fragile joints. Just the same, the first few times he attempted it, the workout left him totally exhausted and out of breath after walking less than a few hundred yards. Such was the lowly state of physical fitness into which he had fallen. His youthful body, though, battered as it was, quickly adapted and with each passing day grew stronger. Though his walks were more work than pleasure, they served his purpose, and that was fun enough.

When the frittata was ready, Rick set it on the table along with some Italian bread, said a quick prayer, and gestured to Fabio to begin eating. Fabio reached for the salt shaker, but when he gave it a shake he heard only the sifting of the grains of rice inside; no salt came out. He tried again, only this time with more effort, but with the same result.

"There no more salt?" he said, regarding the shaker curiously.

"Ha! That's just August in New England," chuckled Rick. "The salt shakers don't work anywhere around here when the muggy weather comes in. Get a toothpick from the cupboard and try giving the holes a poke. That usually does the trick...at least for a while."

As Fabio went to the cupboard, Rick eyed him with a modicum of concern. It was clear to see that a very positive change was taking place in his nephew. One could see it right away in his posture, the way he held his head up, and simply the air of confidence, so sadly lacking in the past, that he suddenly exuded. At home and at work he had become pleasant, almost gracious at times. It was remarkable. It was as if the young man had come back to life after wandering around half-dead for so long. It was of course a wonderful thing to behold, but at the same time Rick suspected that the inspiration for this rebirth of sorts most likely came from his feelings for a certain female student of dance.

Therein lay his concern.

Our hopes and dreams, Rick understood, occupy a fragile place in our hearts. Fabio, he rightly surmised, was in love and, as with most young men in that state, saw only what he wanted to see, not necessarily what was really there. How much validity that view might have in this particular case, Rick could not say, but he wanted desperately to explain it to his nephew, to keep that fragile place inside him from breaking—and the rest of him as well. The question was how.

Fabio returned to the table with a toothpick in hand. The saltshaker unclogged, he shook some salt on his food and took a bite.

"*Ti piace?*" said Rick.

"Only the English here," Fabio reminded him with a smile. "But yes, I like very much."

Rick gave a chuckle and nodded. Then for a time the two men ate in silence, save for the Vivaldi playing on the stereo.

"So, what do you today?" said Fabio.

Rick did not answer right away, but waited for a time, choosing his words carefully. "Well, like you I'm going to the shop first," he said at last. "And after that I have a few other things around town to do." He hesitated again for a moment before continuing. "There is something on my mind, though, that I've been wanting to talk to you about."

"What that?" said Fabio.

Rick took a sip of coffee and rubbed his chin thoughtfully. "Well, I just wanted to say that I'm pleased to see how well you are doing," he began. "Lately you seem much stronger and happier."

Fabio gave a shrug. "I feel a little better these days," he admitted.

"That's good," said Rick. "I hope you can keep feeling that way. That's why I wanted to talk to you." He paused again, unsure of how to proceed. "You see, Fabio," he finally went on, "I believe that every one of us is here for a reason. Of course what that reason is isn't always clear to us, sometimes never, so we have to muddle along as best we can. Sometimes that's easier to do than at others. Sometimes it's brutally hard. That's just the way life is, all sorts of crazy things happen to us, and things always change. But once you get an inkling of the reason, maybe discover just what it is that you're supposed to be doing, no matter what it is and no matter what else might be happening to you, that can be the happiest moment in your life."

It was Fabio's turn to eye his uncle with concern, for he was not completely following where all this was leading. "Are you no happy, Zio?" he asked.

"Yes, I'm happy," he said with a grin. "At least happy enough, though I have my days just like everybody else."

"Then why all this talk?" said Fabio.

"It's just that I've learned a few things in my years, Fabio," he said, trying to forge ahead. "One of them is that we have to accept who we are and try to see things as they are. And we can't let who we are depend too much on other people. We have to learn how to be happy inside ourselves on our own. Does that make sense?"

Fabio shrugged and nodded yes, though unconvincingly.

Rick gave a sigh for he could think of no way to speak plainly of what was on his mind without hurting his nephew. "All I am saying," he finally managed, "is that we all have hopes, but we need to know that sometimes we can't have the things we hope for. That doesn't mean though that things won't work out all right for us anyway. Sometimes it turns out that the things we hoped for weren't really the things we needed, that we're better off without them. God just had other plans for us. Do you understand?"

Once again Fabio nodded yes, though Rick suspected the opposite. Whichever the case, it seemed that Rick could find no tactful way of broaching the subject any further, so all he could do was hope that Fabio would connect the dots himself. Resigned that he had tried his best, he let that be the end of that particular topic of conversation.

When they had finished eating, Rick began out of long habit

to pick up their plates and silverware. Fabio, however, insisted that he leave them. Then, to Rick's astonishment, he went about cleaning up the kitchen on his own. Rick could only marvel. The change in Fabio had indeed been remarkable.

Later, after Fabio had gone on ahead of him to the shop, Rick sat for a time in the parlor, listening to Vivaldi while he contemplated the crucifix on the wall. He wondered if he had truly done his best for Fabio, if perhaps he should not have worried about sparing his feelings and simply told him the truth, at least as he saw it. Then another thought occurred to him. Perhaps, instead of lecturing his nephew, he should first try following his own advice. Rick dwelt on that notion for some time until he came to a resolution. Then, that afternoon after finishing at the shop, he walked to church and went to confession.

CHAPTER TWENTY-SIX

The time had come.

It was late August, and Fabio saw the days on the calendar slipping away like water through his fingers. More disconcerting still, he had heard rumors that the dance studio might soon be closing, perhaps by Labor Day. If that were true then he had only a few Wednesday nights left.

Wearing just his shorts—he had been on the floor going through a quick workout—Fabio sat on the edge of his bed and considered his legs for a time. He tightened his thighs, noting the improved definition of the muscles beneath the skin. He had done all he could to prepare himself these past few weeks, the hours of stretching and walking, the exercises. All of it had left him remarkably more fit, even if his limbs were still every bit as fragile as before.

Encouraged, Fabio went to the bathroom and gazed at himself in the mirror. He avoided dwelling on his face and misshapen cheekbone—though he had let his hair grow long enough to hide it somewhat if he chose—and instead focused his attention on his upper body. He was pleased to see the improved tone of his chest and arms and his well-defined abdominal muscles. He looked and felt stronger. Even so, he had a knot of nervous tension in his gut as he contemplated his plan of action for the evening.

It was Wednesday, of course. Fabio had gone to work as always that day, but instead of waiting around to see Laura passing by on her way to class as he usually might, he had come straight home after the shop closed to get ready. All day long he had thought about Laura, the very idea of her filling him just as his breath filled the molten glass he worked with every day. Just the same he had been on edge, his mind filled with doubts about what he was hoping to do. Even now, as he gazed at himself in the mirror, those doubts still plagued him. Try as he might there was nothing he could do to dispel them, so at last he gave up trying and simply chose to ignore them. In any case, there was not much time, so Fabio looked away from the mirror and turned on the shower.

Later, after he had toweled off, Fabio sat once more on the edge of the bed and wrapped his legs tightly with Ace bandages. Then, when he had put on a new pair of slacks, a fresh shirt, and slipped his feet into a new pair of shoes, he went to the mirror one last time. He stood there for a few minutes, slowly breathing in and out, trying to calm himself. Suddenly, unexpectedly, he found himself thinking of Enzo.

"*Forza i Conquistatori, amico mio,*" he whispered to himself. With that he looked at himself no more and headed for the door.

It was a sultry, breathless evening when Fabio left the house, and he could hear from all around the whine of air conditioners running as he started on his way through the neighborhood and down to Main Street. Despite the heat, he walked briskly along, anxious to get to his destination. He rounded the corner and passed the pizza parlor where a group of teenagers, as always, was hanging around. He walked confidently by, his head held high, and for once there were no snide remarks, no snickering as he passed. In truth, no one recognized him.

Fabio walked until he reached Vita Glassworks. There he stopped and sat down on the front step. He was not tired, but simply wanted to take a moment to collect himself. Meantime, upstairs across the street, the windows were wide open and the music was playing in the dance studio. Laura had already passed by and class had begun. Fabio had known this would be the case. It was in fact his intention that he not be there on time to see her. He wondered if she had noticed his absence as she passed by the shop. The thought that perhaps she had and had been disappointed not to see him cheered and emboldened him. With that hope in mind, Fabio got back to his feet, took a deep breath, and crossed the street to the other side. He stepped up onto the sidewalk and went straight to the door. There he paused for a moment, letting all his self-doubts have their way with him one last time. Then, in his mind, he brushed them away like lint from his shoulder before he opened the door and walked upstairs to the dance studio.

"One-two-three! One-two-three!"

Elizabeth, the teacher and owner of the studio, was counting out the rhythm of the Blue Danube waltz to which her students, ten or so couples, were dancing—or at least attempting to do so. It was sweltering in the room; apparently the air conditioning was not working, or Elizabeth was trying to save money on her electric bill. Whichever the case, the stifling air was filled with the familiar scent of perfume and sweat when Fabio sheepishly poked his head through the doorway. It was a large, open room he saw, with high ceilings and an old hardwood floor. He stepped inside and, without a look at the couples gliding by, discreetly slipped over to the line of chairs on the side of the room where he promptly took a seat.

"Fabio!" called Laura, smiling at him as she and Mark danced by.

At the sound of her voice, Fabio's heart skipped a beat, and he smiled in return until he saw Elizabeth walking in his direction. She was an elegant middle-aged woman, pleasant looking, but with rather intense dark eyes that gave her a no-

nonsense demeanor. Fabio sat up straight, much the way a grammar school student might at the approach of his teacher.

"May I help you?" inquired Elizabeth with a polite smile while the group continued to dance. "Are you here about dancing lessons?"

"Hello," answered Fabio shyly, trying his best not to lose his courage. "If all right, I would like very much just to sit and watch for a little while." In truth, that was as far out as he had planned things for the evening.

Her countenance warming, Elizabeth nodded. "I understand. That's the way it is quite often for newcomers, especially the men. They can be very bashful sometimes when it comes to dancing. All they want to do is sit and watch. But be careful! Dancing is infectious, you know. After a few minutes of watching everyone else do it, you're going to want to get up and learn how to do it yourself. Then once you start, it's so much fun that you don't want to stop."

"Maybe you are right," said Fabio, smiling inwardly for he understood her meaning far better than she could have possibly imagined. "So if okay, I will sit for now and watch the other people dance, yes? Then someday who knows?"

"Go right ahead," she said. "My name is Elizabeth, by the way, if you have any questions later."

"I am Fabio," he replied.

"Yes, I gathered that from Laura when you came in," she said with a smile. Then, turning back to her class, "Now, if you'll excuse me, Fabio..."

While Elizabeth turned her attention back to her students, Fabio turned his to Laura. She and Mark were off on the other side of the room attempting to complete an advanced twinkle. Mark, however, seemed incapable of properly executing the move and the two became entangled as he awkwardly tried to pass in front of her. The two laughed it off and danced on. Despite their missteps they seemed to be thoroughly enjoying themselves.

Fabio could only sit and watch as Laura and Mark and the other couples glided by, but for the time being he was content to do so. It was the first time that Fabio had been in a dance studio since before the accident, and he was soaking in every bit of the sights and sounds of the place as he could. In another lifetime, Fabio might have been inclined to snicker at the amateur efforts of the dancers, but he was energized just to be around them and he looked on with a glad expression, all the while recalling the many happy, if grueling, hours he had spent in the dance studio as a youngster.

Fabio's thoughts quickly returned to Laura, the only reason he had gone there that evening. In truth he had no precise plan in mind as to what he would do next. This was but a first tentative step into a part of her life, and he had no way of knowing if he would be allowed to stay. He was desperate to tell her of the feelings he had for her and to see, as he hoped, if she shared some of those same feelings for him. What he needed most was the opportunity, but with Mark present there seemed little chance of his getting one.

The music suddenly stopped.

"Okay, everyone, let's take five and get a drink of water," said Elizabeth.

Fabio stood as Laura and Mark came straight over looking a bit wilted but delighted regardless to see him.

"Fabio, it's so nice to see you here!" gushed Laura, her cheeks glistening with a thin sheen of perspiration. "When we didn't see you on our way in, I thought that maybe you weren't working as usual. What made you come tonight? "

Pleased and inspired that she had indeed noticed his absence when they passed the shop, Fabio gave a shrug. "Many months I hear the music play, sometimes see the people dance in the window. I see you go in and you always happy when you come out, so I decide to come and see what it is that goes on in this place."

"Well, I'm so glad you did," she said.

"Yeah, me too, bro'," added Mark, dropping onto a chair. His head dripping with sweat, he reached underneath and tugged a water bottle out of a small gym bag on the floor. He passed it to Laura and pulled out another one for himself while he ran a towel across his face. Then he looked at Fabio, who seemed not in the least bit uncomfortable in the stifling heat. "I know you haven't been dancing," he said good-naturedly, "but it feels like it's a hundred and fifty degrees up here tonight. Don't you sweat?"

"I work all the days next to the furnace," Fabio pointed out. "The heat no bother me so much."

"Well, good," chuckled Mark. "In that case, why don't you give me a break and dance with Laura for a little while?"

Stunned, Fabio hesitated. He did not know what to say, for this was even more than he had dreamed of.

"Yes, come on, Fabio!" pleaded Laura. "It will be fun, just like that night on the sidewalk, only this time you can show us what you can really do."

Though he did his best to conceal it, Fabio was delirious with joy.

"You are sure?" he asked Mark, for he could not imagine why he would let another man dance with her.

Mark downed a gulp of water from his bottle. "Of course," he said easily, wiping his brow once more with the towel. "Go ahead and show me how it's done."

Fabio looked at Laura, who gave him an enthusiastic nod. "Okay," he finally agreed. Then, his insides churning, he sat down to wait.

"See?" said Elizabeth a few minutes later when it came time to recommence and she saw Fabio walk out onto the floor with Laura. "I told you that dancing is infectious and that you'd want to give it a try."

Fabio could only smile. He was ecstatic at his good fortune and, as he took his place on the dance floor next to Laura, it all seemed like destiny to him, that the ordeal through which he had passed had been intended precisely to bring him to this very moment. He had been given a second chance and he was determined to take advantage of it. And so, as he waited for the music to begin, he feverishly tried to work out in his mind something he might say to her while they danced, something to draw out her feelings a little and perhaps express his own.

"Places everyone," called Elizabeth.

At that Fabio confidently slipped his arm around Laura's waist and took her hand in his. Almost dizzy with anticipation at feeling her so close, the pure joy of dancing, long forgotten, but now rising in him anew, he gave her a smile. Laura smiled in return then rested her left hand on his shoulder.

Fabio's heart stopped.

"Laura, you have ring," he gasped.

"Yes," Laura gushed. "Isn't the diamond beautiful? Mark gave it to me over the weekend. We're getting married!"

Before Fabio could open his mouth in reply, the Blue Danube began to play once more and there was nothing left for him to do but dance.

CHAPTER TWENTY-SEVEN

"What will you have?" asked Mark amiably.

Fabio tried his best, with little success, to look interested.

"Anything you have," he finally replied.

They were in a bar down the street from the dance studio. Fabio had wanted to go straight home, straight *anywhere*, just to be alone after class, but Laura and Mark had pleaded with him to accompany them and some of the others in the class out for a drink. Reluctantly sitting at the bar with a bottle of beer in hand, Fabio put on a brave face as the others took turn turns asking him questions about where he had learned to dance. Apparently his waltz with Laura had made an impression on them.

The news that Laura and Mark were to be married had been like a dagger to Fabio's heart. Just the same, when the music had begun to play, he had swallowed hard, refusing to let his face betray the devastation inside. His dreams all turning into nightmares, it had felt—and still felt—like his entire world was imploding and there was nothing he could do to stop it.

And so he had danced.

Round and round the room he had gone, leading Laura about to the gentle flowing rhythm of the music. So effortless and confident did he appear that the others, even Elizabeth, found themselves watching. None could perceive how greatly the dance taxed Fabio's legs. The pain was constant and intense, but he had borne it. Only once did his knee buckle. Even then it was so slight that only a very keen observer would have noticed. The physical pain, however, was a mere distraction compared to the agony Fabio bore inside. He was aching, and yet he had danced through it. All things considered, it was as great a performance as any he had ever given on a dance floor.

Now, sitting at the bar, the performance continued in a different way. Amidst the talk and laughter of the others, Fabio pretended to laugh along with them even though his heart had been ground into polenta. Despite that, there he stayed, perhaps still hoping in vain that he might somehow be able to profess his love to Laura and somehow change her mind. So, as the night progressed and the others eventually went on their way, Fabio remained firm in his seat, determined to stay so long as Laura and Mark stayed, till at last it was just the three of them at the bar.

"So, Fabio," said Mark, who had consumed more than one beer. "Have you heard that Elizabeth will be closing the studio in the fall?"

"I hear something, but I no hear why," said Fabio.

"She's moving to Westerly," said Laura, pouting. "I heard she found a space there that was cheaper than this one, and she's planning to open a new studio. I'm going to miss her. I love taking her class. Don't you, Mark?"

Mark was noncommittal.

"I suppose so," he replied with a grin. "But what I'm mostly worried about is how I'll learn to dance in time for our wedding."

"I know," Laura kidded him. "And you really need the help."

"Hey, I have an idea," exclaimed Mark. "We'll go to Fabio!"

"Me?" said Fabio.

"Sure, you can give us some lessons out on the sidewalk," laughed Mark. "It will be great—except in the winter of course."

"He's just being silly," said Laura to Fabio. "But you know it would be wonderful if you could help us a little when the wedding gets close. You dance so beautifully."

Fabio felt his heart sink ever lower at the mere thought of such a prospect. Just the same, he shrugged and said maybe. A little while later, Laura and Mark left, but Fabio stayed behind at the bar and did not leave until he had emptied his wallet.

*

The night air was still warm and sticky much later when Fabio walked unsteadily out of the bar and onto the sidewalk, but he barely noticed it. A little extra discomfort from the weather was not a matter of great concern. His head awhirl, he staggered down the sidewalk until he reached the front of Vita Glassworks. There he paused for a few moments, fumbling through his pocket for his keys, before finally letting himself in.

It was only fitting that he had gone there. How many times had he done the same whenever he needed to escape the demons that had relentlessly tormented him, to quiet the voices in his head? Only at the furnace was he able to do so. It had been his sanctuary, the only place left for him in the world where he could find peace, or at least the hope of it. For how many long, lonely months had he been, if not content, then at least resigned to barricading himself there where the world could not find him?

It had not been until he first saw Laura that he finally began to find the courage to reach out once more to the world. In her he had seen a way to hope not just for peace, but for love. He craved it desperately, and the hope that he might somehow win her had brought the light back into his life.

Now, though, that light had been snuffed out like a candle's flame. The darkness that descended in its wake was far heavier, far more profound than the one that preceded it, so much so that when he stepped through the door and into the shop, Fabio knew with certainty that even this place no longer held any peace for him.

He looked about. All was still inside the shop, the glassware on the shelves faintly illumined by the low lighting always left on at night for security's sake. Fabio stood in the middle of the floor, compassed round about by the glass. The beauty of it all, though, brought him no comfort. Instead, it seemed to taunt him, and the endless hours he had spent at the furnace now all felt like some cruel joke. The despair he felt about Laura soon gave way to anger and he surveyed the shelves holding his work with a black gaze.

"*Perche`?*" he fumed, looking up to heaven. "Why?"

When no answer came, Fabio reached for a broom leaning against the wall behind the counter. He stood, holding it for a time, the anger welling up in him as he gazed at the glass. Then, seething, he lifted the broomstick and began to swing.

CHAPTER TWENTY-EIGHT

With Zio Rick asleep upstairs in the house, Fabio climbed into the truck and started the engine.

He understood everything now. He no longer needed to ask why he could not have Laura; why his dreams of dancing had been crushed; why his friends had been taken away from him.

He understood it all.

As the fog began to roll in, he sped out onto Main Street and before long was careening down the highway at alarming speed, pounding his fist against the dashboard to the rhythm of the music blaring from the radio. But the loud music could do nothing to quell the voices now screaming in his head, all the pain and bitterness, the demons that had all come out to eat him alive. Yes, Fabio understood everything now, and as the sign for Prospect Road came into view up ahead, he knew exactly what he had to do.

When he reached the road, Fabio barely slowed the truck as he sent it swerving around the corner. Soon he was at the crest of the hill where the road began the long steep plunge that led down to the wall by the river. How much like the road down to *il muro* it was, how fitting.

Fabio saw now how things were supposed to end. No matter what he did, he could not knit up the raveled cloth of his life because his life was already over. He should have died in the crash with Caterina and Enzo. Fate had allowed him to survive only to toy with him, to taunt him, but Fabio had made up his mind to be taunted no more, and so he stepped on the accelerator and pushed it to the floor.

Down the hill, down through the fog, faster and faster the truck hurtled, down toward the wall at the end of the road. In an instant, it seemed, the truck reached the end of the descent where the hill bottomed out just before reaching the stop. It was there, in that precise moment, that the fog ahead cleared just enough for Fabio to see a figure in white standing across the road directly in his path. For an instant his addled brain perceived it as a statue of some sort, but a sobering millisecond later he realized that it was a woman walking a dog.

Fabio gasped and stood on the brake.

There came a screech of tires against the pavement, the truck fishtailing first one way then the other before going into a spin. Then came a soft, ominous thud as the truck went sideways up onto the thin stretch of grass along the wall before finally coming to a halt. It was that final sound, the soft thud, that sickened Fabio most as he frantically threw open the door and jumped out of the truck. Certain that he had hit and probably killed the woman in white, he hurried about, trying desperately to find her, but she was nowhere to be seen. For a terrible moment he was convinced that he had hit her and that she had gone over the wall, but then he heard a voice from the other side of the truck.

"No, I'm not dead."

Fabio whirled around and saw the woman, safe and sound, standing with her dog a few yards away. An old, but fit-looking woman, her hair almost as white as her clothes, she stood there glaring at him with arms crossed while the little dog milled about at her feet. Mortified at what he had done, Fabio came closer and stood before her with hands folded in supplication. He was afraid to look directly at her, but found he could not resist, for the old woman's eyes were riveted on him.

"I so sorry," he told her in a pleading voice. "So sorry I do this and frighten you."

Backing away slightly, the woman looked at him with the eyes of one who had seen more than just a little of life, and had not been entirely pleased by what she had beheld. In her gaze alone he felt her rebuke.

"Frighten me?" she said with a sneer. "You almost killed me! What kind of crazy stunt was that? I should call the police!" She paused and leaned closer, giving him a sniff. "Oh, of course," she said, shaking her head, "you've been drinking. What a surprise."

Fabio rubbed the back of his neck sheepishly and looked away, wondering how to explain himself. "I very sorry," was all he could manage to say again as he turned back to face her once more. "I...I going through bad time. My life—"

Fabio never saw the hand coming. Like the tail of a whip, it came lashing out and slapped him hard across his face. So stunned by the blow was he that he stood there for a moment dumbfounded.

"You're going through a bad time?" said the woman, her voice dripping derision, her words stinging far more than the slap. "Welcome to the world, you idiot, we're all going through a bad time, in case you hadn't noticed! What makes you think that you're so special that you don't have go through it like everybody else? And who told you to get drunk and ride around like a maniac to accomplish God only knows what and maybe put an end to someone else while you're doing it? What's the matter, nothing to say now? Answer me!"

Fabio had no reply, but could only stand there mute, his head bowed in shame. For a brief time neither spoke, the silence broken only by the chirping of the crickets and the low hoot of an owl coming from the nearby woods.

Softening, the old woman took a deep breath and heaved a weary sigh of exasperation. "What is it with you young people," she lamented. "Why are you so careless and reckless? You have your whole lives in front of you."

The tears suddenly welled up in Fabio's eyes. "That," he said, finally finding the courage to look at her, "is problem."

The old woman cocked her head to one side. "You mean *the* problem?" she said.

Fabio gave a sigh of his own. "Yes," he said, grudgingly. "*The* problem."

The woman folded her arms once more and regarded him thoughtfully for a time. "What's your name?" she said.

"I am Fabio," he told her.

"Uh-huh," she said with a nod. "And where are you from, Fabio, with that accent?"

"I come from Italy."

"Well let me ask you a question, Fabio from Italy," she said. "Whatever it is that you've got going on in your life, tell me how is hurting yourself or someone else going to make it any better?"

Fabio made no reply. Wiping his eyes dry with the back of his hand, he gave a shrug and shook his head.

At seeing the doubt and remorse in his eyes, the old woman sighed once more and gave him a kind smile. "Listen to me," she said gently. "Whatever it is you're going through right now, just keep on going till you're all the way through it."

"How?" asked Fabio earnestly.

"You know how," she said. "Just have a little faith. Don't give up on life and it won't give up on you. Do you understand?"

Fabio nodded yes, even though he was not completely certain that he truly did.

"Good," said the woman. "Now, if you'll excuse me, I'd like to get going before some other drunken fool comes barreling down that hill." With that she looked down at her dog. "Come on, you," she told it. "It's time to go home."

She started on her way, but then stopped and looked back at Fabio. "And it's time for you to go home, too," she told him, "but if you want my advice, you'd better not get behind the steering wheel of that truck right now. You got lucky once tonight, chances are you won't get lucky twice. Why don't you just sleep it off and drive home in the morning."

"I drive no more this night," Fabio assured her.

"Good boy," she replied. "God bless you." Then she turned and walked away.

Fabio stood and watched her go. "*Signora!*" he called after her. "Thank you!"

He hoped that he might hear her call back, or see her wave in acknowledgment, but in the next moment she and the little dog simply vanished into the darkness.

Left there alone, Fabio scratched his chin and looked at the truck. The old woman had given him sound advice. Sleeping off his drunkenness probably was the best idea, but her slap had awakened something inside him and in a way sobered him up far more than a few hours of shuteye would. He realized then that he could not afford to sleep just now; he had work to tend to at the shop. He looked once more at the truck and bit his upper lip in indecision for just a moment before making up his mind. He had promised the old woman that he would not drive, and he could not go back on his word, and so he locked the truck and started the long walk back to Vita Glassworks.

Chapter Twenty-Nine

"Fabio, wake up!"

Fabio opened his eyes and found Zio Rick standing over him. It was early the next morning at the shop. After trudging some six miles back to Wakefield the night before, Fabio had craved his bed, but instead came straight there and set about cleaning up as much as he could of the havoc he had wrought. He accomplished very little before exhaustion overcame him and he collapsed to the floor just before dawn. There he had remained, curled up asleep, until his uncle's voice awakened him.

"What's all this?" said Rick, looking about aghast. In every direction lay shards of glass. "What happened here? Who did this?"

His head throbbing, Fabio sat up and looked about at his handiwork with forlorn eyes. He had knocked over all the shelves holding his glasswork, every piece smashed to bits. It was only a minor miracle that had kept him from destroying his uncle's work as well. "What a mess I make," he sighed disconsolately.

"You mean *you* did this?" gasped his uncle.

Tears coming to his eyes, Fabio bowed his head. "I so sorry,

Zio," he said. Then he confessed what he had done.

"But why?" cried Rick when Fabio had finished. "What in Heaven's name were you thinking?"

"I no know," Fabio admitted. "I drink very much at bar last night and become very mad at all things. Then everything becomes the blur."

As to what had precipitated his going to the bar in the first place, his ill-starred romantic aspirations regarding Laura, Fabio chose to say nothing at all. That particular humiliation he decided to keep to himself for the time being.

"But this is monstrous!" bellowed Rick. "How could you do such a thing!"

It was the first time that Fabio had heard his uncle speak in true anger, and the sound of it struck him with startling effect. "I so sorry, Zio," was the only reply he could come up with. "I no know."

"You don't know?" griped Rick, growing red in the face. "Well do you know how much time and energy you put into creating everything that you just destroyed? All that sweat and effort wasted. And do you know how much time and sweat and money *I* put into running this place so that you could create it? I've tried my best for you, Fabio. How could you do something like this to me, how could you be so irresponsible?"

"I make things up to you, Zio," Fabio quickly vowed. "I work for no pay until everything made good again."

Still fuming, Rick shook his head in dismay and stood in silence, and Fabio found his silence far worse than his words of anger. But after a time, Rick's ire at last began to abate. He squirreled up the side of his mouth and threw up his hands in what Fabio interpreted as a gesture of resignation.

"Well, it is what it is," he said somberly, rubbing the back of his neck. "I suppose it could have been worse." Then, clearing his throat, he added, "Though I doubt it could have been by very much. But at least you didn't break one of the windows, or anything I made, so I suppose that's something to be thankful for." He paused a moment and looked about the room before adding with a sigh, "And I guess it really *is* only sand."

"I make all up to you," Fabio vowed once more.

"I know you will," answered Rick. He stooped and picked up a broom, the same one Fabio had used to lay waste to the glass. He passed it to Fabio and gestured to the floor. "You have a lot of work to do, my friend. For now you can start here."

By the time Elise showed up at the door to start work, the shelves had been set back upright and much of the broken glass already swept up.

"What happened—where's all the glass?" she cried in shock at seeing the empty shelves.

Fabio had dreaded her coming; the thought of the look on her face when she discovered that he was to blame was more than he could bear. All the same, he swallowed hard and was about to make his confession when Rick preempted him.

"We were vandalized," he said quickly, his eyes briefly meeting Fabio's. "We're just cleaning up. There's another broom in the back near the furnace. Would you mind getting it for me?"

"Of course I'll get it for you," said Elise at once.

Off she went to the back room. When she was out of earshot, Rick fixed his gaze on Fabio and gave him a nod.

"Later on we'll go get the truck," he told him. "Meantime we'll keep all of this between you and me, *d'accordo?*"

"*Si, d'accordo,*" said Fabio.

Then he went back to sweeping up the glass.

In the days that followed, Fabio worked with contrite diligence at the furnace, trying to re-create as many of the works he had destroyed as he could remember. Eschewing the music he normally listened to, he worked in silence, choosing instead to listen to his own thoughts instead of perpetually trying to drown them out. Quite often he found himself thinking about the advice the old woman had given him, that he needed to find a way to put things behind him and start all over again. The question was how, but no matter how long he worked away at the furnace, or floated lazily on his surfboard, or lay in bed staring at the ceiling, the answer eluded him.

One afternoon at lunchtime, he and Elise were sitting out back at the picnic table. It was a sunny, breezy day with just the hint of a brisk nip in it. It was the first time that Fabio had noticed it, and he knew right away that August was all but finished. He liked it. He had had enough of the summer and was ready for autumn even though he knew that the hard cold of winter would be right behind it. It was time for a change of seasons.

"*Grazie*," said Elise, holding up the sandwich Fabio had purchased for her.

"*Niente*," replied Fabio with a nod.

Elise turned her face to the sun and gave a contented sigh.

"It's such a beautiful day today," she said. "What's it like where you come from in Italy this time of year?"

Fabio gave a shrug and swallowed a bite of his sandwich.

"Still very hot sometimes," he finally answered. "Hotter than here, but pretty soon it start to change like here, get a little cooler."

"It *gets* a little cooler," Elise corrected with a mischievous gleam in her eye.

"Yes, yes, it *gets* a little cooler," said Fabio. Then, before biting into his sandwich he added, "You know, maybe you need be more nice to me. I buy lunch after all."

"I'll try to remember," said Elise with a sweet smile.

They sat for a short time without speaking. Fabio was content to idly soak in the sun and listen to the breeze whispering through the alleyway while he ate his lunch. But then his thoughts turned once again to the old woman and he wondered anew about what she had told him that night.

"Do you miss home?" said Elise, unexpectedly breaking his reverie.

"Home?" said Fabio puzzled.

"You know, your home in Italy," she said. "You tell me little things about Italy every now and then, but you never really talk about your home."

"There not really very much to say about it," said Fabio with a shrug. "It not very much of a place."

"Oh sure," she said teasingly, "I bet it's really beautiful."

Fabio gave another shrug and stared into space for a moment.

"Some parts, like the mountains, are beautiful," he admitted. Then, the memories of Enzo and Caterina flooding his mind, he added, "But other things not so pretty. So this place okay with me for now. That's why home I no miss much."

Elise gazed thoughtfully at him for a time.

"Have you ever been back?" she asked.

The question drove a stake of fear into Fabio's gut. He did not answer, but simply shook his head.

Elise eyed him for a moment before saying, "Maybe it's time you did."

Fabio turned away and looked once more into the distance. Suddenly everything that the old woman had said became clear to him, and for the first time he knew what it was that he had to do.

"Maybe," was all he murmured.

After that he said very little.

Later that night, Fabio came downstairs from his apartment to talk to Zio Rick. He found his uncle sitting in the living room, reading a book of essays by G.K.Chesterton. At seeing him come through the door, Rick closed the book and put it aside.

"*Buona sera*," said Rick with a smile. For one reason or another he had relaxed his English-only policy, if only just a little, ever since the incident at the shop.

"*Buona sera*," Fabio replied. He hesitated for a moment and stood there awkwardly, unsure of where to begin.

Rick gestured to a chair across from him. "Why don't you

sit," he said. "Then you can tell me what's on your mind."

Fabio sat and took a deep breath. He had rehearsed what he wanted to say, but now that the moment had come, the words he had so carefully prepared were elusive.

"Zio," he finally began, "I am very sorry for what I did at shop."

Rick looked at him kindly. "I know you are," he said. "But why are you bringing it all up again? It's time to move forward."

"That is why I come and speak to you," said Fabio. "This is my problem all the time that I am here. I no move forward because of what is behind me. Do you understand?"

"I'm not sure," admitted Rick, shaking his head. "What exactly is it that you're trying to say?"

"What I try to say," said Fabio, "is that I must go back."

"Back where?"

"Back home," said Fabio. "Home to *l'Italia*."

Rick made no reply at first, but only nodded thoughtfully to indicate that at last he understood, the same way he would three weeks later when he bid his nephew farewell at the airport and Fabio boarded the plane for Rome.

La Bella Cosa

CHAPTER THIRTY

Liliana sat down at the table on her little terrace, poured herself a glass of mineral water, and looked out over the rooftops of Mont'Oliva and down to the valley below. It had been a scorching hot day, but now a pleasant breeze had kicked up and the air was cooling nicely as the sun slowly began to slip behind the mountains. She took a sip of water and enjoyed for a moment the freshening air. A moment of enjoyment of any kind, however small, seemed all she ever allowed herself these days. Anything more brought with it feelings of guilt and restlessness, so she quickly downed the rest of the water in the glass and stood once more.

Still looking out across the distance, she could see a bus making its way along the road through the valley. She watched it for a time as it dipped in and out of view behind the rolling terrain. She was about to turn away, for Pasqualina had invited her to dinner, when she noticed the bus slowing until it came to a stop at the bottom of the road leading up to the piazza. A few seconds later the door opened and out stepped a young man carrying a suitcase.

At first Liliana paid no heed to the young man; from that distance there was nothing recognizable about him. But when she saw the odd gait of his legs as he started to walk up the hill toward the piazza, her heart almost burst.

"*O, Dio!*" she cried.

By the time she reached the piazza, the young man had already made it up the hill. At seeing her there he dropped his suitcase and rushed into her open arms.

"*Mamma,*" was all Fabio could say as the tears came.

"*Figlio mio,*" cried Liliana over and over again, squeezing him tight until at last she released him and led him home.

Back at the house, her invitation to dinner at Pasqualina's forgotten, Liliana put a pot of water on the stove to boil some linguine while she made a quick garlic and oil sauce. Fabio meantime sat at the table, watching his mother. The pleasing aroma of the garlic brought back the memory of countless meals she had prepared for him. How many times had he sat in that same chair, watching her cook, listening to her prattle on about this or that? The memories, though, seemed like they came from the ancient past, almost as if they were those of another person entirely; it felt as though a thousand lifetimes had passed since he was last there.

"You know, you could have written to your mother once or twice," said Liliana over her shoulder.

"I know. I'm sorry, Mamma," he said truthfully. Then he asked, "How is Zia Pasqualina?"

"Fine," said his mother while she added some red pepper to the sauce. "I was supposed to have dinner at her house, so she's probably wondering where I am. But I'm sure that by now most of the town knows that you're here, so she'll probably come by before you know it." Then, looking over her shoulder once more she asked, "So, was it a long ride here from Roma?"

"I didn't come here from Roma today," said Fabio. "I came from Pescara."

"Pescara?" wondered Liliana aloud. "But why?"

No sooner had she asked the question when the answer suddenly came to her. Despite her joy at having him home, she looked at Fabio with sadness in her eyes.

"You didn't need to go, you know," she said.

"Yes, I did," answered Fabio.

"What happened?" she said barely above a whisper.

Fabio did not answer, but simply shrugged and gave a yawn from the jetlag. He had gone to Pescara to find Caterina's parents two days earlier almost immediately after flying in to Rome from Boston. He had owed them an explanation of what happened the night of the accident. The guilt of not having given it to them for so long, the pain it must have caused them, weighed so heavily on him that he did not want to waste a single minute more. Nothing else mattered to him until he accomplished it.

It did not go well, at least not at first. Fabio managed to find their phone number and called ahead to ask permission to visit. When he arrived the next day at their door, Caterina's parents, Rafaele and Stefania, greeted him with distinct coolness. They invited him into their parlor, but offered him nothing to eat or drink, not even a simple glass of water. Fabio had been prepared for such a greeting, in fact he had felt that it was entirely warranted. And so he had wasted no time in beginning to tell them about how he and Caterina had met and how she came to be in the car that fateful night.

Stefania had burst into tears and demanded that he leave the moment he began, but it was Rafaele who soothed her, saying, "No, no, he must stay. It is good for us to hear everything."

It struck Fabio through to see how greatly they still suffered from the loss of their daughter, so he told them everything he could about that night, determined to be truthful while still using some discretion in explaining why they had been going to Enzo's apartment after leaving the night club. He answered all their questions, and was relieved when one in particular had not been posed. He had feared that they would ask if Caterina had died instantly and not suffered, and he had struggled with what he would tell them. When the question never came, he decided not to broach the subject, letting that horror be his alone to bear.

Later, when the couple walked him to the door, Rafaele stopped and stared at him with red-rimmed eyes. "Tell me one thing," he said to Fabio, his gaze piercing right through him. "Did you love my daughter?"

Till that moment, Fabio had been composed, but then his own eyes welled up. "Yes," he had told him. "I loved Caterina very much, and I wish I could have been the one to die in the car instead of her."

Rafaele breathed a heavy sigh and put a hand on his shoulder. "It's not what God wanted," he said.

Then the two parents had thanked him for coming and Fabio had gone on his way, not happy, but at least satisfied that perhaps he had been able to ease their pain just a little.

Now, sitting in his mother's kitchen, anticipating the bowl of linguine that would soon be in front of him, breathing in the delicious smells, Fabio became acutely aware of how fortunate he was, despite it all. He was equally aware that his mission was not finished. As hungry as he felt, he had one more stop to make before he could even think about enjoying a meal.

"Where are you going?" said Liliana anxiously when she saw Fabio stand. "I was just going to put the linguine in the water."

"I cannot eat, Mamma," he told her. "Not just yet."

Liliana gave a sigh and looked at her son again with that same sadness in her eyes. "Must you go just now?" she said. "Can't it wait a little while?"

"No," said Fabio simply. Then, promising to return soon, he left the house.

Maria blanched when she opened the door and found Fabio standing there outside. Just the same, she smiled and embraced him warmly before tugging him inside. At seeing him come in, Giovanni, who had been sitting at the kitchen table, reading the newspaper, jumped up and embraced him as well. Then the three went to the parlor to sit down and talk. Fabio took a seat by himself while Giovanni and Maria sat together on the sofa.

Fabio looked about the room and swallowed hard. Everywhere he turned was a photograph of Enzo, several of the two of them together. He paused to look at one in particular of himself and Enzo as teenagers, standing by the fountain on the piazza. The two looked so strong and confident and happy.

"He loved you like a brother," said Maria, wringing her hands as she watched Fabio gaze at the photograph.

"I know," said Fabio. "We *were* brothers."

At that Maria caught her breath and began to weep, but she quickly composed herself and wiped the tears from her eyes. For his part, Giovanni put on a brave face, but it was clear that he too was on the verge of tears, and there ensued a long moment of silence.

"So," said Giovanni, finally breaking it, "tell us what you've been doing in America, Fabio."

Fabio told them about Zio Rick and learning how to blow glass. He told them about Rhode Island and living in Wakefield. And he told them about the beaches and how he enjoyed spending time on his surfboard. All the while as he spoke, Giovanni and Maria listened and watched him closely. They were paying attention, but it seemed to Fabio that there was something on their minds that they were hoping to say.

When he had finished, they sat for a time once more in silence. Again it was Giovanni who broke it.

"Fabio," he said. "We're so happy you have come to see us, that is we're both happy and sad at the same time. We're happy to see how much better you are doing since you left for America. You look stronger again and more like yourself. But we're sad too because we know that you didn't go to America for the reason you wanted. That is why we've been waiting to tell you something for a very long time, something that we've needed to say."

For the life of him, Fabio could not imagine what it might be that they wanted to tell him. In truth, it was he who needed to talk to them.

"*Cos'e'*?" he said. "What is it?"

"Fabio, we just wanted to tell you how sorry we are," said Maria.

"For what?" said Fabio.

"For everything that happened to you," answered Giovanni. "You had great plans, great dreams of going to America, and we're so sorry that they didn't come true for you the way that you wanted. We know that it was Enzo's fault."

"What?" gasped Fabio.

"It was Enzo's fault, he was the one driving," said Maria. "How in the world he missed the turn, we don't know, but we hope you can forgive him."

In that instant, the memory of Enzo's eyes in the rearview mirror flashed through Fabio's mind.

"No!" he cried, putting a hand up to make them stop. "You have it all wrong. That is why I came to you, to tell you that what happened was not Enzo's fault at all, it was mine! I was in the back and I...I distracted him for just a second. I didn't mean to, but it was so foggy and the road so dark and...and..."

Fabio broke down and began to cry.

"Enzo...Caterina!" he sobbed. "It was all my fault. You mustn't blame Enzo. It was me. I'm so sorry. I wish it was I who died in the car instead of him!"

Inconsolable he buried his face in his hands.

"Fabio, Fabio *calmati*," said Maria gently, rushing to his side.

Fabio looked up into her eyes and those of Giovanni. In them he saw what seemed to him relief, but also compassion.

"I'm so sorry," he said, trying to gather himself. "Please forgive me."

At that Giovanni reached out and put a steadying hand on

his shoulder. "Fabio," he said very calmly. "Listen to me and understand. We have always worried because we were afraid that you blamed Enzo for what happened to you. But however true what you just told us might be, you cannot blame yourself. It was an accident, a terrible accident." He paused, then with his voice quavering, said, "There are a million reasons why it happened, and a million reasons why God wanted you to live instead of the others, but there's no way for us to know them. Do you understand? So, it's time to let it all go now and move on."

"He's right, Fabio," said Maria. "That's what Enzo would want you to do."

Fabio heaved a heavy sigh and wiped his eyes dry. The jet lag and the emotions all had overcome him. He was totally exhausted, but somehow, somewhere deep inside, a part of him had healed.

"*Dio*," he said with another sigh.

"That's right," said Giovanni. "Just leave it with Him."

Maria must have phoned ahead to Liliana after Fabio left for when he arrived back home the linguine was already in the water, boiling. Trudging into the kitchen, weary beyond words and hungry deep in the pit of his stomach, Fabio exchanged a nod with his mother before plopping back down into his seat at the table.

"How did it go?" asked Liliana as she stirred the pasta.

"They are the best people in the world," said Fabio simply.

It wasn't long before Fabio had a bowl of steaming linguine and a glass of wine on the table before him. He sprinkled some grated cheese on it and breathed in the aroma of the garlic before reaching for his fork. He stopped first, though, and looking down at his food, made the sign of the cross by way of giving thanks before he took his glass of wine and lifted it toward his mother.

"*Salute*," he said.

"*Salute*," she replied.

Then he took a sip of wine and settled down to eat the meal

his mother had prepared for him. And somehow, in those simple things, it finally felt to Fabio like life really was meant to go on.

CHAPTER THIRTY-ONE

Fabio stayed three and a half weeks in Mont'Oliva. He spent most of his days relaxing at home and letting his mother fuss over him. He ate, it seemed to him, more in those few weeks than in the nearly two years he had been away in America. In the evenings, he would stroll up to the piazza and spend an hour or two chatting with his old friends who still lived in the village. Not surprisingly there were few, for most of the people he had grown up with had gone off to other places in search of work. Those who had remained behind acted genuinely happy to see Fabio again, and he was happy to see them. Even Bettina, now married with two little children of her own, greeted him cordially the first time they passed one another on the street.

Most of all, Fabio slept. It seemed there was a bottomless well of fatigue inside of him. In the beginning he thought it was just the jet lag he was feeling, but then he realized that he was simply exhausted and had been for a very long time. He had filled that well of fatigue one anxious, restless night and work-driven day at a time, and now sleep was the only way to empty it. And so he spent many hours in his bedroom, still surrounded by his old ribbons and trophies, slumbering abed. When he was not doing that, he would often sit outside by himself and simply gaze out at the mountains.

The day before he was to leave, Fabio decided to take a walk down to the cemetery just outside the village. To reach it in the most direct way, he would have to pass by *il muro*, and as he descended the road from the piazza, Fabio could feel the knot tightening in his gut. Just the same he continued on; he had known all along that this was something he would have to do and there was no more putting it off. When at last he came to the junction in the road, he stopped directly at the spot where Enzo's car had careened across and tumbled over the wall. He turned and forced himself to look at where it all had happened. For a terrible moment he heard the voices calling to him again, but just as quickly they subsided and a feeling of calm acceptance came over him. He stayed there but a moment or two more then continued on his way.

At the cemetery, Fabio first visited his father's grave. It had been a very long time since he had done so, but the memories of his father were as fresh as ever in his mind. After spending a few minutes there, he knelt and said a prayer for him before moving on to look for Enzo. When he found his friend, Fabio nodded a greeting at the headstone and sat down next to it on the grass. For a long while he stayed there, staring out at the nearby vineyards. As he did so, that same feeling of calm came over him and it felt for all the world as if Enzo were sitting there beside him once again, nudging him in the side, asking him what great plans they had for the evening. How strange life seemed to him at that moment, how inexplicable. All the dreams he had chased, all the torments he had endured, all the love he had lost, all the hope he had regained, everything good and bad, all to that point had led him to that resting place of the dead. It was as if he had always been trying to catch the wind. As he sat there, reflecting on these things that made up his life, Fabio realized that they could never be truly understood, but all the same he realized that he was glad that his place was still with the living. And so, when his time there was finished, he bid his father and

Enzo a farewell, promising to visit again, and looking forward to that day, whenever it came, when they would all laugh together once more. Then he walked back past *il muro* and up the long hill back home.

Later, that evening, Zia Pasqualina came by the house and sat with Fabio and Liliana out on the terrace. It was a pleasant evening, the air comfortably warm while the top edge of the sun dropped like a weary eyelid closing behind the mountains. Down below in the village the church bells were ringing the hour and from the houses all round came the murmur of the voices of people getting ready to sit down to supper.

"So, *bellissimo*," Pasqualina said brightly, "you are going back to America after all tomorrow."

"*Si*," said Fabio with a nod.

"And what are you plans for when you get there?" she asked. "Do you think you will stay working for Zio Enrico?"

"I don't know what else to do right now," he said with a shrug. "But Zio has been good to me and taught me a lot, and I'm pretty good with the glass."

"*Bravo*!" said Pasqualina

"*Bravo*?" scoffed Liliana. "Don't you think he would be better off staying right here at home with his mother?"

Fabio feigned a sigh and rolled his eyes for Pasqualina's benefit, for this was a conversation he had already had with his mother numerous times during the preceding three weeks. He gave a little laugh and patted her hand. "Please, Mamma," he told her gently, "don't worry so much about it. Besides, wasn't it you who wanted me to go to America in the first place?"

"That was before!" cried Liliana, throwing her hands up. Then, composing herself, she sighed and said, "I know, I know. It's just that you're doing so much better now. Maybe you could stay just a little while longer."

"I need to go, Mamma," said Fabio gently.

"He's right, Liliana," said Pasqualina. "He does need to go."

She turned to Fabio.

"So, like I told you once a long time ago, *nipote mio*," she said, "go back out there into the world and find whatever it is that you're looking for. Finish whatever it is you have started in America, and just keep going. Forget about this place and everything that happened here. It's time for you to move on. And don't worry about anything, we'll always love you and we'll always be here for you if you need us."

Though tears were welling in his eyes, Fabio smiled and reached out to take his aunt's hand. "Then it would be all right if maybe I came back to visit every now and then?" he asked jokingly.

"Ayy, you had better!" exclaimed his mother. "And don't wait two more years like you did this time."

"I won't," promised Fabio.

He got to his feet and gave his mother a kiss on her forehead. Then, while she and Pasqualina went to the kitchen to prepare supper, he went upstairs to collect his things and finish packing.

Morning the next day, Liliana walked with Fabio down from the piazza to the main road to await the bus. It was a cloudy, moody morning and for a time neither mother nor son spoke, the silence broken only by the whisper of the breeze through the trees, the occasional passing car, and the sporadic sound of shotgun fire coming from down in the valley where some men were out hunting.

"Are you sure you packed everything you need?" fretted Liliana, finally breaking the silence. "You looked under the bed to make sure you didn't forget anything?"

"I didn't forget anything under the bed, Mamma," said Fabio patiently. "But I did leave something for you on top of it."

"For me? What is it?"

"It's nothing," said Fabio with a shrug. "Just something I made for you."

"And you've had it all this time?" said his mother. "Why

didn't you give it to me before when I could have opened it with you here?"

Fabio gave a half smile and shrugged again.

It wasn't long before the bus came, and when it did there was little time for goodbyes. When the moment came for Fabio to get on board, he quickly turned and embraced his mother one more time.

"*Ti amo*, Mamma," he told her.

"*Ti amo, figlio mio,*" she said, heaving a heavy sigh. She reached up and put her hand on his face. "Listen to me," she told him quickly. "Find a way to be happy, because in the end that's the only thing matters in this world. Do you understand?" With that she gave him a gentle shove toward the bus. "Now go," she told him. "And *sta attento!*"

Fabio simply nodded and, without another word, kissed her hand, turned, and hurriedly stepped up into the bus. The door hissed closed behind him and in the next instant the bus roared away leaving his mother standing alone at the side of the road.

Feeling shattered inside, Liliana walked back to the village with tears rolling down her cheeks. Back at the house, she sat at the kitchen table and quietly wept for who knows how long. At last she calmed herself and, when her breathing had finally steadied, she got up from the table and poured herself a glass of water. She downed the drink and for a time gazed out the window.

"*Dio*," she sighed to herself as she wiped her eyes dry with the back of her hand. She turned and looked all around her. How empty the house suddenly felt to her. It was a feeling with which she had learned to live those long months when Fabio had been gone, but now that he had come home and left again, she felt it all the more acutely. She was brooding on the lonely days to come when suddenly she remembered Fabio's bedroom.

The package Fabio had left was there waiting for her on the middle of the bed when Liliana came into the room. She sat down on the edge of the bed and took it in her hands. Of moderate heft, whatever lay inside was wrapped in layers of newspaper. Fabio had obviously carried it to Italy inside his suitcase and somehow managed to keep it out of sight the whole time he was home. Liliana carefully peeled away the paper until she found what lay hidden inside. To her surprise it was an exquisitely beautiful heart of glass. Crafted, though she could not have known it, from the broken glass Fabio had been saving in his uncle's shop, it was infused with every color imaginable, swirling and twisting and dancing delightfully. Dazzled, she turned it over and over, admiring it from every angle. It was a treasure—and it was perfect.

At the sight of it, Liliana caught her breath and the tears once more came to her eyes. But this time they were tears of joy, for she understood what her son was trying to tell her. That beautiful thing inside of him, the part of him that she had once adored so much and feared was lost, was not dead after all. It was alive! Somehow it had come back to life in a new and different way, one that she would never have imagined. The thought of it all caused her to rejoice inside, and in that moment she knew for certain that her boy was truly going to be all right. And so it was that, later that day, Liliana Terranova went to the church where she knelt for a good long time and at last gave thanks.

CHAPTER THIRTY-TWO

Fabio did not tell his uncle of his plans to return that day. When the cab from the airport dropped him off at the house, he went up to his apartment and left his bags. The temptation to lie down on the bed was great, but he resisted and instead headed straight back out the door.

It was late in the afternoon of a lovely autumn day when Fabio left the house. Strolling down Main Street, he took his time as he made his way toward Vita Glasswork. He stopped and said hello to Eddie as he passed the bike shop and later waved a greeting to Joe, who was out wiping off the chairs in front of the sandwich shop. As he looked about at the trees and the buildings, and breathed in the crisp air, he realized that everything felt somehow different to him. *He* felt different, but in a way that he could not quite understand. Whatever it was, it filled him with a sense of optimism that he had not felt in a very long time. He had almost forgotten what is was like to have that feeling, wherever it sprang from, but he resolved to try to hold onto it for as long as he could.

Zio Rick was sitting with Elise, looking over some papers at the counter, when Fabio finally walked into the shop.

"Fabio!" Elise cried in delight.

Rick turned quickly. At seeing his nephew walk in, his face

lit up in surprise and he jumped up to embrace him.

"Well, welcome back to America," he said warmly, patting his back. "I was beginning to wonder if you would ever return. When did you get back?"

"Just a little while ago," Fabio told him.

"You should have let me know you were coming. I would have come up to Boston to get you."

"Sorry, Zio," said Fabio, "but I no want to bother you."

"Eh, what bother?" said Rick with a dismissive wave.

Fabio turned to Elise, who looked as if she wanted to run over and embrace him as well. The two regarded one another for a moment and exchanged smiles.

"*Ciao*, Elise," he said.

"*Ciao*, Fabio," she replied. "I'm so glad you're back."

"Me too," said Rick. "So, tell me, how are things back home in Mont'Oliva?"

Fabio did not answer straightaway, but took a deep breath and let it out. Then he gave a little shrug and nodded.

"Things much better," he said simply with an air of tranquility.

Rick eyed him thoughtfully in that way he had that made it seem as if he could see and understand everything. "That's good," he finally said.

"So, how are all the things here?" said Fabio with uncharacteristic enthusiasm. "How is Virgilio?"

"The same," lamented Rick. "As temperamental as ever. Lately he's been a real pain in the glass, if you know what I mean."

It took a moment for it to register, but when Fabio understood the pun he smiled and gave a healthy laugh.

"Well, Mister Terranova, I do believe that is the first time that I ever heard you laugh," said Rick, looking mildly impressed. Then, very seriously, he added, "I guess it really was a good trip home after all."

Fabio only nodded.

"So, *nipote mio*," Rick continued, "what are your plans now that you are back in Wakefield, Rhode Island?"

"I like to go back to making the glass, I guess," said Fabio. "If that is okay with you."

"Hmm, that would be fine, I suppose," replied Rick. "I mean, after all you do have a very great gift for it. But I had another idea that I thought you might consider, something perhaps that you could do at the same time."

"What is your idea?" said Fabio, curious.

Rick exchanged glances with Elise and gave her a wink. Then he walked to the front window and beckoned for Fabio to come over.

"Take a look across the street," said Rick.

Fabio did as his uncle asked and looked out the window though he had no idea of what exactly he was supposed to see.

"Notice anything different?"

"No," said Fabio at first, but then he looked a little higher to the second floor. It was then that he noticed that the sign for the dance studio was gone. "Oh," he said a little sadly, "the dance studio close."

"The week after you left," said Rick. "I heard the rent got too high for Elizabeth, so she moved. Too bad, she was there for a long time. But it does leave an opportunity, that is if you are interested."

"What you mean?" said Fabio.

Rick gave a little laugh. "Do you remember that day back in the winter when you said that maybe I wasn't meant to be a priest?" he said.

"Yes, Zio," Fabio replied. "But I no—

Rick held up his hand to cut him off. "The reason I bring it up," he said, "is because while you were gone I got to thinking that maybe *you* just weren't meant to be a dancer. You were meant to be something else—and not just a glassblower."

"What then?" said Fabio.

"Maybe you weren't meant to be a dancer," answered Rick, "but maybe, just maybe you were meant to be a dance *teacher*."

"A teacher?" wondered Fabio aloud. "But how do I do this thing and where?"

"There are no other dance schools in town anymore," noted Rick. "But if you were looking for a place to start one, why not take a look upstairs. We've just about finished clearing it out. It's quite spacious up there actually, and I think you'd find the rent very reasonable."

Taken completely by surprise, Fabio stood there not knowing what to say. The idea at first seemed so farfetched, but then, little by little, it began to take hold of him like the embrace of a long lost friend.

Just then the little bell on the door handle jingled and in walked a smartly-dressed older woman, the very same one who had visited the shop the day before Christmas.

"I hope it's not too late," she said sweetly. "I'm going to a party this evening and I just need to pick up a quick gift for someone."

Fabio and Elise exchanged knowing glances as Rick, smiling from ear to ear, hurried over to help her.

"You're not late at all," he assured the woman. Then, turning back to Fabio, he quickly said, "Why don't you go upstairs and have a look around, and we'll talk later."

"I'll come with you," said Elise, sharing a smile with Fabio.

The two went to the bottom of the stairs and lingered there long enough to watch Rick go over to assist the woman.

"I do hope I'm not causing any bother," she said.

"No bother at all," he said genially. "My name is Rick, by the way."

"I'm Helen," she replied.

"Well, Helen, let's see if we can find what you're looking for," he said, and the two walked off together to look at the glass.

At that Elise gave Fabio's shirt sleeve a tug and nodded for them to go upstairs. "Come on," she whispered. "Let's leave them alone."

As they climbed the stairs together, Fabio's heart began to race, but not from the exertion of the climb. With his uncle's idea whirling around in his head, he was filled with a strange mixture of anticipation and anxiety. Could he really do it? Fabio was not sure. When they came to the top of the stairs, he stood there, suddenly aware of how very close Elise was standing next to him.

"Mister Rick told me that you were a great dancer in Italy," she said. "What do you think, would you like to teach?"

Fabio hesitated, not sure of what he should do until Elise unexpectedly nudged him into the room.

"Go on," she said gently. "Have a look around."

Fabio took a few tentative steps inside. He saw that Zio Rick was right, it was indeed a very spacious room, more than large enough for a dance studio. As he gazed about at it, Fabio could hear in his imagination the music playing and see the couples whirling by as he called out instructions. A rush of excitement came over him as he envisioned it all, but just as quickly he was once more filled with doubt.

"What's the matter?" said Elise at seeing the look on his face.

"This could be good idea," said Fabio. "But not so easy to do all alone."

Elise beamed a beautiful smile at him. Then, to his astonishment, she stepped close, brought her face to his, and softly kissed his cheek.

"You don't have to do it alone," she told him as she pulled back. "Don't be afraid, I can help you. I could be your apprentice." She gave a laugh. "But I can't dance, of course, so first you'll have to teach me a few steps. I'll be your first student."

With that Elise took his hand and led him to the center of the room. Fabio let himself be pulled along, all the while a thousand wonderful dreams suddenly gushing like fountains in his head. As he looked around at the room and back to Elise, he was too overwhelmed by these new possibilities for his life to turn away from them. He was too thrilled.

"So, what do you say, Fabio?" said Elise. "Could you do it, could you be a teacher?"

Fabio grinned and kissed her hand.

"Yes," he told her, all doubts and fears allayed. "I can be teacher—but not just *a* teacher. I will be the best!"

Then he took her in his arms and the first lesson began.